Mavis was about to wheel herself back down the hallway when the other woman bent toward her to whisper, "You're new here. You'd better watch your step. There's all sorts of things going on."

Lord have mercy! Mavis thought. Does she know something about the murders? Trying to appear calm, she asked, "What kind of things? Is there danger?"

"Of losing your mortal soul!" Swannie said. "Don't tell me you haven't seen it? How can you be so blind?"

"Seen what?"

"The lustful looks, the secret glances."

Mavis sat up straighter. "I can't rightly say I've noticed anything," she said. "I've been here only one night."

"That's the worst time! I hear them sneaking up and down the hallway, the doors opening and closing. It's a regular sex ring. I wrote letters to the police, but I'm sure they were intercepted. You get out while you can, or you'll end up a white slave like the rest of 'em."

Also by Robert Nordan
Published by Fawcett Books:

RITUALS
ALL DRESSED UP TO DIE
DEATH BENEATH THE CHRISTMAS TREE

DEATH ON WHEELS

Robert Nordan

FAWCETT GOLD MEDAL • NEW YORK

A Fawcett Gold Medal Book
Published by Ballantine Books
Copyright © 1993 by Robert Nordan

All rights reserved under International and Pan-American Copyright Conventions. Published in the United States by Ballantine Books, a division of Random House, Inc., New York, and simultaneously in Canada by Random House of Canada Limited, Toronto.

Library of Congress Catalog Card Number: 92-97255

ISBN 0-449-14842-4

Manufactured in the United States of America

First Edition: April 1993

for Steve Gilbert

Acknowledgments

The author would like to thank Douglas Rhone, M.D., Bonnie Friedman, and Vassi Minervino for their help in relation to this book.

Chapter One

"Zeena Campbell, if you can't pay more attention to your driving, you just let me out of this car right here and now. I'd like to get where we're going in one piece, thank you, ma'am, and not end up scattered across the road."

Mavis began to pull on her gloves. Ever since Zeena had honked the horn loudly out in front of the house (late, as usual—Mavis had been ready and waiting for at least twenty minutes when Zeena finally pulled up), Mavis had regretted accepting the ride. "Come help me with my costumes," Zeena had begged her last Sunday after church, and Mavis, thinking about the long bus trip she'd have if she went by herself, said, "Well, all right, you just tell me what time."

"Mavis, honey, I'm sorry. I'm just so *excited*, I don't know what to do." Zeena slowed down; the car behind them honked loudly, pulled out, and passed, and they could see the driver's mouth working wildly up and down. Mavis was glad she couldn't hear his words. "We've been practicing for this performance for *months*, and now that it's here, my stomach is all tied up in *knots*. What if I mess up? The other girls would never forgive me if I ruined the show."

Laying down her gloves, Mavis turned to look at Zeena. Well, my goodness, she thought, she *does* look like she's about fifteen years old and just made the cheerleading squad. Zeena's eyes gleamed and her skin shone (helped along by goodness knows how many expensive creams and lotions), and Mavis had to admit that Zeena looked quite trim in the

1

designer sweatshirt she wore, its multicolored spangles reflecting the early afternoon sun that shone through the windshield. It was her hair, of course, that gave her age away. Black as a crow and bright with lacquer, it looked just like a wig. Zeena must have spent half the morning downtown at Shirlee's Beauty Shoppe getting it done up that way.

"Now, don't you worry," Mavis said, touching the neat gray curls on the back of her neck. "You'll do just fine." She let out a deep breath, relieved that Zeena had slowed down and wasn't looking around at the backseat every other minute to see if the costumes were okay. They hung there on a pole in plastic bags, with Zeena's cowgirl boots and matching hat carefully placed on the seat beneath them. "Y'all ought to be able to perform your little number in your sleep," Mavis said, "much as you've practiced. Every time I've been over to the senior center for my exercise class, I've seen you there kicking up your heels with the sweat pouring off your backs. If it had been me, I'd have dropped dead sure thing."

"You should have joined."

Mavis looked at Zeena as if she'd lost her mind. "Lord have mercy, no! I will have to admit that the exercise class has helped my arthritis—and I have you to thank for talking me into going there in the first place—but as for joining The Markham Merry Makers, it's not for me. Why, I could barely get myself to go out of the house in a pair of sweatpants when I first started to exercise. Never in this world will you find me prancing around a stage dressed in cowgirl fringe and waving pom-pons. No, I'll be part of the audience, and that will be just fine."

For a while after that, they drove in silence. Now that Zeena had calmed down a little, Mavis could enjoy the ride. The Lakeview Nursing Home, where Zeena and her group were to perform at the Fall Festival Bazaar, was located in an older section of Markham. The houses there were set well back from the street—two-storied, most of them, brick, with white trim and gleaming windows—a few with pumpkins already by the door and Halloween decorations on display. The lawns were as trim and neat as pictures in a magazine, with cascades of late-blooming chrysanthemums in beds and only a scattering of leaves from the trees that arched, golden in the sunlight, overhead. At the curb, neatly tied leaf bags sat ready for the collection truck that would come later in the afternoon.

A shame, really, to have the leaves taken away by the garbagemen. Even though they said it was better for the environment, Mavis missed the scent of burning leaves in the fall. Used to be, when John, her husband, was still alive, the two of them would work in the yard together on fall days like this one, while their daughter rolled in the dry piles of leaves, her laughter ringing out like bells in the still warm air. "Daddy, Daddy," she would say, "bury me!" (oh, how could either of them know then what was to come?), and John would stop his raking and go over and spread the leaves over the child until she disappeared from view, while Mavis would stand watching them, her heart filled with joy. When she bent again to her task—planting pansies ready for the next spring's flowering—their bright colors would be blurred by her tears. Now fall always had a tinge of sadness to it, a time of change, of death. Her daughter had been killed on a bright fall morning.

"Lord, look at the cars!"

Mavis gave a start at the sound of Zeena's voice, then peered through the windshield past her friend's pointing finger. Every space in front of the nursing home's main building looked to be taken. "This is a right big event," Mavis said, "the Fall Festival Bazaar, I mean. The volunteers organize it every year, and people come from far and near. It's a good cause. They make money for their activities and keep the residents busy the year long preparing things to sell. I've been coming as long as I can remember."

Zeena drove past the drive that led up to the entrance. "They said we could park in the employees' lot out back," she said. "I hope there's still room." Suddenly she turned at a small sign that said LAKEVIEW NURSING HOME—EMPLOYEES in front of a car coming from the other direction that had to swing to the middle of the street to avoid hitting her. Lord, Mavis thought, I'll be glad to get my two feet on the ground again.

The main building of the Lakeview Nursing Home once housed the country's tubercular sanatorium. Years ago when Mavis was just a young girl, she had driven by and had seen the patients sitting outside on the veranda that stretched across the front of the long, low building, and that picture had remained in her memory. Each one solitary and alone, young and old alike, they had sat there bundled up against the cold of a winter's day, with pale sunshine coming through the barren tree limbs overhead. No one moved, no one appeared to speak, and they had looked as remote as if they had settled upon the surface of the moon. Dear Jesus, don't let me ever get sent there, she had prayed as she went on her way.

Later, of course, they found drugs to cure that disease, and eventually the sanatorium was closed. It stayed empty for a while, then was used for county offices, until finally it was sold to the owners of Lakeview, who had remodeled it extensively, adding a whole new wing. Mavis had to admit that they had made a nice job of it. The lobby was warm and inviting, the hallways spotless, and the rooms spacious and bright. But still, every time she visited people there, Mavis left with a sense of sadness. . . . Most of them, she knew, would never go home again.

The road dipped down behind the new wing, where the dining room and activity rooms were located on the ground level. Zeena parked in a spot marked with someone's name, but that little fact didn't seem to bother her. "Well, here we are," Zeena said, and her voice sounded as if she'd caught something in her throat.

I do believe she's got stage fright, Mavis thought, and she reached over, patted Zeena on the arm, and said, "It's going to be fine, honey. You just relax." She opened the door. "Come on, let's get this stuff inside."

Getting out, Mavis looked up the embankment to the lawn where a platform had been erected with a blue and white tent stretched across the top. Rows of tables fanned out from it, piled with goods, and people were already strolling up and down the aisles. "My goodness," Mavis said, "they're getting fancier every year. Just look at that." She pointed.

"It might rain," Zeena said, and sounded almost as if she hoped it would.

"Now, you just hush," Mavis said. "You've been practicing half the year to get ready for this shindig, and now you're talking about rain spoiling it. You ought to be ashamed. Think of the others and how disappointed they'd be. It's not going to rain one drop." But when she looked up, past the tables and the far reaches of the lawn to the sky, she saw a low gathering of clouds just above the stand of trees rimming the small pond that gave Lakeview its name. She might have to eat her words.

"I'll carry the hat and boots," Mavis said, "and you take the costumes. I don't want to get blamed for any wrinkles."

As she clutched the garment bags to her, Zeena's excitement seemed to return. She beamed. "Wait till you see them, honey. We'll do the cowgirl number first; then comes something slower that we wear long skirts for, covered in feathers. The patriotic part is last, with all of us marching around waving red, white, and blue pom-pons and doing splits at the end, while LaVerne Peebles does cartwheels across the stage. She had a hip replacement last year, and now she's as good as new."

Mavis followed Zeena across the parking lot to the entrance, feeling a little foolish carrying the big white cowgirl hat and the fringed boots. She certainly hoped no one she knew saw her and thought she was going to make a fool of herself up on that stage. When she went through the door, she almost stumbled, blinded by the sudden dimness of the hallway after coming from the brightness outside. Reaching out, she caught herself on the doorframe, and thought, Zeena will never forgive me if I smash her fancy hat.

"Hey there!" The voice rang out all smiles, and Mavis, steady now, peered through the gloom to see who in the world it belonged to. "I'm Kimberly Collier, the activity director here at Lakeview," the voice said. "And *you* must be one of the Merry Makers."

The woman rushed forward and tried to take the garment bags from Zeena, but Zeena hung on to them. Mavis, her eyes adjusted, stood and watched them tug back and forth for a minute. Kimberly wasn't a bad-looking girl, she thought, but she had too much hair and too many teeth, and her bright voice could drive a person crazy. Finally she let go of the bags and turned to Mavis. "Are *you* one of the Merry Makers, too?" she asked.

Mavis could feel Kimberly's eyes sweeping over her navy blue dress with pocketbook to match, and her white gloves (maybe they *weren't* as festive as Kimberly's brightly printed skirt and satiny blouse, but that outfit had gotten Mavis through a lot of funerals and afternoon teas down at the church), and she knew that Kimberly didn't think for a moment that Mavis was going to be cavorting on any stage. "No, ma'am," she said, shifting the hat in her arms. "I just came along for the ride and to help Zeena with her things. I've got a visit to make upstairs—Miss Elgie Skinner from down at the church is a patient here—and then I'll wander around and see if I can find something to buy."

Kimberly smiled and turned back to Zeena. "Y'all come on in," she said, her voice a little softer. "The Merry Makers have the employees' locker room to change in, and the others are using the activity room."

"What others?" To Mavis, Zeena's voice sounded a little miffed.

"Why, the other *entertainers*," Kimberly answered. "We've got the New Harmony Quartet that sings just beautifully a cappella, and the Christian Youth Bellringers from Ebenezer Baptist Church—they'll do hymns. But the Merry Makers are really the stars of our show, no doubt about it."

Zeena walked ahead with Kimberly, and Mavis followed them down the hallway. Then Kimberly turned and opened a door on the right, and immediately a swirl of excited voices spilled out. There stood a dozen women in various stages of dress, with their bright costumes hung on hangers on the doors of open lockers and laid across the dirty laundry hampers at the back of the room. "Zeena, honey, we thought you were *never* going to get here," a voice called out. "We couldn't go on without you."

"I almost didn't make it, I got so scared. If it hadn't been for Mavis here, I might have turned right around and gone back home."

The women smiled at Mavis. She recognized some faces she had seen at the senior center when she went there to do her exercises, and she smiled back. Then she set Zeena's boots and hat on a bench between the lockers. "I guess I'd better be going," she said.

"Stay and help me get my costume on," Zeena said as she hung up the garment bags.

"Looks like you won't need any help," Mavis answered, smiling at the others. She tucked her purse under her arm. "I want to go see Miss Elgie before everything starts up."

"Give her my love," Zeena said, her voice muffled by the sweatshirt she was struggling to pull over her head without messing up her hair.

Mavis didn't answer her; she turned and walked out the door.

The crowd had grown on the lawn in front of the wooden stage. People milled about, a few of them already with packages under their arms. Later, after her visit, Mavis would try to find something among the tables she didn't mind too much putting out money for. Probably, if she went home right now and looked at the bottom of her cedar chest, she would find all the embroidered pillowcases and handwoven guest towels she had bought over the years at such events. But that was all right—the home could use the money, and anyway, it would give the residents pleasure to think that someone wanted to buy their handiwork.

She began to walk slowly up a set of stone steps by the side of the new wing. Halfway to the top, she had to stop and get her breath. Two girls, giggling, dressed in identical bright pink dresses with white ruffles around the collars and the hems of the skirts, ran past her and almost knocked her down. Two of the Christian Youth Bellringers, she'd bet anything in the world, probably chasing after some boy. She shook her head, looked up, and noticed that the clouds had grown larger above the trees. If a storm came up, nobody would be performing that afternoon. She began to climb upward again.

At the top, a gently sloping ramp led up to the veranda where the tubercular patients used to sit. Mavis gave a sigh of relief. In spite of her exercise classes at the senior center, she was still winded after climbing a flight of stairs, and the backs of her legs ached a little. But at least she could still get around on her own, and that was something to be thankful for.

"Can I help you?" the young man at the information desk asked Mavis as she came through the entranceway. He had soft dark brown eyes, pretty as a girl's, and his hair, pulled back in a ponytail, hung halfway down his back, curling at the ends. He was dressed brighter than a bantam rooster. Lord, how things changed! A few years ago, no self-respecting man would ever have taken a job as a receptionist, much less get himself up in such a garb. But maybe it wasn't such a bad thing after all, giving folks a little more freedom to do what they wanted. She smiled at him and set her pocketbook in front of her on the desk.

"I'd like to visit one of your patients," she said. "Miss Elgie Skinner. She's been here a right long time."

The man smiled at her with those pretty eyes, looked back down, rapidly typed something on a computer keyboard, then looked up at her again. "Room 210," he said, "in the new wing." He pointed past Mavis, and she had to turn to follow his finger. "Go through that doorway there, and you'll find the elevator. It's one floor up, and you'll see signs indicating the room numbers."

Mavis picked up her purse. "Thank you," she said as she started to walk across the soft carpet to the doorway.

"Yes, ma'am," he said. "You have a nice day."

The hallway was shadowy, quiet; Zeena and that bunch must be on the floor right below, no doubt making enough noise to raise the dead, but here you couldn't hear a sound.

When the elevator came, the doors opened with only a slight *whoosh,* and Mavis didn't realize at first that it was there.

The second-floor hallway was just as gloomy, but as she stood trying to read the numbers on a sign in front of the elevator, Mavis began to hear little sounds—rattly coughs, snores, muted laughter on TV game shows, then the sudden ring of a telephone at the nurses' desk at the end of the hallway. The arrow to room 210 pointed in that direction, and Mavis began to walk toward the desk very carefully, afraid that she might mar the surface of the highly polished floor. Room 210 was halfway down on the right.

At first she thought no one was there. The room was dark, with only a thin, sharp line of sunlight showing beneath the pulled-down window shade, the bed covers stretched taut and smooth. But then, peering closer, Mavis could see Miss Elgie's slight form beneath the spread, not much bigger than a whisper, one single tuft of fine white hair spreading on the pillow. "Honey, are you asleep?" she called out softly, afraid that she would startle the woman. She waited, holding her breath in anticipation of the answer.

None came at first, and Mavis had the sudden horrible thought that Miss Elgie might be dead. Surely not . . . the nurses must check on the patients every little while. When a tiny hand emerged from the sheet and plucked at the wispy hair, Mavis gave a great sigh of relief. "Yes?" Miss Elgie said. And Mavis rushed to the side of her bed, almost upsetting the metal nightstand.

"It's Mavis Lashley," she said, and realized her voice was too loud in the somber room. "From down at the church. We were in the same Sunday-school class. You remember?"

Miss Elgie raised her head slightly. Her skin, caught in the slight glow that came from the window, looked transparent, like thin paper covering a photograph in an old book, but her eyes were sharper than Mavis would have expected, bright blue. "Sure do," she said. "There every Sunday, rain or shine. I sang in the choir, too, till my voice gave out."

"Why, that's right," Mavis said. She could close her eyes right now and see Miss Elgie in her white-collared robe standing in the front row of the choir loft—perky little thing, always had a good word for everybody. Back then, Miss Elgie had worked for the county, a telephone operator for years in one of the government buildings, and she must have received a pretty good pension after she retired. Her house, which, the neighbors said, she kept neat as a pin, was only a few blocks from Mavis's own, and sometimes, when Mavis went for a walk after supper on a summer evening while it was still light, she would pass Miss Elgie's house and she would be sitting on the porch, and they would wave. But Miss Elgie faded quickly after her retirement, had to go into the home (Mavis wondered what had happened to the house), and here she was now, no bigger than a minute, lying in the darkness. Mavis said a little prayer that she would escape such a fate.

"Can I get you something?" Mavis asked. "How about some nice ice water?" She looked at the stand for a glass.

"No, ma'am. It hurts my teeth. They'll bring in a snack in a little while. Always poking food or something to drink at you."

"You have to keep your strength up," Mavis said, but Miss Elgie gave no answer.

"Wouldn't you like for me to raise the shade? They're having the Fall Festival Bazaar out on the lawn, and there's all sorts of people there. Going to have entertainment, too."

Miss Elgie sighed. "I reckon not. Folks on this floor don't get around much. Upstairs, now, that's different. They're the ones that go on trips and make stuff down in the activity room. I don't have the strength."

Mavis didn't know what else to say. Some folks visiting in sickrooms could talk your ears off, go on about every sort of foolishness and tell somebody dying they looked *real good* and would be up again in no time at all. But Mavis had never been one to do that, and if Miss Elgie didn't want to talk now, she was content to let her be. They had known each other for years, and Miss Elgie knew that Mavis would do anything in the world she could for her. With a little rush of love, Mavis reached out and took Miss Elgie's hand (no bigger than a child's, dry and blue-veined) and clasped it in her own. Miss Elgie gave a slight squeeze back, and Mavis knew she understood.

"What are you two ladies doing here in the *dark*? Let's get some light in this room."

Mavis jumped and dropped Miss Elgie's hand. She wouldn't have been surprised if the voice had rattled the metal stand. Turning, she saw a flash of white pass from the door to the window, a hand reach out and jerk up the window shade. The bright light blinded Mavis, and she could not see the woman who stood there, outlined like a cutout silhouette.

"Now, isn't that better?" the woman said, her voice not quite so loud. She walked around to the other side of the bed, bent over right in Miss Elgie's face, and said, "How's our sweet little lady today?", then looked up at Mavis before Miss Elgie could give an answer. ESTELLE OVERBY, R.N., NURSING SUPERVISOR said the pin on the front of her uniform. Its heavily starched creases looked sharp enough to cut. "Are you kin?" she asked, patting Miss Elgie's head.

"No, ma'am. Just a visitor. Me and Miss Elgie went to the same church, have known each other for years. I came out for the bazaar today and thought I'd pay a little visit."

"Well, that's real sweet of you," the nurse said. "Miss Elgie doesn't have many visitors." She stood up and started tucking the covers even tighter around Miss Elgie with square, capable hands, the nails blunt-cut and unpolished. A tall woman, she had thick brown hair that hung straight to her shoulders and was parted on the side. She wore no makeup, and her heavy eyebrows shaded her eyes, the kind of woman, Mavis thought, who took little interest in her appearance, except for cleanliness, and had no patience for anyone else who did. Wherever she lived, you would be able to eat off the floor, but she would have few visitors. This job was her only life. "Your snack will be coming in a little while," she said when she had finished with the bed. "I want you to eat every bit of it." She turned, and without saying a word to Mavis, walked out the door into the hallway.

"Bitch," Miss Elgie said under her breath, and Mavis's mouth almost flew open in surprise.

She stayed only a few minutes longer. Miss Elgie lay with her eyes closed against the light and did not respond when Mavis asked her if she wanted her to lower the shade again. There was nothing left to say. Bending, Mavis gave Miss Elgie's forehead a quick little kiss and said, "You take care, now; I'll come again," and then left the room.

She started to turn toward the elevator, but she saw the lit desk at the other end of the hall and began to approach it instead. This end of the hallway was brighter, a large sun porch opening off it at the end past the desk, though even its brightly printed sofa and chairs looked a little dull.

Nurse Overby was writing in a chart and did not look up as Mavis came to the desk. After Mavis propped her pocketbook on the edge and cleared her throat, Miss Overby finally said, "Yes?" but Mavis still could not see her eyes beneath the shaggy brows.

"You mind telling me how she is? Miss Elgie, I mean."

Nurse Overby let the chart drop to the desk. Her voice sounded exasperated. "I won't beat around the bush," she said. "She's given up. You can just look at her and tell. After that, they don't last very long a-tall."

Mavis, tears in her eyes, gathered up her purse and walked quickly down the hallway, heels clicking on its polished surface, no longer concerned about marring its perfect shine.

Chapter
Two

Lord, it looked even more like rain. Mavis looked out through the trees in front of the main entrance and saw that the sky had grown grayer, only a single rim of sunlight visible at the western horizon, as if the clouds had a slight tear in them. The air felt cool now, and she was glad her dress had a little jacket, providing some warmth on her arms.

But still people were coming to the bazaar. Out in the field past the area where the tables were set up, cars were parked on the grass, and more kept turning in from the street. The volunteers were busy with customers at the tables, and a little crowd was beginning to gather in front of the stage, drawn by a few preliminary squawks from the sound system. They'd better hurry if they wanted to get their show going before a storm came up, Mavis thought. Wouldn't Zeena and the others be disappointed if they didn't get to do their act.

Avoiding the stone staircase this time, Mavis walked down the gently sloping lawn toward the tables, smiling at the people she passed. A few faces looked familiar—maybe she had seen them at church or shopping in a store downtown—but most were strange to her. So different from what it used to be. Not all that long ago, anywhere she went, she would see half a dozen people she knew well enough to stop and talk to. That was half the enjoyment of going shopping, knowing that she would run into somebody she hadn't seen for a while and could stand and talk and catch up on the news, maybe go have lunch at the nice cafeteria in Burke's Department

Store. Now, with so many new people moving into town (every cornfield had a subdivision), and the malls draining off all the shoppers, every person Mavis passed downtown looked to be a stranger, and she avoided going there as much as possible. Every night in the paper you could read of a purse snatching in broad daylight.

The aisles between the tables were crowded, people buying things right and left, though Mavis didn't see a single thing she couldn't do without. Crocheted toilet tissue covers in the shape of hats, painted plaster figurines as gaudy as a prize from some carnival bingo stall, fancy aprons with appliquéd flowers and cute little sayings embroidered on them, pale jams that would be thin as water when you peeled off the wax seal—they would all be put away at the back of a closet when people got them home, perhaps to be retrieved again when a grab bag gift was needed for a Christmas party. But no doubt about it, the residents at the home had been working all year long on the items for sale (some now sat behind the tables in wheelchairs, smiling to beat the band when someone praised their handiwork), and Mavis would have to buy a little something just to be charitable. She finally decided on a wooden plaque with a Bible verse and a pair of praying hands painted on it that she could hang next to the window above her kitchen sink. There could be worse things to look at. "Thank you, ma'am; I know you'll enjoy it," the volunteer said as she put the plaque in a bag and handed it to Mavis. "It'll be real inspirational."

"Hold it, Miss Mavis. I want a picture of that for the paper! 'Miz Mavis Lashley seen at the very popular Lakeview Nursing Home's annual Fall Festival Bazaar'—I can just *see* the caption now."

Mavis turned, almost dropping her package; her hand went to her hair to see if it was in place before she even thought. Then she saw who it was. "Dale Sumner, you nearly scared me to death! I've got a good mind to give you a spanking right here."

He kissed her on the cheek. "Now, that *would* make the

news, wouldn't it? 'Grown man beaten by woman at bazaar.'
Your reputation would be ruined.''

She laughed. ''I expect when it's your own kin, people
wouldn't even notice.''

Dale was Mavis's nephew, her sister Florence's boy.
Though Florence had been older by four years, it had seemed
when they were growing up that their ages were reversed:
Mavis was the responsible child, the one who made sure the
two girls' beds were made in the morning, checked to see if
Florence's hair ribbon matched her dress, carried both their
lunches—Florence was just flighty. And when, at age nine-
teen, she announced she was going to get married (a man
years older than herself, red-gold hair piled high in a pom-
padour and a flashy new car, not paid for, it later came out),
everybody said it wouldn't work. They were right. In two
years, he was gone and Florence was pregnant, and she had
to move back home with her mama and daddy to stay till she
had the child.

But to Mavis, the boy, Dale, made up for everything that
had happened. Hair light and fine as corn silk, eyes so blue,
it almost hurt to look at them, he had the disposition of an
angel. And in those early years, Mavis spent more time with
him than Florence did. Even after she was married and had
her own child, she found excuses to have Dale come over
and spend the day with her and her daughter, relishing his
quick laughter. After Florence died, she needed no more
excuses. Dale had sought her out himself, saying, ''You're
all I've got now; we need each other,'' and she'd had to wipe
away quick tears.

Dale had drawn her aside between two of the tables. ''What
a crowd,'' he said. ''Have you ever seen so much tacky stuff
in your whole life?'' He swept his arm around.

''You be nice,'' Mavis said. ''But what in the world are
you doing here?''

''Honey, don't you remember? This is what I do for a
living.'' He pointed to the camera in his other hand. ''I get
to photograph all the very *smartest* social events around town
for the paper. If there's an opening at a mall, a ground break-

ing for a new Sunday-school building, a pie-eating contest, Dale Sumner is there to record it for posterity.'' He rolled his eyes. ''It's enough to make you throw up!''

''Hush!'' Mavis said, looking around to see if anyone had overheard. ''It's not always that way, and you know it.''

''What do you mean?''

''The police. You know.''

''Oh, that. . . . Well, maybe. But things don't happen all that much.''

''Enough,'' Mavis said, remembering some of the pictures she and Dale had looked at together in the past. When the police photographer was busy or out of town, Dale was sometimes called in to photograph the scene of a crime. He always made copies and brought them over for Mavis to see, and the two of them would pore over the prints, looking for clues. It was even more enjoyable than reading the mystery novels they also shared.

''Well, I don't think it's likely there'll be any bodies around here to photograph this afternoon. Not unless a couple of ladies get in a struggle over some cute little candy dish and one cracks it over the other's head.''

''Now, you *behave* yourself,'' Mavis said, and gave Dale a little tap on the arm, but when she looked into his bright eyes, still as blue as they were when he was a baby, she couldn't help but smile.

''Oh, Mr. Sumner, *there* you are!'' It was Kimberly Collier, the activity director, pushing through the crowd. If she remembered meeting Mavis, she didn't let on. ''They said you were here, but in this crowd I couldn't find you. We're so *pleased* to have somebody from the paper to photograph our little festival. You finding your way around all right? Anything you need? Our entertainment will be starting up any minute now, and I just *know* you'll be able to get some good shots of the performers. You march up there right in front of the stage and get yourself a good spot.''

She gave Dale a big smile, and it looked to Mavis as if Kimberly might grab his arm and drag him away. Mavis knew what Dale was thinking: pushing thirty, and with an empty finger on her left hand you know she's desperate for a man—and anything in pants will do. Well, with Dale, she'd soon learn she was barking up the wrong tree, no doubt about that. Kimberly Collier was about the last person he'd be interested in. Stepping closer to Mavis, he said, "I'm doing just fine. Don't you worry, I'll get a place near the stage. But I've got to say good-bye to my lady friend here first. She'd be mad as fire if I ran off and left her."

Kimberly looked as if she'd been dumped in water, all wilted. Then she gave herself a shake and said, "Let me know if we can help with anything," and walked away without looking back.

"Lordy, that was a close call." Dale pretended to wipe sweat from his forehead. "I sure wouldn't want to get tangled up with her the rest of the afternoon."

"She's just trying to do her job."

"You know better. Not unless her job is to latch on to every stray man she can find. I know the type. I'm glad you were here to protect me."

Mavis laughed. "I expect you can protect yourself. You've done it long enough."

Dale squeezed her hand. "I guess," he said. "And I guess I'm going to have to strike out on my own again." He pointed toward the stage. "Looks like they're getting ready, and since I'm here, I suppose I ought to do my job. You want to come up front and stand with me?"

"No, thank you! They have everything so loud these days, it hurts my eardrums. I'll stand back here, and it'll be just fine. You go on." Dale gave her hand a final squeeze, turned, and walked between the tables toward the stage, his bright head bobbing up and down, plainly visible.

The stage was crowded now. Off to the side stood the a cappella quartet, four men dressed in powder blue tuxedos and white patent leather shoes, with enough pomade on their hair to grease a jet plane. Heads bent close, they looked as if they might be tuning up, but without a microphone on, you couldn't hear a sound. Opposite them, lined up, stood the Bellringers, the girls in their ruffled dresses and the boys in jackets and ties, each one holding a silver bell with the clapper held down so it wouldn't sound. The Merry Makers must still be inside, awaiting their turn.

Just then, a man dressed in a navy blue suit walked from the back of the stage to the microphone up front and tapped it twice. The sound was sharp, almost like a gunshot, and the crowd instantly quieted, people straining forward to see. Mavis moved a little closer. Who in the world is that? she wondered. Kimberly hadn't said anything about a solo performer. Certainly he didn't look as if he'd perform any magic tricks or sing, that prissy little man with a wide forehead and thin lips, two little pouches on the sides of his mouth, as if he'd just popped candies inside. He straightened his rimless glasses, tapped once more, and then began to speak.

"Ladies and gentlemen," he said. "My name is Clifford Joyner, and I'm proud to say that I'm the administrator of Lakeview Nursing Home. It's my privilege to welcome y'all here this afternoon and to thank you kindly for coming. Our employees thank you, our volunteers thank you, and our residents thank you. They've made all those wonderful items you've been buying, and they'll be the ones to benefit from your *generous* donations. Now, I'm not going to take up much more of your time—I know all of you are just dying for our entertainment to get started—but I *do* want to say one special word of thanks. Kimberly, you come on up here." He turned around and looked toward the back of the stage. "Miss Kimberly Collier, our activity director, made all this possible. She's worked like a *dog*, and now I want to give her a hand." He began to clap, his hands too close to the microphone, so that the sound was deafening.

Kimberly came up then, smiling and blushing, mouthing thank-yous as the crowd applauded. My goodness, she does look pleased, Mavis thought, and felt a little sorry for Kimberly. Poor girl, she probably lived for this moment all year long, not much of a reward for all her efforts. No wonder she seemed so anxious to latch on to some man.

"Thank you, folks. I'm sure Kimberly appreciated the applause." Clifford Joyner did not look at her as she moved,

still smiling, toward the back of the stage. "Now it's time
for some music," he said, and pointed to the four men in
their light blue suits. "The New Harmony Quartet, with some
of your favorite songs. Let's give them a big hand."

Quickly the men moved up to the front of the platform,
the lead singer took the microphone, and with a "One,
two, three," they began to sing, bodies swaying, feet
tapping. Lord, what a noise, Mavis thought, the men's
high-pitched voices rising up in a squeal that the speakers
amplified and carried across the lawn. But nobody seemed
to mind. The crowd up front was smiling, and some kept
time with the music, clapping their hands and waving their
heads. They probably had hearing loss from walking
around with speakers plugged in their ears all day long
and couldn't hear much anyway. Mavis herself wasn't
about to risk ending up with a hearing aid.

The Bellringers weren't much better. The quartet finished
(they gave three encores, and Mavis prayed after each one it
would be the last), and the girls and boys marched up. After
a signal from their leader, they began dingdonging "Abide
with Me" on their silver bells, so slow, anybody would think
they were leading a funeral procession. Mavis wondered what
the sick folks inside thought when they heard it. From the
audience came the bright pop of flashbulbs as relatives took
pictures, but the Bellringers gave no indication that they were
aware, looking straight ahead, with not a sign of an expression on their faces. Sure as anything, as soon as they got off
the stage, they'd get out of their dress-up clothes and head
out to the mall, where they'd take up all the benches so nobody else could sit down, playing radios as loud as they
would go. You couldn't go anywhere in peace anymore.

Finally they were finished. They bowed, filed off the stage,
and when somebody dropped a bell and it went clanging
down the stairs, the crowd laughed and applauded all over
again. Parents closed their cameras and put them away. It
was time for the Merry Makers.

Mavis moved forward. After all, she'd come out here to
see Zeena and the others do their number, so she might as

well get a good look. But, Lord, they'd better hurry, she thought as she looked up suddenly at the sky. It was a solid mass of clouds now, darkest in the west above the treetops. The little pond was black, with not a ripple on its surface, though Mavis thought she felt the chill of a breeze on the back of her neck. Don't let Zeena break her leg, she prayed to herself, and a little rustle of sound went through the audience as if they, too, whispered to themselves.

But when the Markham Merry Makers came marching on, Mavis forgot all her worries. Didn't they look cute! Smiling to beat the band, their white cowgirl hats cocked to one side, the fringe on their uniforms dancing, they marched in to the sound of "Hooray for Hollywood" blaring from the loudspeakers. Even if no one quite knew what cowgirl outfits had to do with Hollywood (surely it wasn't a tribute to Dale Evans), the crowd loved them, and whistles and shouts rang out as the Merry Makers lined up across the front of the stage doing high kicks. For a minute Mavis couldn't spot Zeena, but then she found her in the line, perky as the rest, and looking as if she was having the time of her life, even though Mavis knew she had to be panting for breath.

It was at that moment that the first clap of thunder came, a sharp, deafening crack that blotted out the music. People looked around, unsure whether the noise came from the amplification system or the sky. Suddenly they heard another sound coming from the hillside by the pond. No words to understand at first, just a wail, but one of such heartbreak that the crowd became suddenly quiet, the dancers stopped, and every head turned toward the hill.

There, gesticulating wildly, stood the figure of a man, old certainly, white-haired, his movements stiff and jerky, mouth moving frantically. A second clap of thunder sounded as he began to run down the hill toward the crowd. Now they could hear his words: "Help me!" he cried. "My wife! There's been an accident! Please, somebody come!"

For a moment no one moved, as if they were all caught there in some awful dream and could not awaken. But then the rain came, sudden, violent, and the man on the hill became only a blur of flapping clothes, his words drowned out by the cries of the crowd, suddenly released, as they rushed to find shelter. Mavis did not know which way to run, but suddenly she felt a strong arm around her shoulders and heard Dale's voice saying, "Come on, honey, let's run for it. My car's just over there in the employees' lot. I guess maybe we were wrong about finding a body here after all!"

Chapter
Three

The rain poured straight down in torrents for a few minutes but then stopped as suddenly as it had come. The tables were flooded, puddles standing on the sheets of plastic the volunteers had managed to throw over the items for sale, and streams of water ran between them down an incline toward the lawn where the cars were parked. Most people had scattered, racing to cars or the shelter of the building, but the Bellringers ran around like a bunch of ducklings, faces held up to the rain, mouths open. The girls' sodden ruffles clung to their legs, and their hair was plastered down in darkened strands; the boys' red bow ties were bleeding into their shirts like wounds. On the platform, the Merry Makers huddled in a corner, hats slightly askew, no doubt afraid their makeup would run. The grass was squishy.

But even though people sighed in relief when the sun came out, the figure did not disappear. Closer now, standing at the bottom of the hill, the old man still called to them, "Help me! It's my wife!" and pointed back toward the pond, his face wet with the rain and with his tears.

Kimberly Collier got to him first. Rushing between a row of tables, she ran toward the man with such a look of concern on her face that Mavis, watching her through the turned-down window of Dale's car, thought, I have misjudged her. She's not all smiles. When Kimberly finally reached him, she took the old man's hand and tried to calm him, as if he had been a frightened child, but they could not hear her words. "What in the world do you think's going on?" Mavis asked Dale. He shrugged his shoulders, intent upon his camera, trying to wipe the moisture away with a Kleenex that Mavis had found in her purse. "I'm going to get out," she said, and opened the door.

Others were beginning to venture out into the open. Someone shushed the Bellringers, and they quieted down, standing close to one another as if for warmth, soaked to the skin. The quartet quickly went down the stairs behind the platform and hurried to the entrance of the building, and the Merry Makers cautiously walked to the edge of the stage. They watched what was going on at the bottom of the hill as if it were a little play.

Kimberly seemed to have calmed the man. He stood now, his pale green sport shirt soaked through so that the others could see a dark patch of hair on his scrawny chest, his head down, as if he had no more strength left to scream. Kimberly stood with her arm around his shoulders, still whispering in his ear. All of a sudden Clifford Joyner, the administrator, called out from somewhere behind the platform, "Hey, Darnell, Olin, you go down there and help Miss Kimberly," and two men dressed in uniforms—one black, one white, attendants, no doubt, from the home—rushed out the doorway of the building and started across the lawn. Lord, Mavis thought, their britches will be covered with mud.

Kimberly talked to them for a minute, pointing behind her toward the pond. Some of the young people in the crowd began to move closer, but she called out to them, "You stay back. We don't need a bunch of folks getting in the way." Withdrawing her arm from the old man's shoulders, she said something to the attendants, and they took his arms, one on each side, and almost carried him back up the hill toward the pond and the stand of trees. Slowly Kimberly turned and began to walk back toward the tables, face impassive, as if she might find it hard ever to smile again, and when Clifford Joyner called out, "You want me to call the police?" she wearily nodded her head yes.

Dale, who had come up behind Mavis while she was

standing in the parking lot watching the scene at the bottom of the hill, said to her, "You stay here. I'm going over there." And before she could turn around and tell him to be careful, he had run off with his camera dangling from his neck. It was one of the few times she wished she were younger and could follow.

"Poor thing."

The voice came from just behind Mavis's left shoulder. She turned and saw a black woman standing there, arms folded over her ample bosom. Dressed in a pink uniform with white collar and cuffs, she wore an artificial red rose in her pulled-back hair, and when she spoke again, Mavis saw a flash of gold in her mouth. "Mr. Dixon, he gonna just about *die* if something happen to Miss Luna."

"Dixon? Mr. *Jesse* Dixon and his wife?"

"Yes, ma'am—you know them?"

"Why, sure I do. They used to go down to my church . . . before Miss Luna got so bad." Mavis had turned, facing the woman now. She saw soft, dark eyes, and she smiled at their warmth, even though the sad sight on the hill had not gone away. "Are they living out here now? I hadn't heard."

"Sure thing," the woman said. "Got one of them little apartments over on the other side." She pointed vaguely toward the building. "I saw them this morning bright and early. They always come in together to eat breakfast, him wheeling her like she was the most precious thing on this earth."

"You work here?" Mavis wondered if she was being too forward.

"Yes, ma'am, in food service. I take trays around to folks that can't leave their rooms for meals. And some just don't want to, so we humor them, too. Worked here for ten years now. My name's Daisy Norris. Do I know you, ma'am?"

"I reckon not. I'm Miz Mavis Lashley. I come out here to Lakeview quite a bit to visit the sick—you know how it is when you get older; half the people you know have got something wrong with them—but I never was around during mealtime."

"That's nice." Daisy flashed a smile. "A lot of folks don't

have visitors a-tall. Mr. Jesse and Miz Luna, they never had no children, but Mr. Jesse's got this niece that comes out to see them right regular in the little while they've been here; nobody much else, though. Still and all, they didn't seem all that lonely, not with each other around. They look like they just love each other to death.''

At the word ''death,'' Mavis's hand flew out as if she might be able to catch it and hide it before they realized what it might signify. Daisy looked horror-struck. ''Oh, Lordy, what did I say?'' Tears sprang to her eyes. ''I just don't want to think about anything happening to her.''

''Has she been worse lately?''

''No, ma'am, not that anybody knows of. She's got the Alzheimer's, and I guess you just go downhill kind of gradual with that, nothing sudden. When I saw them in the dining room this morning, I said, 'Hey, there, look at you,' talking to Miss Luna, 'that's a pretty new dress. I ain't seen that one before.' She just smiled. Sometimes she knows you and sometimes she don't. Mr. Jesse, he spoke up and said, 'Got her all dressed up today, you know, for the festival. But we won't be around when the crowd comes. It'll just upset her.' He patted Miss Luna on the shoulder, but she didn't take no notice. 'We'll go on a ride over to the pond and back. It's restful there.' ''

Daisy moved just a little to the right of Mavis and peered over her shoulder. Mavis turned and followed her gaze. Over on the hill, the two attendants were just disappearing behind the trees with Jesse Dixon between them, and Dale wasn't far behind. They watched for a moment. Then Daisy turned back. ''It *is* pretty over yonder,'' she said. ''If it ain't rained and made the pond all muddy, it looks bright as a mirror, and the trees give a lot of shade in summer, makes it cool. I heard Mr. Jesse say it reminded him of the cabin they used to have up at Lake Junaluska. Went there every summer without fail. He fished, and Miss Luna would read or whatever. They had to sell the place when Miss Luna got bad. He said, 'Going over there on the hill brings back memories. I even think Luna knows, too. She seems calmer there, more content.' ''

Mavis frowned. "It's so sad," she said. "They were such wonderful folks down at the church—so dedicated. For years they ran the nursery on Sunday mornings so people could leave their young-uns there while they attended services. Everybody knew Mr. Jesse and Miss Luna—never called them anything but that—and they were truly *loved*. Babies grew up and went away and then came back with *their* babies for them to take care of. Why, the church gave them this big celebration for their fiftieth wedding anniversary just before Miss Luna started getting sick."

"Yes, ma'am, I know. Mr. Jesse has this scrapbook with just about a zillion pictures of babies in it, and he showed me the write-up of that shindig. There was a picture, too, both of them looking sweet as sugar."

"My nephew took that picture! He's the one that went hightailing it up the hill a few minutes ago." Mavis turned and pointed, but Dale was nowhere in sight. "He said it was a real pleasure for him to take a picture of such nice folks. That's not always the way."

Daisy shook her head, but before she had a chance to say more, a loud bleat came from the loudspeaker system on the platform. "Come on," Mavis said. "Maybe they're going to tell us something." She started to move away in order to get a view of the stage.

Daisy looked at her watch. "I better not, Miz Lashley. Them folks eat early, and we got to get them trays ready, no matter what. I don't want nobody saying I'm shirking my part." She smiled at Mavis. "You take care now, you hear? I enjoyed our talk. We can both pray nothing real bad has happened." She turned and went across the parking lot to the entrance to the ground-floor level, and Mavis headed for the stage.

Clifford Joyner was there, fumbling with the microphone. His puffy little cheeks were bright red, and his mouth was set in a severe line. Mavis wondered if he'd be electrocuted if he touched a wet wire. Finally the microphone came on with a popping sound, and he began to speak.

"Well, I guess you folks know we didn't order this

weather." He tried to smile. "But the storm's over now, and we're going to go right on with the festival. Soon as the volunteers get the tables cleared off, you can go right back to buying the unique crafts our residents and friends have made. We don't want to disappoint them, now, do we?"

He paused a moment but then looked as if he was about to go on when somebody shouted out from the audience, "What's going on over on the hill?"

Clifford Joyner's cheeks got a little redder. "Seems like there might have been a little accident," he said. "We're investigating, and an ambulance has been called. No need to worry. We'll take care of everything just fine now that the storm's over. Y'all go ahead and enjoy yourselves." He turned as if to leave the stage, but apparently saw the group of Merry Makers standing huddled at the rear, and came back to the microphone. "I'm real sorry to have to say it, but our friends the Markham Merry Makers won't be able to finish their act. This stage is just too wet, and we don't want any *more* accidents today. But you ladies come on up and take a bow. We'll have you back next year mighty sure and certain."

Carefully, as if suddenly aware of their own fragility, the women walked to the front of the stage, hooked arms, and gave a bow; the audience applauded loudly. Then, removing their big hats, they filed down the stairs to the parking lot and headed for the building to change. Loud music came up suddenly on the sound system, and people began to move through the aisles of tables again, trying to avoid the puddles in the grass.

Mavis decided she'd just as soon not ruin her good shoes. She'd bought all she intended to buy (and where was her package? She must have left it in Dale's car when they took shelter from the storm), and the show was over. She might as well go inside and help Zeena pack up her costumes again. Still, she did wonder what was happening over on the hill. Shielding her eyes with her hand, she peered out over the lawn, but the figures had disappeared. The trees burned red in the late afternoon light, and the pond glistened like silver.

She walked across the parking lot to the entrance. Several of the Bellringers stood there, still wet, hair plastered down. Tomorrow they'd be sick as dogs with colds. Inside, the hallway was deserted; Kimberly Collier and Clifford Joyner must have gone upstairs to tend to business. From the food service area came the rattle of pans, and Mavis smelled the scent of cooking food, slightly nauseating to her. She'd had only a light meal this morning, and too much excitement this afternoon—no wonder her stomach was turning over.

When she opened the door to the employees' locker room, where the Merry Makers would be changing, she expected a burst of noise, all of them chattering like birds. But the group of women there, looking as bedraggled as the Bellringers even though they had been protected from the worst of the rain, was nearly silent, turned away from one another as they pulled on their clothes and packed their costumes. Their boots were splashed with mud, and their cowgirl fringe was limp. "Oh, Mavis, honey," Zeena said when she saw Mavis in the doorway, and looked almost as if she might cry.

"I thought you might need a little help getting your stuff together," she said. A few of the women looked around but did not speak.

Zeena shrugged her shoulders. "I guess so. It doesn't matter much now. Everything's ruined. First the rain, and then whatever else has happened out there on the hill."

"Well, it's not the end of the world," Mavis said.

"No, but it was our *debut*, and we were all so excited. I saw you talking to Dale—I bet he didn't get a single picture of us before it started raining."

"There'll be another time."

Zeena shrugged and sighed. "Yes. We're going to be out at Cherry Hills Shopping Center next Saturday when the new Piggly Wiggly opens, and they've asked us to participate in Variety Night at Ridge High School, but somehow this was more special, with all those people out there, and pictures for the newspaper and all."

"Lordy, Zeena, I didn't know you were so vain. The Bible says it's a sin."

"I'm not. But we worked so hard, we wanted some notice, that's all. You don't need to be so critical."

Just then they heard the wail of an ambulance in the distance, and everyone was silent. They listened, almost as if they held their breaths, and the sound stopped, then resumed again after a few minutes and gradually receded until they could hear it no more. Almost at the same time, though, another siren sounded nearby, almost surely a police car. The women bent back to their packing, hurrying now, anxious to be away. "Here," Zeena said, and handed Mavis her hat and boots. "Let's get going."

Outside, the crowd had thinned, and at some of the tables the volunteers were packing up what was left of the goods in bags and boxes. The stage was empty, though the music played on, softer now, as if, somehow, the power had faded. Zeena headed for her car, but Mavis stopped her. "Look," she said, pointing to the hill by the pond. "Something's happening."

The scene was no longer empty. Another act in the little drama there was taking place. Figures moved between the trees, and someone seemed to be circling the pond. "It must be the police," Zeena said. "There's a road leading to the pond that turns off down the street a ways. That must be the way they came. I wonder what in the world has happened."

Mavis stood still, trying to see if she could identify Dale's pale head, but he was nowhere in sight. She wondered if she ought to worry about him. Then, out of the corner of her eye, Mavis saw a spot of pink and, turning, recognized Daisy Norris, the red flower in her hair drooping to one side. "You wait," Mavis said to Zeena, and Zeena looked too surprised to ask Mavis where she was going.

"You heard anything?" Mavis called out. Then she noticed Daisy had been crying. She touched her arm and said, "Poor thing, what in the world's the matter?"

Daisy choked back tears. Her dark brown eyes looked as if they were melting. "It's Miss Luna," she said. "She's dead. I heard the police talking to Mr. Clifford and Miss Kimberly upstairs." She looked as if she might begin to cry again. Then she clenched her fists and drew a little nearer to Mavis, as if she might give her some explanation of what had happened. "But that's not the worst of it," she said, eyes wide in disbelief. "They're claiming Mr. Jesse done it. They've taken him away!"

Chapter Four

Mavis decided to ride home with Dale. After she had gotten Daisy Norris quieted down ("Don't you worry," she had told her. "They won't keep Mr. Dixon long at the police station. Anybody in the world would know he wouldn't kill his own wife and then announce it to the world. You go on back to work."), she had been helping Zeena hang her costumes in the car when Dale came up behind her and asked her if she wanted a ride home.

"I wouldn't mind," she said quickly, before Zeena had a chance to say anything. Lord, Mavis thought, Zeena could hardly keep her mind on her driving on the way out—what *will* she be like on the way home after all that's happened?

But when Zeena spoke, her voice sounded brighter, almost relieved. "Well, Dale, honey, that would be real nice," she said. "I certainly don't mind taking Mavis right to her door, but it *is* a little bit out of the way, and I'm just *exhausted*. I can't wait to get home and get out of these tights and step into a hot bath." She batted her eyes at Dale, and Mavis knew she'd be all right. Soon as she got out of the tub, she'd be on the phone telling everybody in town what had happened.

"I'm sorry I didn't get to snap your picture this afternoon, Miz Zeena. The rains came before I had a chance."

Zeena smiled sweet as could be and said, "Well, there'll be a next time. Maybe you can come out to Cherry Hills Shopping Center when we open the new store there."

"I'll try," he said, and winked. "If the newspaper sends me, I'll come."

They left Zeena still arranging things in the back of the car, walked over to where Dale's little sports car was parked, and Dale helped Mavis inside. "I don't know whether I could do it by myself," she said every time she rode with him. "I have to practically fold up double as it is. These foreign things weren't made for old ladies." He laughed and said that she was only as old as she thought, and to just imagine she was out riding with her boyfriend and she wouldn't mind at all.

Dale pulled out of the parking lot up the drive to the road. While he was waiting for a break in the late afternoon traffic, Mavis looked over at the front entrance of Lakeview and saw that two police cars still sat there. Lord, she had almost forgotten what had happened. Once Dale had turned out into the traffic and they were going along and he still hadn't said anything, she asked, "Well?" and gave him a hard look.

"Well what?"

"You know. What happened over on the hill? I still can't imagine. Somebody back there said one of the patients was dead and they'd taken off her husband to jail. I know them— Mr. Jesse and Miss Luna Dixon—you do, too. You took a picture of them for the paper when the church gave them a fiftieth anniversary party."

"Now I remember," Dale said, snapping his fingers. "He *did* look familiar, but in the rain, and with so much going on, I didn't make the connection. Poor things. It was sad to see."

"Well, what *did* you see? Start at the beginning and tell me."

Dale took a breath. "You witnessed part," he said. "When they called out the attendants, I just followed right behind. Nobody said stop, and I probably would have gone right ahead even if they had. Those two disappeared for a minute or so, but then I came up on that little rise near the pond, and I could see 'most everything. It was strange, being over there and looking back, like I was in some sort of picture with everybody watching."

"We were," Mavis said, "or, at least, I was. I was a little worried, too, afraid something might happen to you."

Dale waved his hand. "Wasn't anything to worry about. I just felt odd, cut off. Once you go behind those trees, it's like country, just the pond and a marshy area by the dam and a road leading off through the bushes. You'd never know you were still in the city a-tall."

"But what was happening?" Mavis asked. "What were the others doing?"

"Well, when I got there, the attendants were still half carrying the old man under the armpits, like he was about worn-out and couldn't take another step without them. They were up on the hill by that rim of trees, just standing at first, but then one of them pointed and started running down toward the water. I couldn't see what he was pointing at, so I took off again. When I finally got there and looked down, I knew something bad had happened. 'Oh, dear Jesus,' the old man kept saying over and over. It was the most pitiful thing you've ever seen."

"Poor Mr. Jesse," Mavis said, shaking her head. "Where was Miss Luna?"

Dale gave Mavis a quick look, then turned back. "Darnell—he was one of the attendants, black guy—he was standing just at the edge of the water. When I looked, I could see a broken wheel sort of off to the side in some cattails growing in the marsh. I didn't see the body at first, but when Darnell bent down and reached out, I saw her and knew right away there was no hope. She was spread out there almost as if she floated on the water, face turned up, and Darnell didn't even try to pull her away. 'She's gone,' he called up to us, and Mr. Dixon sort of sagged down, fainted, I guess. Olin was the other attendant's name, looked strong as an ox, and he just picked up Mr. Dixon like he didn't weigh more than a bag of groceries, and I scrambled down the hill to where the body lay."

"What an awful thing—to end up in such a way." Mavis's vision blurred for a moment.

"Yes, ma'am, it was sad, her just lying there. Later, Jesse told us he had turned her over, and you could see traces of muddy water on her face, like some child's tears. A place on her forehead was already darkening, I reckon from where she fell. Darnell and I just looked at each other. There didn't seem to be much else to do.

"Then we heard a siren, far off in the distance at first— we weren't even sure it was headed to where we were at— but the sound came closer and then we could see the lights of the ambulance flashing through the trees. It stopped on the road that crosses over the dam, and two people got out almost in a trot, with a stretcher already swinging between them.

"I don't know what made me look down just that moment, but I did and saw my camera hanging around my neck, and I started taking pictures before the ambulance people could move the body away. I got several close up and then moved back a little to survey the scene. After all that's happened, maybe it wasn't such a bad idea, though I don't think the ambulance folks took to the idea too kindly. They shoved in front of me and Darnell, bent down and examined her, and then one of them asked, 'How long she been this way?' And when Darnell told them it had been at least fifteen minutes, maybe more, since Mr. Dixon had appeared on the hill shouting to the crowd, they said it wouldn't be any point in making heroic efforts, and they set down the stretcher on the ground and picked up the body with no strain at all.

"It was a sad sight, them carrying the body away. Her clothes were sopping wet and trailed after her on the ground, a pale rose color, though the fabric was streaked with mud. Up on the hill, Mr. Jesse gave a little cry, and he would have fallen if Olin hadn't held him up again. He struggled a little bit—thought he ought to go after her in the ambulance, I guess—but then he just sagged down like all the wind had been knocked out of him and he didn't have another ounce of strength left."

Dale's voice had grown softer and then was silent, as if the whole picture still sat before his eyes and he would see it again in his dreams. He always was a sensitive boy, Mavis thought. Why, when he was just a child, a scary tale from a storybook—even if it had a happy ending—would worry him for days, and if he saw a dead baby bird lying on the sidewalk, you'd have thought it was a member of the family, such tears were shed. Though he never talked about it, Mavis knew he still mourned his mother's death, and each year, after the two of them went out to the cemetery on the anniversary to put fresh flowers on her grave, it would be two or three days before he would be his bright self again. Mavis turned to him and patted him on the arm, and he gave her a little smile.

"I might as well tell you the rest," he said. "As soon as the ambulance drove away, a police car came up screeching. Darnell and I went back up to the hill to where Olin and Mr. Dixon were standing, and this detective got out of the car and came over. Another officer was driving. You could tell he was as mad as a wet hen just by the way he walked, short guy, stocky, built like a brick you-know-what—he sort of bounced along. I'd seen him a time or two down at the station when I was delivering pictures or something, and nobody much had anything good to say about him. Wilton Early's his name. I guess he thinks he's pretty important.

"He didn't exactly know who was who, so he asked just sort of generally, 'Where's the body? We got a call from the home there'd been a death.'

"Olin stood Mr. Dixon up a little straighter and said, 'They took it away. Didn't you see that ambulance when you came down the road?'

"Detective Early looked like he would bust a gut. 'You let them take the body *away*? Didn't you know it had to stay here? We've already called the lab people—what'll they do once they're here if there's no body?'

" 'I reckon they'll just have to look around there,' Darnell said, and scratched his head with his eyes open real wide. You just knew he was putting on an act.

''Then the detective looked at me. 'What about you?' he said. 'You didn't have enough sense, either, to tell them to wait?'

''I shrugged my shoulders, playing dumb like Darnell. 'I guess we didn't think past it was an accident. Poor man there, he ran all the way from here over to the home to get help for his wife. We surely didn't think he'd done anything to her. She was obviously gone by the time we got here, and we couldn't have interfered with the ambulance folks, anyway. They'd have called the police on *us* if we'd done that!'

'' 'What about him?' the detective said, pointing to Mr. Dixon, like he'd just seen him for the first time.

'' 'This here's Mr. Dixon,' Olin said, pushing him forward just a little bit, like he might have been some shy child. 'He's her husband, the lady who was here. He's the one came and got us.'

''The detective gave a sort of smart little laugh, then said, 'He left his wife lying here while he went running way off yonder to get help?'

'' 'Won't nothing much else he could do,' Darnell said. 'Ain't no telephone hanging on any of them trees, is there?'

''I thought the detective might haul off and hit him, but he just bounced up and down on the soles of his feet a minute trying to look taller, and that kind of got him calmed down. Finally he said to Mr. Dixon in a halfway decent voice, 'You tell me what happened out here before you left to get help. You take all the time you need.'

''Mr. Dixon didn't answer at first, still leaning against Olin, looking like he might start shivering any minute. But then he straightened up, his eyes cleared, and he took a deep breath. When he began to speak, his voice was cracked and dry, as if all that hollering had rubbed his throat raw. It was painful to hear, just the sound of it. And *what* he had to say was even more painful.

'' 'It had started out to be such a nice day,' he said. His wife woke up real perky, and for a minute or two, he thought, she seemed to know him—got a real big smile on her face when he wished her a good morning. 'Not that she's ever any trial, mind you,' he told us right quick, 'but she has her good days and bad, like most folks.' After that, he'd gotten her dressed up in a brand-new outfit his niece had gone shopping for, pants and top in a rose color she'd always liked before she got sick. When they went over to the dining room, one of the ladies there said didn't she look *pretty*, and Miss Luna seemed to get a big kick out of that. She ate well, even wanted a second piece of toast, and he told her, joking, that she was going to get fat as a pig. Even though he knew it wasn't true, he said, the thought went through his head, Maybe she's getting a little better, maybe it won't end up so bad after all.

"After breakfast, he rolled Miss Luna out onto the veranda and let her sit while he read the paper. It was real peaceful there, quiet, with birds singing in the trees, and Miss Luna seemed content for a while. But then cars began to pull up, people started to set up the tables for the festival, they were trying out the sound system, and she got kind of restless. 'Let's take a walk,' he told her, and he put away the paper and wheeled her down the lawn past the employees' parking lot out across the field to the pond. They could look back and see all the activity, he said, but couldn't hear a thing, like watching a picture on TV without the sound.

"They stayed there an hour or more, didn't go back for lunch. It was only going to be sandwiches, anyway, because of the festival, and he always carried a few treats for Miss Luna in a bag on the back of her chair—a candy bar, some crackers. He sat down on the grass beside her chair, and they ate. 'It's just like old times,' he said he told her, 'like being up at Lake Junaluska and having a picnic.' She seemed to know the name—*Junaluska*—and gave him a real hard look when he said it.

"That was when Mr. Dixon noticed the clouds rising up behind them. It looked like it might pour, and there they were without an umbrella or anything. He jumped up, put away the little bits of food they had left, and then turned

Miss Luna's chair back toward the home. But all at once, he said, she made the most pitiful sounds, like a baby crying, and put her hands on the wheels of the chair so that he was afraid to move it, afraid he'd scrape her palms. 'All right,' he told her, 'we'll take a little stroll around the pond as far as the dam, but then we've got to get back.' She gave him a big smile, and he knew that's what she wanted all the time.

"It was slow, pushing her up the hill to where the trees are, and he was sweating by the time he got there. 'Lord, let me get a rest,' he said out loud, and then took out his handkerchief to wipe his face. That's when it happened. He let go of the chair, closed his eyes just one minute, and then when he opened them again, Miss Luna was flying down the hill. Maybe he didn't lock the wheels, maybe she unlocked them herself—he didn't know. All he remembered was seeing her rolling faster and faster toward the pond, that big smile still on her face, like she was a child again, riding some ride at the fair.

"He got to her as soon as he could, but by then the chair had already flipped over, one wheel still spinning, and Miss Luna was lying with her face down in the water. He turned her over and called her name, but she didn't answer. He couldn't pick her up. Since she got sick, she'd put on a few pounds, and he knew he'd never get her back to the home, even if he could lift her, soaking wet, out of the pond. 'It was awful, leaving her there,' he said, but he couldn't think of anything else to do. So he kissed her and told her, 'Honey, I'll be right back,' and then lit out across the hill, headed for the crowd and calling out. But the rain caught him like some hard slap across his shoulders, and it wasn't until the storm was over that he could make anybody understand. By then, it was too late."

Dale gave a deep sigh, then looked over at Mavis. A ray of late afternoon sun slanted through the window of the car and shone directly in her eyes, and she knew that it illumined her tears. "If that's not the saddest story I ever heard," she said. "That poor man."

"We thought so, too, standing out there on the hill with Mr. Dixon. Even that detective, Wilton Early, was quiet for a minute or two before he started up again. Then he asked, 'It looked that way to you? The body, I mean? Is that how you found it before those fools in the ambulance took it away?'

"He looked from one of us to the other, waiting, and finally Darnell pointed to me and said, 'Him and me went down to the pond while Olin held on to Mr. Jesse up here. It was like he said, Miss Luna lying there just at the edge of the water with her face turned up to the sky. Ain't that right?'

"Mr. Dixon answered him back real quietly. 'Yessir.' You could hear in his voice how tired he was getting.

"Wilton Early just couldn't let go. 'But she'd just rolled down the hill that minute and turned over, right?'

"Mr. Dixon answered him, 'Yessir,' again.

"The detective looked at us. 'That don't make any sense a-tall,' he said. 'Nobody could have drowned in that short a time.'

" 'Maybe it wasn't no drowning,' Darnell said.

"That perked Wilton Early right up. 'What do you mean?' he asked.

"Darnell put his hands in his pockets and shrugged his shoulders. 'Had a bump on her forehead, already turning dark. Must have happened when she fell. A rock.'

"The detective looked like he was going to ask him something else, but then all of a sudden he got this funny look on his face, and he bent over toward Mr. Dixon again. 'What was wrong with your wife?' he asked. 'Why was she in a wheelchair to start with?'

"Mr. Dixon answered him without a pause. 'She had Alzheimer's,' he said. 'She wasn't able to get around on her own anymore.'

" 'She was getting worse then?' I don't know how he did

it, but that Detective Early almost made those words sound obscene.

"Mr. Dixon looked down, then said, 'Yes, you could tell. Oh, sometimes I fooled myself, like I said, but I knew she drifted away a little more each day. In her mind, that is—physically she was in fine shape, the doctor said. Could have lived for years.'

" 'That bother you, the idea she'd keep on getting worse but still live on?' Detective Early kept at Mr. Dixon like a dog gnawing a bone. It was plain as day he was after something, but we didn't know what until he asked his next question even before giving Mr. Dixon a chance to reply.

" 'Did you decide to do something about that on your own?' he said, thrusting his face into Mr. Dixon's. 'Maybe you just couldn't stand it anymore and decided she'd be better off dead.' He pulled back a little bit and looked at us. 'There are stories about that kind of thing in the paper all the time,' he said. 'Mercy killing. Some people think it's just fine, but it's still murder, and folks still get charged for it. What about it, Mr. Dixon? You roll our wife out here and decide to push her down the hill while all the commotion was going on back at the home? Might as well tell us if you did.'

"Well, you should have seen Mr. Dixon, bless his soul. He perked up like something that's run down and then been wound up again. I thought he was going to punch that detective right in the face. 'Don't you dare say such a thing!' he shouted, pushing away from Olin, who was so surprised he didn't even try to hold him back. 'I love my wife with all my heart, have for over fifty years. She wasn't in no pain, wasn't no bother to anyone, least of all me. Why would I want to kill her? She was all I had. I'd have killed myself before I'd have harmed a hair on her head.'

"For just a minute, Detective Early might have felt ashamed—his face kind of flushed. But then he rocked back on his heels and said, 'I'm sorry, sir, but we'll have to take you down to city hall and get a sworn statement. You, too, maybe,' he said to the three of us. 'We'll call later if we want you to come down.'

" 'You taking Mr. Jesse away right now?' Darnell asked.

" 'Might as well get it over with,' Detective Early answered. He took hold of Mr. Dixon's arm, and Mr. Dixon didn't resist. For a minute I thought Olin might hold on to him, but he looked at me and shrugged his shoulders and patted Mr. Dixon on the back.

" 'Don't you worry,' he said to Mr. Dixon. 'They ain't got no reason a-tall to hold you. You'll be back in time for supper.' Mr. Dixon didn't answer but walked beside Detective Early over to the car; the two of them got in the backseat, and the driver turned around and took off back up the road with the siren blaring. Before we even had a chance to say to each other wasn't it awful what happened, a van came down the road and four or five lab people piled out. We showed them where the body had been and told them a little bit about what had happened, and then Olin and Darnell and I just came on back to the home. There didn't seem to be much else to do.' '

Mavis shook her head. "I just can't believe it," she said. "That detective taking away poor Mr. Jesse Dixon. Why, anybody in the world would know he couldn't have murdered his wife, much as he loved her. And *he'll* probably die of pneumonia if he doesn't get some dry clothes on soon. Talk about police brutality—I've got a good mind to write a letter to the paper.''

"It just might help." Dale smiled at her. "And your tonight's paper is lying right up there on your walkway.''

Mavis looked out the window. She had been so upset, she hadn't realized that they had driven up to her house and stopped in front. "Lordy, I'd better calm down.'' Reaching in the backseat for her package, gathering up her pocketbook and gloves, she turned to open the door. Then she had an idea. "Why don't you come on in," she said to Dale. "I'll fix us a little supper.''

"That would be too much bother," Dale said.

"No bother a-tall or I wouldn't have asked you. But I expect you've got something better to do than spend the evening with an old woman."

"Shoot," he said, taking the keys out of the ignition. "I can't think of anybody I'd rather spend it with. And you're a lot younger than plenty of people I know half your age. Come on."

Chapter
Five

In spite of all that had happened the day before, Mavis awoke refreshed the next morning, no dreams to mar her sleep. When she had asked Dale to supper, she had expected him to run off as soon as they ate, but he had stayed till nearly bedtime, talking about poor Mr. Jesse Dixon.

Mavis had fixed a good meal. Before she had started to get ready to go out to the festival with Zeena, she had taken a chicken out of the freezer to thaw, and she had fried it and made pan gravy and mashed potatoes, about Dale's most favorite thing to eat in the whole wide world. While she was cooking, he had sat at the kitchen table stringing some late pole beans she'd found at the store, and it had seemed like old times, the two of them there together. When he was just a little child and Florence would drop him off for the day to play with Mavis's daughter, Dale would want to help her cook. "Show me," he'd say, and she'd let him stir a pot or scrub a potato. Her daughter never took any notice at all—funny how things turned out. He had eaten two helpings of everything and would have had a third dish of ice cream if she hadn't told him he was going to get as fat as a pig. "Lord forbid!" he had said, and pushed his bowl away.

They had sat, then, at the table till long after dark, drinking coffee and discussing what had happened. Over the years, they had shared mystery novels with each other and pored over newspaper articles of real crimes, looking for clues and coming up with explanations of their own. But this time it was such a sad story that they hadn't even felt like speculating on what had happened. Mr. Dixon was a good man. . . . Surely he wouldn't have done anything to his wife. It was all in that detective's head. "Still and all," Dale had finally said, "I've got to get those pictures developed. They might help, and the paper will certainly want to use one for a story." He had gotten up from the table, kissed Mavis on the forehead, said in a teasing voice, "I thank you kindly for the meal," and then gone out the front door. She had watched him through the window until he had gotten into his car and driven off, and then she had switched off the porch light.

The dishes hadn't taken long, and after she had finished them and undressed, Mavis had listened to the eleven-o'clock news. The big story was that two tornadoes had touched down in neighboring counties (as usual, turning over a bunch of trailers and blowing off a few roofs) at almost exactly the same time that the rains had flooded out the Fall Festival at Lakeview. Lord, they'd been lucky. At the end of the broadcast, they had mentioned Miss Luna's death briefly, just to say that there had been an accident at the home and the police were still investigating, not a word about Mr. Jesse. After she had gotten into bed and said her prayers, Mavis had added a special little prayer for him, poor man, all alone in his grief, or worse, sitting in a jail cell downtown.

And now, even though the thought of him had not disturbed her sleep the night before, she could not get Mr. Jesse Dixon out of her mind. As soon as she had gotten up and put the coffee on, she went to the front door, checked to see if anyone was about (since she was still in her robe), and then quickly opened the door and picked up the paper from the stoop. It came encased in a blue plastic bag, dry and neatly folded, delivered by someone in a car she'd never seen; and though that was much to be preferred over scrambling around beneath damp shrubbery to find the paper wadded up there, thrown by some neighborhood boy on a bike, she wondered where children would learn some sense of responsibility with no more chance for them to have a paper route. No wonder so many of them ended up on drugs.

It was spread all over the front page of the paper: WOMAN DIES MYSTERIOUSLY AT BAZAAR, HUSBAND HELD. So they had put poor Mr. Jesse Dixon in jail after all. Shaking her head at the shame of it, she walked back to the kitchen, peering closely at the paper to see the details of the photograph next to the story. The pond was there, a fringe of trees beyond, and the upturned wheelchair. On the marshy edge lay Miss Luna's body, half-hidden, thank goodness, by a stand of cattails. What an awful way for such a sweet lady to end her days.

Mavis didn't feel like reading the story just yet. Pouring herself a cup of coffee, she took a sip, then set down the cup and began to fix her breakfast. Once a week she allowed herself a real treat—eggs, bacon, butter on her toast—completely different from her usual breakfast of cereal with skim milk and sometimes a little fruit. She didn't tell her doctor. You're in good health, keep it that way, he'd say with a frown. But she couldn't give up *everything*. What was the use of living if you couldn't indulge in a few of life's little pleasures?

She sat down at the table with the plate in front of her. The eggs had turned out perfectly, scrambled light and foamy; the bacon wasn't too crisp. With the paper propped up beside her, she ate her first bite and then began to read:

Yesterday, at the annual Fall Festival Bazaar of the Lakeview Nursing Home, one of the residents, Mrs. Luna Dixon, met her death. According to the woman's husband, Mr. Jesse Dixon, also a resident, he had taken his wife in her wheelchair to a secluded area behind Lakeview where a small pond is located. Mr. Dixon told police that he let go of his wife's chair for just a brief period and it went careening down the hill to the pond, where it turned over and the victim was thrown out into the water. As soon as he could get to her, Mr. Dixon claims, he turned his wife over but was unable to revive her. At that point, he hurried back to the festivities at Lakeview and returned with two attendants and a photographer for this paper, who determined that Mrs. Dixon was dead.

Detective Wilton Early, who was the first to arrive on the scene after the police were called, was quoted as saying that death by drowning in so short a time was unlikely, and since the body bore other marks, Mr. Dixon was being held in the city jail until a complete investigation could be made. According to Lieutenant Early, Mr. Dixon has refused to have a lawyer or to answer any further questions. An autopsy has been scheduled.

Mavis put a spoonful of strawberry preserves on her last bite of toast, ate it, and sighed. She could just see Mr. Jesse down at the jail behind bars, and she felt guilty about indulging herself. Why, an accident like that could happen to anybody, even her and John, though she was glad she had never been a burden to him. Why did the police think it was murder? Surely by now they would have learned what fine church folks the Dixons had been all their lives, how devoted they had been to each other. They must be blind as bats.

Mavis got up and began to wash the dishes at the sink, only half-aware of what she was doing, her mind still on Mr. Jesse. When a cup slipped from her hand and would have been broken if she hadn't caught it just in time, she said aloud, "I just can't stand it," but smiled, knowing at that moment exactly what she was going to do. Drying her hands, she went over to the cabinet where she stored her cookbooks, pulled down the one in which she kept the clippings she had collected over the years, and began to flip the pages.

The cake had turned out well. Mavis looked at it cooling on the counter. Lemon juice and grated rind—that was the secret. Otherwise, it would be just a plain pound cake. Mavis had discovered the recipe years ago in a magazine, and anytime she served it, she got compliments. Not too rich, easy to digest—it would be the perfect thing for Mr. Jesse. Maybe it would cheer him up. She had never seen a man yet who didn't like sweets. Lord knows what they gave the prisoners down at the jail to eat—greasy hamburger and french fries, most likely, with no sign of a vegetable on the plate. She'd give the cake to Charles Morgan, the one person she knew on the police force. At least *he* wouldn't think she'd baked a file in it to help Mr. Jesse escape.

She dressed quickly. When she had gone out earlier for the paper, she could tell the day would be warm, surprising since Halloween was next week, so she chose a dark cotton dress, burgundy and blue, and low-heeled patent leather shoes. With just a dab of lipstick and her hair tucked under a sheer net that was hardly visible, she was ready to go. She put the cake in a tin (from Christmas, but that was all she had), set it carefully in a shopping bag she had saved from her last trip to the mall, and walked out the front door. My, what a pretty day, she thought, the sun shining, the trees dappled with gold. She took it as a sign from the Lord that she was doing the right thing.

The bus stop was just up the street. No one was about. What few of the old neighbors who were left sat inside all day with their noses stuck to the TV set, and the young folks who had moved into the neighborhood all worked. Only on weekends did Mavis ever hear the sound of children's voices, and she thought how sad it must be for them to be dropped off each morning at a baby-sitter's and then to be picked up by a tired mama or daddy each night. At least she had the memory of all her child's young days. There was always something to be thankful for.

In less than five minutes the bus came, and Mavis climbed up, glad she didn't have to stand too long in her dress-up shoes. To her surprise, the driver said, "Afternoon, ma'am," and didn't sit frowning while she fumbled in her purse to find her senior citizen's discount card. Except for one man on a rear seat who looked to be sound asleep, Mavis was the only person on the bus, and she sat just behind the driver in case the man was drunk and woke up and got rowdy.

Downtown, too, seemed nearly deserted. On the benches the city had installed when they tried to make Main Street into a mall, a few people who looked as if they might be homeless sat around, and though she felt sorry for them, they frightened her a little, and she was never sure whether or not she should give them some change. Half the ladies she knew didn't go downtown anymore for that very reason—afraid they'd be attacked. Mavis wasn't to that point yet. She could yell even if she couldn't run very fast.

She went upstairs to Charles Morgan's office in the city hall building, smiling as she passed an officer on duty who was a perfect stranger to her, though he didn't try to stop her. The hallway was shadowy and cool after the warmth outside, and she waited a moment for her eyes to adjust. Then she walked to the clouded glass door that had LIEUTEN-ANT CHARLES MORGAN, DETECTIVE printed on it in big black letters, knocked, and went in without waiting for an answer. "Well, my goodness, Miz Mavis, what brings you down here?" Charles Morgan said, sitting up so suddenly from his reared-back position that his desk chair squawked. "This is a real nice surprise."

Mavis had known Charles since he was a little boy. Back when she taught a Sunday-school class in the junior department down at the church, he was one of her pupils, a large-boned, clumsy child, always bigger than the other boys. They seemed neither to especially like him nor to exclude him, and though his wide face seldom had a smile, he was never one to start real trouble. Later, after he'd come back from the army only to have to take care of his parents till they died, Mavis would see him at church occasionally and they would speak. He always seemed remote then, his eyes a little sad. No doubt about the reason—he'd been left standing at the altar by the one girl who had been able to bring a little life to his face, and after she had run off to seek fame and fortune, he became the old Charles again.

"Don't you get up," Mavis said as she pulled up a chair to Charles's desk, wiping off the seat before she sat down. She set the shopping bag with the cake carefully beside her on the floor. If Charles noticed it, he didn't let on, bending toward Mavis with his elbows planted on the surface of the desk. "Well, now, it's been a long time, hasn't it?" Mavis said. "I haven't seen you down at church in a month of Sundays."

Charles gave what, for him, was a smile and said, "Still keeping an eye on us, aren't you? When I was little, if I ever whispered in church, I'd look up and expect to see you watching me. You didn't miss a thing."

Mavis laughed. "Well, I miss a lot these days. Age does that to you. I can barely keep up with my own self, much less watch over anybody else."

Charles's lips turned up just slightly at the edges again. He waited for a minute or so and then said, "What brings you down here to see me? I expect it's not just a friendly call to ask me why I haven't been in church lately."

Mavis felt herself about to blush. "Well, I guess I *am* sort of trying to take care of somebody else's business." She looked down at the shopping bag on the floor. "It's that Mr. Jesse Dixon. I know he's been locked up. It was in the paper this morning. I was out at the bazaar yesterday when it all happened, and I can tell you right now, there's no reason in the world to have Mr. Jesse sitting in a jail cell."

Charles's eyes brightened. "Death seems to follow you around, doesn't it, Miz Mavis?"

"Charles Morgan, what an awful thing to say! I was out there on a charitable mission, and you accuse me of bringing death."

"I'm sorry," Charles Morgan said. "I shouldn't tease about such a thing. But *were* you involved?"

Mavis leaned back in her chair and placed her pocketbook on her knees. "Only indirectly," she said. "My nephew, Dale, was out there taking pictures for the paper—you know him—and he was one of the ones who found the body after Mr. Jesse came over the hill yelling for help. He took pictures of that, too."

"I've heard." Charles Morgan shook his head. "Lucky he was there since I guess everything else got messed up, the ambulance attendants taking the body away and all."

"How were they to know? From what Dale said, it sure looked like an accident. In fact, about the only person who thinks it wasn't seems to be that police lieutenant—I've forgotten his name. Too bad you weren't there.''

"I was off duty for a change. And Wilton Early isn't so bad.''

Mavis sniffed. "Dale indicated that he was just a little too big for his britches.''

"He's young, wants to make a good impression.'' Charles leaned back and put his hands behind his head. "In a little while he'll mellow out. You have to on this job or it'll get to you in the end.''

Mavis wasn't sure she wanted to ask him any more about what he meant, and she changed the subject. "What are they going to do with him? Mr. Jesse, I mean.''

"Nothing right now. They're just holding him. He hasn't been very cooperative. Just sits there, they say, and claims it was an accident, but it doesn't make sense.''

"Why not?''

Charles bent forward again, picked up a pencil from the desk, and began to doodle on a pad there. "Well, if she drowned—and that seems to be the likeliest thing to have happened—it couldn't have been in just that little bit of time Mr. Dixon says passed before he got down the hill and turned his wife over. And if it turns out that bruise on her head comes from a deliberate blow, rather than the fall, it's going to look even worse for him. We'll just have to wait for the autopsy report.''

"Well, I still don't believe Mr. Jesse would ever do anything to his wife.'' Mavis gave her pocketbook a little shake. "They were just devoted to each other. Anybody who ever knew them would tell you that.''

"That's what *she* says.''

"Who?''

"Mr. Jesse's niece. She's his only kin. She was downstairs visiting him a while ago when I came in.''

"My goodness,'' Mavis said, a little flustered. She had gone to all the effort of making Mr. Jesse a cake, and here he was having all sorts of visitors, no doubt bringing food. She tucked up the hair on the back of her neck that had escaped from the net. "Well, I guess I'll give you this," she said, pointing to the bag on the floor. She started to get up.

"What is it?" Charles leaned farther forward across the desk to see.

"Just a little something for Mr. Jesse. A cake. I thought he might be hungry."

Charles stood up straighter and made a little coughing sound that Mavis realized was an outright laugh. "Well, you *do* take care of folks, don't you? Come on," he said. "You carry that cake down yourself. Mr. Jesse isn't such a dangerous criminal." He walked around the desk, picked up the shopping bag, and took Mavis by the arm.

They passed only one other person in the hallway outside, a woman wearing a loud print dress and too much jewelry, who called out, "Afternoon," to Charles Morgan but didn't look at Mavis. Once inside the elevator, Charles said, "I hope you won't hear anything that shocks you down there. Some of the men can talk kind of rough."

"I've lived long enough to have heard just about everything," Mavis said. "Even back when you were little, I knew what you boys whispered to each other. I wasn't shocked."

Charles gave his strange laugh again and opened the door.

Mavis wasn't sure what she expected. On TV, police stations always seemed to be such frantic places, people running around and criminals being dragged away. But here it looked not much different from some business offices—a wide hall; on one side a long, narrow room with a few desks where two men sat working; on the other a barred door leading to cells beyond. A stale odor of perspiration and cigarette smoke filled the air, and Mavis would have been careful had she been invited to sit down.

Just then a policeman in uniform appeared behind the bars and began to unlock the door. He came through, apparently unaware of Mavis and Charles at first, but then looked up and smiled broadly, his face bright red. Mavis knew he drank. "Hey there," he said, and looked as if he might have recognized Mavis, but she knew she had never seen him before in her life. "Who's your lady friend?" he asked Charles, but before Charles could answer, the policeman turned and stood aside so that someone could pass him out of the barred doorway.

Well, isn't she the prettiest *thing*! was Mavis's first reaction. The woman who stood there was tall, slim, dressed in a soft blue sweater and skirt to match, dark hair cut short but naturally curly so that it swung in soft waves around her head, like some heavy flower on a stem. Her eyes were the same blue as her sweater, and though they glistened even here beneath the dulling fluorescent lights, they looked sad to Mavis—the brightness possibly the remnants of tears. "Miss Warren," Charles said when he saw her, and his voice was as warm as Mavis had ever heard it before.

"Detective Morgan," the woman said. "I didn't realize I would see you again so soon." She smiled, and Mavis thought she saw the sadness in her eyes ease a little.

"This is Miz Lashley, Mavis Lashley," Charles said. He set down the shopping bag he was still carrying and motioned toward Mavis at his side.

"I'm real happy to meet you," Mavis said, extending her hand. "I bet you're Mr. Jesse's niece. Charles was just talking about you."

"I'm Elizabeth Warren," she said, and touched Mavis's hand with cool fingertips. "You knew them? My aunt and uncle?"

Mavis smiled. "I sure did, went to the same church. But everybody in Markham knew Mr. Jesse and Miss Luna. That article they had about them in the paper a few years ago was right inspiring."

"I know. Whoever would have thought it would end this way?" Elizabeth Warren looked down, silent for a moment, then looked up again. Charles moved toward her.

"Miz Mavis made a cake for your uncle," he said. He pointed to the bag. "I'm sure it'll be good. Miz Mavis always was a fine cook."

"It's not much," Mavis said, trying not to look too pleased. "I just thought it might make him feel better. I'm sure the food here isn't fit to eat."

Elizabeth reached out and touched Mavis on the arm, then drew back as if she had been too forward. "That was so sweet of you," she said. "I bet Uncle Jesse hasn't eaten anything a-tall. He'll appreciate it."

"You want to take it inside?" Charles looked at Mavis.

She shook her head no. "I guess not this time. Let the poor man have his privacy. I don't know if I could find words to say standing in a jail cell."

Charles picked up the bag and gave it to the policeman who still stood there. "Here," he said, "take that to Mr. Dixon, and if he wants a knife to cut it, you get him one. But watch and take it back when he gets through. We don't want him doing anything to himself."

"Oh, Lord!" Elizabeth said with a stricken look. She put her hand up to her face. "I never thought of that. It would be just awful!" Charles looked as if he, too, was in pain, standing there with his long arms dangling.

Well, *do* something, Mavis wanted to tell him, but he didn't move, so Mavis went over to Elizabeth and put her arm around her shoulders. "It'll be all right, honey. Don't you worry." With a sudden inspiration, she motioned with her head for Charles to move away and said to Elizabeth, "Why don't you and I go have us a little something to eat. Burke's Department Store is just up the street. They have the nicest little sandwiches, and we can have some tea. How about that?"

Mavis felt Elizabeth's shoulders relax. "I'd like it," she said, and smiled. Charles looked wistfully at them from the cell door.

Chapter Six

Mavis had shopped at Burke's Department Store since before she was married. Back when old Mr. Ed Burke was alive, he pranced around the store with a fresh boutonniere in his lapel every day, greeting ladies with a big, "Well, how are *you* today, ma'am?" and the store had remained a family institution, despite offers from the big chains to buy it out. His sons still strolled the floors with ready smiles, and the clerks, too, seemed like family, employed there for years, so different from the shops out at the mall, where you practically had to knock down some teenager to get them to wait on you. As she walked through the main floor to the elevator with Elizabeth Warren at her side, nodding to people she knew and acknowledging their smiles, Mavis felt her spirits lift. The jail had been so depressing. No wonder poor Elizabeth had tears in her eyes.

"It won't be crowded this time of day," she said to Elizabeth as she pushed the button for the third floor. "Not many people shop downtown anymore, and though they do a good business at lunchtime, what with all the office buildings around, about the only folks you'll ever see at night are senior citizens who come in for the Early Bird Special. And they don't linger. With so much meanness around, they want to get home before dark."

Elizabeth smiled. "I'm glad you invited me," she said. "Lunchtime just slipped by, I was so worried about Uncle Jesse. Now I'm famished."

54

"Well, I could eat a little something, too. I just nibbled while I was making the cake since I'd had a big breakfast. I'm surprised I didn't get a headache, not eating like that."

They moved through the line. "Can I help you, ma'am?" the ladies behind the counter all said, just as nice as could be. Mavis saw one of the Burke boys—gray-haired now, he looked a lot like his daddy—checking on the iced-tea container, and she smiled at him and waved. "These salads look good," she said to Elizabeth, selecting a plate with a large portion of chicken salad surrounded by slices of hard-boiled egg and tomato wedges. "They have the best blueberry muffins you ever put in your mouth, and you can have as many cups of coffee as you want. This'll be enough for me."

At the cashier's desk, Elizabeth tried to pay for Mavis's food, but Mavis told her, "You'll do no such thing. I invited you, and it's going to be my treat. Now, you just put your money away." Mavis paid the woman at the counter, then led the way to a table in the No Smoking section by the wall. She didn't want anyone eavesdropping on their conversation.

They ate in silence for a little while. Elizabeth had gotten a big chef's salad, the blueberry muffins, as well as a big piece of pecan pie (it did look good, but Mavis thought it might be too rich for her digestion), and she ate in quick little bites. Poor thing, Mavis thought, she was nearly starved. Well, she'll feel better now with something in her stomach.

Elizabeth seemed to know what Mavis was thinking. She laid down her fork and said, "Excuse my manners. I guess I was hungrier than I'd thought. When Uncle Jesse called this morning, I was just getting myself a cup of coffee, and I was in such a hurry to get down to the jail to see him, I didn't take time to have anything else."

"You didn't know till then?"

"No, ma'am. I was doing some work around the house last night, so I didn't hear the news, and the morning paper was still lying outside the door when the phone rang. I didn't know who in the world it could be calling that early. I still can't believe it, him being held for Aunt

Luna's death. He'd be the last person in the world who'd do anything to harm her.''

"Don't you worry, honey," Mavis said, buttering a piece of muffin. "He'll be out in no time. Everybody knows it was an accident.''

"Not that policeman, the one who's investigating. He asked me some questions, and he made it sound just like Uncle Jesse was halfway to the electric chair.'' Elizabeth's eyes sparkled again. She sighed. "I haven't even *thought* about Aunt Luna, about arranging for the funeral and all. They'll release the body after the autopsy.''

Mavis reached over and patted Elizabeth's arm. "You'll have a lot of help. Just call the preacher, and he'll get things going. Why, they were so good to so many people over the years, everybody will want to do something to pay them back.''

Elizabeth looked away for a moment, then brushed her eyes with her napkin. "They were certainly good to *me*,'' she said. "Actually, they're my *great*-aunt and uncle. My mother was Aunt Luna's sister's daughter. Mama died when I was young, and Uncle Jesse and Aunt Luna sort of adopted me, especially in the summertime. We lived up in the mountains, my daddy and I, but every spring we'd get a letter with a bus ticket in it for me to come here to spend the summer. I couldn't have been happier, and I guess it was a relief for my daddy to have a growing-up girl off his hands for a little while.''

"They always did love children," Mavis said. "Couldn't have any of their own." She became silent. In her mind she saw a vision of a young Elizabeth Warren in a thin summer dress running across a hot, bright field with hair ribbons streaming behind her, seeds and insects scattering from her feet, and her own daughter's face merged with Elizabeth's features. She almost gasped: This might have been her daughter, all grown-up and sitting here with her now. A woman with her own life, losses, hopes—if it hadn't been for a skinny teenager in a rattletrap car who had snapped out her life before Mavis even had a chance to scream, Watch out!

"You all right, ma'am?" Mavis could see Elizabeth's blue eyes peering at her.

"Oh, yes," she said, taking a drink of water. "I was just thinking about the past."

Elizabeth smiled. "I have so many nice memories of those summers—we had such good times. Uncle Jesse and Aunt Luna would take me out to the park to ride on the merry-go-round, and sometimes they would let me swim in the pool, though I know they were always a little worried, afraid something might happen to me. When the county fair came, we'd spend a day out at the fairgrounds, and Uncle Jesse would take me on all the rides. 'Never get me on one of those things,' Aunt Luna would say, and Uncle Jesse would tease her, call her a fraidycat, but she'd stand her ground. If we passed one of the girlie shows, she'd tell us, 'Keep moving,' and wouldn't even answer Uncle Jesse when he'd say, 'Hold on, let me get an eyeful of those hootchy-kootchy girls,' and laugh up a breeze. By the time we would get home at night, I'd be worn out, asleep before I touched the bed."

They talked on. Elizabeth told Mavis how, after she came to Markham to go to the university, Jesse and Luna Dixon had looked after her—invited her to dinner several times a week, made her take food home, even offered to do her laundry. And after her father died, they were even closer. "Sometimes I felt guilty that I couldn't do more for them," she said. "But if I mentioned it, they'd only say, 'Your just being here brightens up our days. Don't you worry about anything else.' "

"You're at the university?"

"Yes, ma'am. In my second year in the social work program. In a way, Uncle Jesse and Aunt Luna are responsible for that, too."

"What do you mean?"

"Oh, they were always involved, trying to help people. Every time I was at their house, I'd hear some pitiful story sad enough to make your heart break. I guess I felt that I had to try to help others, too, and that seemed a good way."

"I certainly hope you can help your poor uncle."

Elizabeth sat back, fiddling with her fork. She looked worried. "I don't know," she said. "He's got a real stubborn streak. Aunt Luna used to say it was his only fault. He's not being very cooperative."

"Why? What does he say?"

"Probably no more than what you've read in the paper. Says he took Aunt Luna out behind the home for a little ride in her chair to keep her away from all the excitement of the bazaar. He let go just a minute, she went flying down the hill, and the chair turned over so that she fell into the edge of the pond. When he couldn't revive her, he went for help. Every time he gets to that point, he begins to cry, and I don't have the heart to keep on after him."

Elizabeth sat up straighter, her hands balled into fists. "But I know he didn't kill her!" she said. "That detective is trying to make it out to be a mercy killing, but a thought like that would never cross Uncle Jesse's mind. He's protected her for so long. Why, he kept what was wrong with her even from me as long as he could. I'd see that she'd forget things, little things like where something was kept, but I didn't think much about it. After a while, it became more noticeable, but Uncle Jesse would cover up for her, try to give her clues about what to say. Finally, when I came in one day and she didn't know my name, he had to tell me. It was one of the saddest days of my life, like losing my mother all over again. That was when Uncle Jesse decided to sell the house and move out to Lakeview."

"Why was that?"

"He was beginning to see there'd come a time when he couldn't handle her alone, and a lot of places won't take somebody in if they're in too bad a shape to start with. He hated to sell the house, though. They'd worked for it so many years, and it had a lot of memories attached. For me, too—I'd spent half my life there, seemed like."

"He couldn't keep the house?"

"No, he needed the money. That's part of the deal out at Lakeview—you sign over all your assets, and they promise to take care of you as long as you live. I guess that's some sort of guarantee, but I'm not sure I would want it.''

Mavis shook her head from side to side. "Me either!" she said, thinking how awful it would be to give up everything you owned and be at somebody else's mercy. "I hope I never come to that.''

"Uncle Jesse didn't complain all that much. They had their own little apartment and could use their own furniture if they wanted to. Of course, not everything would fit—forty years in one house and you accumulate a lot of stuff. But Uncle Jesse had his lounger, and Aunt Luna had her sewing table—not that she could do much anymore—and they bought this huge TV set that took up half the living room. Aunt Luna soon got to the point where the sound seemed to hurt her ears, so she would look at the picture in silence half the time while Uncle Jesse read the paper. It could have been worse. Uncle Jesse couldn't boil hot water, and at Lakeview they got three good meals every day, and medical care if they needed it. Seemed like they were set for a while, until all this happened.''

"Sometimes it's hard to understand the ways of the Lord," Mavis said. "We just have to trust that we are in his hands and he knows best.''

Elizabeth didn't answer. She put her napkin on the table. "I reckon we'd better be going," she said. "Can I give you a ride home?''

"Oh, no, you don't need to bother," Mavis said. "It's probably out of your way.''

"Well, you don't know that for a fact, and even if it is, I don't mind. All I've got to go home to is an empty apartment and a lot of studying for a course I don't even like.''

Mavis looked at her watch. It would be the beginning of rush hour, and the bus would probably be packed. Lord knows, nobody would get up and offer her a seat, no matter how hard she stared at them. "All right," she said, and smiled. "I accept.''

They spoke little on the way home. Elizabeth turned on the radio to get the news, but there was nothing about Luna

Dixon's death. When they got to Mavis's house, Elizabeth stopped, then leaned over and took Mavis's hand for a moment. "Thank you so much for all you've done," she said, "the cake and everything. And for listening to me. With Aunt Luna gone and Uncle Jesse locked up, I don't have anyone around to talk to who's like family. Even though I haven't known you more than a few hours, you seem like somebody I can trust. I appreciate that."

"Lord, honey, I wish I could do more. You call if you want to talk again. And I'll say a special prayer tonight for Mr. Jesse and Miss Luna. Maybe the Lord will help." Mavis got out of the car, went up the walkway, then climbed slowly up the front steps. At the top, she turned back toward the street just as Elizabeth was pulling away. Mavis raised her hand in a final gesture, and Elizabeth smiled back and waved in return.

For a moment she stood there, watching the sun drop golden behind the treetops. Now, isn't she about the *nicest* thing you've ever met? she asked herself. They don't make girls much like that anymore. All of a sudden Charles Morgan's face loomed in front of her against the light. She laughed aloud. Wouldn't that be something? Him and Elizabeth Warren. As far as she was concerned, there couldn't be a better match. She'd have to see what she could do about it!

Chapter
Seven

Mavis was just sitting down to supper when the phone rang. As soon as she picked up the receiver and recognized the voice, she thought, Well, I might as well forget about eating. It was Iva Mae Johnson from Mavis's Sunday-school class. She'd talk for the next hour. "Iva Mae, honey," Mavis said, "how in the world are you?"

In spite of her chicken salad plate and the blueberry muffin she'd eaten down at Burke's with that sweet Elizabeth Warren, Mavis had felt hungry when she had gotten home. After changing her clothes, she had made macaroni and cheese (from a mix—Lord, she'd die if anybody knew, but it was a whole lot easier), fixed a nice little salad, and cut up some fruit for dessert. She was all ready to sit down and enjoy it when Iva Mae called.

"I'm a little poorly," Iva Mae said. "This weather is so changeable. I'm afraid I'm taking a cold. Wasn't that the awfulest storm we had yesterday?"

"Mercy, yes," Mavis said. "A gully washer."

Iva Mae gave a little cough and waited, but when Mavis didn't say more, she went on. "I just hope there won't be rain for the funeral."

"What funeral?"

"Oh, you mean you haven't heard the sad news?" Iva Mae sounded a lot sprightlier.

Well, I reckon not, Mavis thought to herself. Whoever had a chance of getting the news faster than Iva Mae? If the Lord ever decided to flood the world again, Iva Mae would have her bathing suit packed, waiting for the ark, before the first drop ever fell. Mavis could see her right now at the other end of the phone, lavender curls bobbing around her face in excitement, eyes wide with nothing to stop them, since Iva Mae had almost completely plucked her eyebrows off. "Who?" Mavis finally asked. "Who died?"

Iva Mae's voice dropped just slightly as if in deference to the dead. "Miss Elgie Skinner," she said. "Died early this morning out at the Lakeview Nursing Home."

"Lord have mercy!" Mavis exclaimed, and almost dropped the phone. "I just saw her yesterday. We had a nice little visit. I can't believe it."

"Well, you just never know, do you? The Lord can take you in a minute."

"Yes, but usually there's a warning. She looked fine to me."

Iva Mae was quiet a minute. Then she said, "You must have been one of the last to see her alive."

"Why was that?" Mavis wondered if Iva Mae sounded a little jealous.

"They said she didn't have any visitors last night. Ate her supper, the woman who takes trays around said, then had the TV on for a while. They checked her around ten o'clock, and she seemed just fine. It wasn't till they came in the morning that they found her."

"Who told you?"

"Ardella Wiggins called me late this afternoon when I was just getting up from my nap. You know her—her daughter works in the office down at the church. Little Angela. Prettiest thing a-tall, but never that swift in school, so they found a job for her a few hours in the church office, licks envelopes and things. Well, Angela comes home today telling how the preacher got back from his visitation of the sick this morning and said he was as surprised as could be when he walked into Miss Elgie's room and they were getting ready to carry her out."

"The preacher saw her there after she'd passed away?"

"Well, honey, I guess he's used to that. Think how many funerals he's preached in all these years. I don't see why it makes any difference whether they're in a casket or not. Anyway, he said she looked real pretty, all made-up and with her hair curled."

The memory of her visit to Miss Elgie (her poor little form lying under the covers of her bed) came into Mavis's mind. "Made-up?" she said. "Now, that's a surprise. When I was there, she didn't have a bit of color in her face, and her hair was all mashed down."

"I don't know," Iva Mae said a little sharply, as if she thought Mavis doubted her word. "It's what Ardella told me, and Angela hasn't got sense enough to make up something like that."

"Do you know anything about the funeral yet? When is the visitation at the funeral home?"

Mavis could almost see Iva Mae shrug her shoulders. "I don't know that there'll even be one," Iva Mae said. "Ardella called up the preacher after Angela told her little story, and he said that as far as he knew, the only kin Miss Elgie had was a brother who was worse off than she was up in the mountains somewhere. There may not be any money."

"Why not?" Mavis asked, but went on before Iva Mae could answer. "Miss Elgie worked for the county must have been forty years, and she should have had a good pension. She owned that little house she lived in, I'm almost certain, and it would fetch a right good price."

"She had to sell it when she moved into Lakeview. That's what they do when you go there to stay permanently, make you sign over everything you've got."

"Well, I certainly hope they can spare some of what they made off her to give her a decent funeral." Mavis knew that her voice sounded angry. "Another person dead and all their money gone. At least Miss Luna Dixon has Mr. Jesse to see to it that she gets a respectable burial. Poor Miss Elgie has nobody a-tall."

There was a gasp at the other end of the phone. Mavis realized that it had occurred to Iva Mae that Mavis must have been out at Lakeview when Miss Luna's accident occurred. "Mavis Lashley, you mean you were out at Lakeview yesterday for all the excitement and didn't call me? Well, I never! You should have known how concerned I'd be." Her voice dropped almost to a whisper. "Do you think it was murder?"

"No, of ourse not," Mavis said, trying to keep the exasperation out of her voice. "You know how devoted to each other Mr. Jesse and Miss Luna were. As for Mr. Jesse, they took him off down to the jail, and if he's said a word since, I don't know about it." She was silent then. Not for the world would she tell Iva Mae about her visit to the jail and her talk with Elizabeth Warren.

For a minute, Iva Mae, too, was silent. Mavis knew she was trying to decide which was more important—trying to pump Mavis for more information or calling up a dozen other people that night to tell them that Mavis Lashley had been out at Lakeview Nursing Home yesterday when Miss Luna Dixon had met her death—murdered maybe—and was acting like it was nothing at all. Finally she said, "Well, it's all so sad. I guess we'll just have to wait and see what happens. You take care of yourself, Mavis honey. And give me a call if you hear any news. 'Bye now." Iva Mae hung up.

Mavis stared at the phone, then got up from the living room sofa and went back to the kitchen. Her supper sat on the table, the macaroni congealed on the plate, shiny in the light, the salad limp and browning around the edges. All her appetite was gone. Quickly she scraped the food into the garbage can, got down a box of cereal, filled a dish and spread the fruit on the top, and ate it without tasting it at all. Soon after, she went to bed. And though she fell asleep almost immediately, she had strange, disturbing dreams of Miss Elgie's face floating in front of her like a moon against a dark sky, cheeks rouged, eyes shadowed, lips painted the red of a harlot's smile.

Chapter
Eight

Early the next morning Mavis received another phone call, but this time she began to smile as soon as she heard the voice. "Why, Charles Morgan," she said, "what a nice surprise. Seems like it's feast or famine—I go for months without hearing from you, and then it's two days in a row we talk." She laughed, but Charles Morgan sounded serious when he spoke again.

"I hope I'm not disturbing you," he said. "It's kind of early to call."

"Don't you worry about that. I was up, had already eaten breakfast and was finishing the dishes when the phone rang."

"I've got a favor to ask."

"You go right ahead."

"Can I come over in a little while? I've got something I want to talk to you about if it's not too much trouble."

Mavis smiled. Poor Charles. He was so polite, you'd think he was eight years old and asking his mama for money to buy a candy bar. "Of course you can," she said. "Just say what time."

"Ten-thirty too early?"

"Not a-tall. You come ahead. I'll be ready." She hung up the phone and started back to the kitchen. Now, isn't *this* something, she thought. Company coming, and me still in my gown-tail. It only goes to show you—sure as you laze around, something's going to happen to make you regret it.

Thank the Lord she had cleaned earlier in the week. The

65

furniture wouldn't be too dusty, and anyway, if a tabletop didn't exactly sparkle, she doubted that Charles would notice. She finished up the dishes except for the coffeepot, which she left on in case Charles wanted a cup, emptied the garbage, then went to the living room, where she straightened up the magazine rack and fluffed up the crocheted doilies on the backs of the sofa and chairs (her own handiwork), and finally, satisfied that everything looked just fine, she hurried into the bedroom to dress. By the time she was ready, she still had fifteen minutes to spare. Remembering that a few last chrysanthemums were still blooming by the side of the house, she went outside, cut them, and brought them inside. She was just placing the vase on the coffee table when Charles Morgan knocked on the door.

"Come on in," she said, holding the storm door open.

Charles took off his hat and walked past her. Beneath his arm he carried a brown paper bag, and when Mavis pointed to the recliner and asked him to sit down, he placed it on his knees in front of him is if it were some sort of special prize. "Thank you for letting me come over," he said. "I won't keep you long."

"Stay as long as you want. I was being lazy this morning, sitting around drinking coffee. You want some? I left it on just in case."

"No, ma'am," Charles said. "I've had a couple of cups already this morning. Any more, and I'll be shaking."

Well, Lord, we don't want that to happen, Mavis thought. Sitting there with that bag on his knees, Charles looked as awkward as he did when he was in her Sunday-school class, as if he might knock over something any minute. She reached out and touched the bright yellow heads of the chrysanthemums. "What can I do for you?" she said finally when it seemed that Charles would never speak.

He thrust out the package. "I brought back your cake plate," he said. "The one Mr. Dixon's cake was on. It would get broken if it sat around down at the station."

"Well, my goodness," Mavis said. "I hadn't even thought about it. But it *is* one of my good plates, had it for years.

cial trip.''

''It wasn't any trouble,'' Charles said. ''Mr. Dixon ate a right good piece and gave the rest to some of the other fellows we have in there. He asked me to tell you he appreciated your thoughtfulness. That's about the most words he's said the whole time he's been locked up.''

''Poor man, it's such a shame. They should have let him go already.''

Charles shook his head. ''It's not likely. Wilton Early seems bound and determined to prove Mr. Dixon did it. He'll have to indict him soon, though. Can't keep him in there much longer.''

''There must be somebody that he'd talk to. Did his niece come back? Elizabeth. She's about the sweetest thing I've seen in a long time.''

Mavis wondered if Charles blushed, but she couldn't tell in the low light of the living room. ''Not this morning,'' he said, ''but I expect she'll be there later.''

''Well, you make a point of seeing her. She needs somebody to keep that Detective Early from pestering her. You can do the job just fine.''

Charles was silent for a minute or so. Finally he said, ''I have to admit something to you, Miz Mavis. The cake plate wasn't the main reason I wanted to come by today. It's something else.''

Mavis smiled. ''Well, I expect I already knew that. You can't hide a thing. Never could.''

Charles smiled, too. ''I guess so,'' he said. ''You always caught me back in the junior department anytime I got into something.'' His look became serious again. He sat back against the chair. ''Partly, I just don't know where to begin. It's about what's going on out at Lakeview. The deaths and all. There have been a whole lot in the last little while.''

''Well, I don't see why *that's* a surprise. With all those old folks, a lot of them sick, some are sure to pass away.''

''Yes, ma'am, I know. But it seems like there are too many unexpected ones. Like that Miss Elgie Skinner who died yesterday—you know her?'' Mavis nodded her head. "Folks not getting any better, but not likely to take a sudden turn for the worse, either. Still, nobody suspected anything—till lately. The doctors would come in, write down 'Died of natural causes' on the death certificates, the nursing home would call the funeral director, and that would be that.''

"Oh, Lord," Mavis said, a sudden tightness in her chest, "do you think something untoward has been going on?"

"We just don't know. Certainly there's no evidence to speak of. In fact, nothing more than an anonymous telephone call, and that could be anybody with an ax to grind—or just plain crazy."

"What in the world did they say?"

"I wasn't the one who got the call. It came to the desk. A woman, most likely, trying to disguise her voice, saying something like, 'You might want to look into how many people are dying out there at Lakeview Nursing Home. There's too many.' We checked the records, and sure enough, there *has* been a bunch of deaths, most all marked 'Died of natural causes.' Nobody quite knew where to go from there, and then somebody else died during the bazaar.''

Mavis's voice rose. "Charles Morgan, surely you don't think Mr. Jesse Dixon has been out at Lakeview killing off folks all this time! He's not one of those serial killers.''

Charles rubbed his hand over his forehead. "I don't know what to think. It doesn't seem likely a-tall, and he couldn't have killed Miss Elgie Skinner—he was already in jail when she died. But it *would* have to be somebody in the home, now, wouldn't it? I can't see a perfect stranger sneaking in there in the middle of the night and killing people."

"Did the caller say anything else?"

"Well, yes, she did. That was the strangest part of all.'' Charles paused, looked off as if he was seeing something in his head. Mavis wanted to shake him to make him go on. Finally he continued. " 'They were all fixed up'—that's what the woman on the phone said. You know, with makeup and all, as if they were already laid out for a viewing at the funeral home."

"My Lord, that's what Iva Mae Johnson told me last night about Miss Elgie." Mavis saw that Charles looked puzzled, so she explained that Iva Mae was in her Sunday-school class and knew all the latest gossip before anybody else in town. "Why would anybody do such a thing?" she said. "They'd have to be wrong in the head."

"Worse things than that have happened," Charles said. "You see it all the time on TV."

"Not me. Not much anymore. The eleven o'clock news got so bad that I finally stopped watching. Now I listen to the weather report and the Community Bulletin Board on the radio before I go to bed, and that's about all. I sleep better by a long shot."

Charles shifted forward again, as if he might be getting ready to go. "What are you going to do next?" Mavis asked. "You can't just let it drop."

"No, we won't. There'll be an autopsy on Miss Elgie. Maybe that will tell us something. We might even have to exhume some of the others."

"Oh, I hope not!" Mavis exclaimed, pain in her heart. "Those poor folks moved out to Lakeview to spend their last days in peace, and then they end up getting murdered. And now they still won't be able to rest, disturbed in their graves. Surely the Lord will punish whoever has caused them so much harm."

Charles didn't answer. His body seemed tense as he played with the edge of his hat. Mavis suddenly thought, He's got something else to tell me. Oh, Lord, I don't know that I can take much more. When he opened his mouth again, she felt like telling him to hush. "We'd like to ask you a favor," he finally said.

"What?" Mavis couldn't keep the surprise out of her voice.

"Something that would help with the investigation," Charles answered. "Might be real important."

"Well, don't beat around the bush," Mavis said. "Tell me."

Charles bent even closer. His voice dropped. "Would you

consider going out to Lakeview and being a patient for a while?''

"What for?"

"To keep your eyes and ears open and find out anything you can. You never know what you might pick up just being there. The administrative types aren't going to be too eager to talk to the police—they don't want the reputation of the home ruined. And the patients probably say things among themselves they'd never repeat to outsiders.''

Mavis felt a tingle of excitement inside. "So I'd be sort of an undercover agent. Imagine that, at my age!''

Charles gave his funny smile. "Well, yes, I guess so. I hadn't thought about it in just that way.''

"But I'm not sick,'' Mavis said. "They'd know.''

"We had another idea. We can put you in a cast and say you broke your leg and need care since you live all alone. It'll slow you down a little, but I expect you can handle it. And if it gets too bothersome, we can say you have to see the doctor and then get you cut out of it for a rest.''

"Well, my Lord, you've thought of everything. It's like a spy novel.''

Charles looked serious again. "The only thing is, you've got to be careful. If there really is some lunatic out there killing off people, we don't want him to find out about you. You won't be able to tell a soul what you're doing. One slip and goodness knows what might happen.''

"One person has to know.''

"Who's that?"

"My nephew, Dale. He won't tell anybody, and I'll need him as part of the act. Who else would take me out to Lakeview? I couldn't drive up in a police car, now, could I?''

"You're right,'' Charles said. "But nobody else.''

"Absolutely,'' Mavis said, thinking that Zeena and Iva Mae would just *die* when it all came out. "When do I start?''

"Tomorrow, if you want. We'll set it up with a doctor so that you can go out to the hospital and get the cast on in the morning, and they'll make the reservation out at Lakeview for the afternoon. After that, you're on your own, but I'll be coming in to talk to the patients and see you when I do. The administration knows we're starting an investigation. We're just not making it public.''

Mavis was too excited to sit still any longer. She stood, and Charles got up from the recliner. ''You can depend on me,'' she said to Charles. ''If there's anything going on out at Lakeview, I'll find out.''

''That's why we asked,'' Charles said. He reached out and took Mavis's hand. The gesture surprised her. ''But promise me you'll be careful. I don't want anything to happen to you.''

She squeezed his fingers and smiled, and Charles turned away, headed for the door.

Chapter Nine

She called Dale before Charles had pulled away from the curb in front of the house. "Lord, let him be there," she said under her breath, and gave a sigh of relief when the girl who answered his phone said, "Hold on, I'll go get him. He's in the darkroom."

"Hey there," Dale said when he got to the phone. "To what do I owe this pleasure?" Mavis knew he was smiling.

"I'm sorry to disturb you, honey, but I'm going to need your help, and I had to call right away."

Dale's voice became serious all at once. "What is it?" he asked. "Is something the matter?"

"No, just the opposite—I've got the most exciting news!" And before Dale could say another word, she proceeded to tell him all about Charles Morgan's visit that morning to return her cake plate, the suspicious things he said were going on out at Lakeview Nursing Home, and finally, his request for her help. When she finished she said, "Now, don't tell me that's not the most exciting thing you've heard in a month of Sundays."

"Why, Lord, yes!" Dale exclaimed. "You'll be a regular Mata Hari. And you know how *she* got her information, don't you?"

"Be ashamed of yourself, Dale Sumner," Mavis said, smiling. "I've got a good mind not to ask you to help me the way I'd planned."

"I'm sorry, I'm sorry," he said in a little-boy voice.

"All right," she said. "This time." She began to speak very fast. "I need you to take me downtown in the morning to get my hair fixed. Lord knows when I'll have a chance to go again once I'm at Lakeview, and I want it to look halfway decent while I'm there. I've got a little shopping to do, and then I have to get my cast put on and go on out to Lakeview. I know that's a lot to ask, but you're the only one in on the secret. Think you can do it?"

"You just try to stop me," Dale said. "Make your appointment and let me know what time. I'll be there—you can count on it."

Dale picked her up at exactly eight-thirty the next morning, sleepy-eyed, dressed in blue jeans and a rumpled shirt beneath his leather jacket, hair every which way. Mavis didn't ask him what he'd done the night before. Since it was Saturday, traffic was light, and they were downtown in no time at all. When Dale dropped her off in front of Shirlee's Beauty Shoppe, Mavis was twenty minutes early for her appointment. "I'm going to the gym to work out," Dale said as Mavis closed the car door. "I'll be back to pick you up by ten-thirty. That okay?"

"Sure thing," Mavis said. "I'll be ready." Then she turned and walked to Shirlee's front door.

Shirlee had done Mavis's hair for years, and half the people Mavis knew from down at the church went to her, too. "I bet I use more blue rinse than any place in town," Mavis had heard Shirlee say one day, and thought it was probably true—she'd seen enough bright blue heads walk out of there—though she never let Shirlee put anything on her own gray hair, no matter how many times she asked. Shirlee's Beauty Shoppe wasn't like those fancy places out at the mall with mirrors everywhere and loud music piped in and weird-looking operators all dressed in black. Shirlee's was homier, almost like your own living room, except for the color—a deep shade of lavender that might have been more appropriate in a bawdy house. It was on sale when Shirlee first painted the place. You got used to it. "Good morning," Mavis said, and let the door jangle closed behind her.

"Well, look at the early bird," Shirlee called out. As usual, she had a cigarette dangling from her mouth, eyes half-closed against the smoke. Her own hair changed color often, and this morning it was a sort of strawberry red. "I'll be with you in a little while. Rayette," she called out. "Come on and wash Miz Mavis. You can leave that straightening up till later." And through the curtain to the back room where Shirlee kept her supplies came the girl who did the shampoos and brought in the soft drinks Shirlee kept for her customers if they wanted them.

"Morning," she said to Mavis. "You come on here and we'll get you started."

Taking off the lightweight coat she had worn—there had been a chill in the air that morning—Mavis said, "Morning, Rayette," and then sat down in the chair, relaxing already as Rayette tilted her backward toward the sink. Whenever she had her hair washed, she felt like a little girl again, remembering her mother's strong fingers as she massaged her scalp and poured warm water from the kettle over her head into a pan in the kitchen, while a fire in the wood stove warmed the room. She smiled to herself and almost fell asleep.

All the time Shirlee worked on Mavis, she talked about the Halloween costume she was making for her daughter, Bonnielee. "It's going to be the prettiest *thing*," she said through a veil of cigarette smoke, "a princess outfit. I got this material on sale at the outlet mall, white and satiny-looking, and it's going to have tons of it in the skirt. The top's fitted, with a sweetheart neckline and sequins trimming it. And we found a crown at the bridal shop. I'll take pictures and show you next time you come in."

"I'll look forward to it," Mavis said, but thought that maybe a ghost outfit or something a little less revealing might be better for Bonnielee. Last spring Shirlee had talked Mavis into buying a ticket for the variety show that Bonnielee's school was putting on, and when Mavis had seen the girl up on the stage in the school choir, bigger than any of the others, she had thought, Somebody ought to put that poor girl on a diet. She's headed for a lifetime of big ladies' fashions and personal heartache if somebody doesn't do something about her weight soon. She must have gotten it from Shirlee's husband. He was fat, too.

Shirlee had gone on to another subject before Mavis even realized. ". . . and the visitation is going to be down at Sander's Funeral Home tonight, though they say she hasn't got a single relative to be there."

"What? What's that?" Mavis moved her head, and Shirlee pulled her hair.

"Miss Elgie Skinner," Shirlee repeated. "They're having the visitation for her tonight. It was in the paper this morning. I'm going to try to go after work, though Lord knows I'll be tired out after being on my feet all day."

"I didn't get a chance to see the paper," Mavis said, "trying to get down here on time. Did you know her? Miss Elgie, I mean."

"Of course, honey; I've been doing her hair for years. It was real fine—you had to be careful not to burn it off. She was the sweetest little thing, never had a bad word for anybody. It was real sad when she had to go into Lakeview."

Mavis remembered that she was going to be out at Lakeview soon investigating Miss Elgie's death. "She ever buy any of that fancy makeup you're always trying to get me to buy?" she asked, hoping that her voice sounded casual.

"Why, no, ma'am," Shirlee answered. Her voice sounded puzzled, and she stopped pinning up Mavis's hair for a minute. Mavis hoped she hadn't already given something away. But then Shirlee went back to work, saying, "She didn't use a dab of anything, said she'd been brought up in a primitive Baptist church, and you know how they are about makeup— it's worse than adultery—so she never could get used to the idea of painting her face. 'Honey,' I'd tell her, 'you don't need a thing to make you prettier,' and she'd just laugh and say, 'Hush,' but you could tell she was pleased."

* * *

"Well, don't you look nice," Dale said as she got into the car. "Probably nobody in the world would suspect you were a spy."

"Stop your silliness," Mavis said. "And anyway, you're looking pretty good yourself." The sleepiness had gone from Dale's eyes, his shining hair was perfectly combed, and even his clothes looked less rumpled.

"Lord knows I try," he said. "It gets harder all the time." He gave a big sigh and pulled away from the curb.

They were headed for the mall. Mavis had decided she would rather shop there than at Burke's, where she knew most of the salesladies, who might wonder why she was buying three new nightgowns, particularly if they learned later that she had broken her leg the very same afternoon. Now that it was late morning, traffic was heavier, and they had to drive around the parking lot twice before Dale found a spot near Penney's. "I don't want you to have to walk so far," he said.

"Lord, it may be a while before I can walk again," she answered him. "I'd better do it while I've still got a chance." She got out of the car, and Dale locked the door. Looking around, she said, "My, don't they have everything done up pretty." There were stacks of cornstalks all along the covered walkway, with pumpkins and decorative gourds artistically arranged beneath them, and a scarecrow poking up from behind. They'd better have the guards out on Halloween next week, or trick-or-treaters would make a mess of things, Mavis thought. Last year somebody had smashed the jack-o'-lantern she had carved and set on her front stoop.

They spent nearly an hour in women's lingerie on the third floor, going through the racks. Mavis was looking at something nice in flannel (the nights would soon be cool) when she got a tap on the shoulder, and there was Dale holding up a few bits of lace and chiffon on a hanger in front of him, wiggling his hips like a Radio City Music Hall Rockette and saying, "Mavis, you'd knock 'em dead out at the home in this!" Then, before she could give him a smack on the wrist, he danced away and found some other shameless outfit anybody in the world would know was made for a harlot, and draped it around himself. Finally the black woman who had been trying to help Mavis said, "When you-all decide just who's going to wear those gowns, you let me know," and walked away shaking her head.

Mavis finally selected three gowns, two of flannel, one of thin cotton, nicer than the others, with lace around the collar and a pretty bow. Dale had insisted on buying her a robe, and chose one in dark burgundy silk (all his foolishness over with) that she told him was much too expensive. "It's a going-away gift," he said, and winked. "We don't want you looking *tacky* out at Lakeview, now, do we?" She gave him a hug, and they went back out to the car and put the packages in the trunk beside the canvas bag Mavis had packed the night before.

They had lunch at Wendy's and then drove out to the hospital. "I'm just as nervous as can be," Mavis said as they got out of the car. "I feel like everybody in the world can look right through me and know what I'm doing." But when they went inside and asked the woman at the information desk for the doctor whose name Charles Morgan had given her, the woman just smiled an automatic smile and gave them the directions to the waiting room. There a few people sat, but they hardly looked up from the magazines they were reading when Mavis and Dale walked in. Mavis was relieved when the girl at the desk said, "Yes, ma'am, he's expecting you," and didn't give her any papers to fill out. She'd hate to put down a lie in writing.

The procedure was painless. The doctor, a short man with very dark hair, who wore a long, light blue coat, winked at her and said, "Which leg?" and startled her so that she couldn't answer at first. Obviously Charles Morgan had set everything up, and she wasn't going to be asked any other questions.

"The left one," she finally said. "It's the one with the arthritis in the knee. Maybe it'll help to give it a rest."

When the doctor had finished wrapping the cool plaster gauze around her leg, he gave Mavis a pat on the back, laughed, and said, "Now, that's an unusual Halloween costume, isn't it?" and helped her into a wheelchair. He pushed her back outside to the waiting room.

As soon as he saw her, Dale jumped up, his face white as the cast on Mavis's leg. "Lord, it nearly scared me to death," he told her later, "seeing you there with that thing on you. I forgot for a minute it was all pretend and thought you actually *did* have an accident. You just be as careful as you can be from now on," he said. "I don't want to have to do this for real."

They said good-bye to the doctor. He shook Dale's hand and patted Mavis on the arm. "Take care of that leg," he said in a serious voice, but Mavis could see that his eyes were smiling.

Dale pushed Mavis down the hallway back toward the entrance of the hospital, and she became aware, suddenly, of the cast upon her leg—a pressure, a kind of pulling as the plaster dried out. She'd heard that people nearly went crazy sometimes with itching, and wondered if it would happen to her. But most of all she felt helpless. She couldn't run, couldn't walk except with a crutch or with someone else's help. What if something *did* happen out at Lakeview? How would she protect herself? She gave a little shake and said to herself, The Lord will protect me. I have to believe in his power.

"Come on!" she called back to Dale. "This as fast as we can go? You must have worn out those pretty muscles of yours at the gym this morning."

"You just watch," he said, and speeded up, and they went sailing down the hallway.

Chapter
Ten

"Well, what *are* you going to tell folks about how you got hurt?" Dale asked as he got into the car after returning Mavis's wheelchair to the entrance of the hospital. He started up the engine and pulled slowly out of the parking lot.

"I hadn't thought." Mavis shifted in her seat to give her leg more room. "You got any ideas?"

"Well, you could say I took you out dancing at a disco and you were doing a high kick and slipped."

"Don't be silly," Mavis said, frowning. "It's got to be something reasonable. "I can't say I was hit by a car—there'd be more injuries and probably a piece in the paper—and there isn't any ice to slip on. Maybe a home accident. They say more people get hurt that way than any other. I could have been cooking, spilled some water I didn't see on the floor, then slipped so that my feet flew out from under me."

"That sounds pretty good, but we could make it a little more dramatic."

"What do you mean?"

Dale smiled, and Mavis knew that if she could see his eyes, they would be twinkling. "Well, you were lying there for the longest while, then had to *drag* yourself across the floor, finally made it to the telephone and dialed me with your last ounce of strength. I came racing over to save you at ninety miles an hour and got here just in time."

"You've been watching too much TV, honey," Mavis said, patting Dale on the arm. "Let's not dress it up any more than we have to. I'm already feeling guilty about telling so many lies.''

"It's for a good cause.''

"Yes, I know, but it still bothers me. My mama hammered it into me—'Always tell the truth,' she said. I've tried to follow those words all my life.''

There were only a few empty parking spaces at the nursing home. Saturday was a busy time for visitors. Dale pulled in to a spot marked HANDICAPPED, and Mavis was about to tell him he wasn't supposed to park there when she looked down and saw the cast on her leg and thought, Well, if anybody is handicapped around here, *I* am, and then didn't say anything more.

"I'll be right back," Dale said as he got out of the car. Mavis watched him bounce up the ramp and go inside the front door. So much had happened in the past few days since she had gone out to Lakeview for the Fall Festival Bazaar. Still, as she looked at the trees arching over the parking lot, pure gold in the afternoon sunlight, then at the wide veranda where those silent figures of her childhood spent bright, cold days bundled up in deck chairs, she found it hard to imagine that anything evil was going on here. Somewhere in the distance a lawn mower droned, and a few birds, traveling south, twittered in the treetops. It was warm, and she almost dozed.

"Here we go." Mavis looked up with a start. Dale was standing by the car with a wheelchair. He opened the door and helped her out. "You're going to have to get used to this thing so you can get around by yourself," he said. "Look." He showed her how to lock the wheels so that the chair would be steady when she got in and out. "Now you try it just over to the ramp."

Afraid somehow that they would hurt her fingers, Mavis touched the wheels hesitantly but discovered quite quickly that they rolled with little effort, and in no time at all, she was at the foot of the ramp. "Well, I guess I can manage," she said to Dale as he pushed her the rest of the way up to the door. "Although, if there was a fine-looking gentleman like you around to help me, I wouldn't mind at all letting him lend a hand.''

"What would one of those women's rights folks say about that? You're supposed to be independent.''

"That's all right for them, I guess. Me, I don't mind having a man around sometimes.'' Dale laughed, and Mavis joined him as they went inside.

The same young man with the soft eyes and ponytail was at the desk. "How're you, ma'am?'' he said, and seemed to remember her. Mavis gave her name, and after he pushed a few buttons on his computer, he said, "Everything is in order. We're expecting you.'' He looked at Dale with those pretty eyes and gave him a big smile. "Push the chair over there and have a seat. Miss Santucci, the assistant administrator, will need to take down some information. She'll be with you in a minute.''

"Sure thing,'' Dale said, and smiled back, then rolled Mavis over to a row of chairs and sat down beside her.

It was a pleasant room, freshly painted in a pale gray, with rose-colored upholstery on the chairs and glossy dark brown tables in the corners holding magazines. A large plant with shiny green leaves stood in front of the window. No one else was there, and exept for the ring of a phone every now and then behind the counter and the sound of a computer, there was silence. Dale was quiet, flipping through a magazine (strange for him, he usually talked a blue streak), and Mavis wondered if he shared her sudden feeling of apprehension now that she was here. This wasn't a game anymore. People had died, some might have been murdered, and Mavis was here to help find whoever had killed them. She might be in real danger herself! She gave a little shiver, as if a sudden blast of cold air had come from the air conditioner across the room.

"Miz Lashley, this way now,'' the young man behind the counter called out.

Dale jumped, threw down the magazine he had been looking at, got up, and wheeled Mavis over to the counter. "Think you can make it from here?'' he asked. He had an awful look on his face. "I'll go out to the car and get your stuff.''

"Sure I can," she said with a smile, hoping to relieve his anxiety. "I might as well get used to this thing. Just show me the way," she said to the receptionist as Dale went out the door.

"Right through there," the man said, pointing to an archway at the end of the counter. "Miss Santucci's office is just down the hall to the right.''

Mavis thanked him, and then, pushing just lightly on the wheels, moved the chair quickly through the doorway to the hall. Just as she got to the open doorway where BARBARA SANTUCCI, ASSISTANT ADMINISTRATOR was printed in white letters on a sign next to it, a voice called out, "In here, please," in what was surely the thickest Yankee accent Mavis had heard in years. With a sigh, she rolled inside.

One look at the woman sitting behind the desk, and Mavis had to bite her tongue to keep from saying, Well, aren't *you* a sight for sore eyes! She might have been pretty, but who'd ever know? With her eyes made up like Cleopatra's on the Nile, lips painted red as a fox's you-know-what, and black hair darker than Zeena's could ever be, she looked as if she already had on her costume for Halloween. "Welcome to Lakeview Nursing Home, Mrs. Lashley," Barbara Santucci said, holding out her hand, and at least fifteen jangly bracelets slid down her arm.

"Thank you kindly," Mavis said, and clutched her pocketbook to her breast.

Barbara Santucci must have asked her a hundred questions. Where she was born, her parents' names (now, wouldn't any fool know they'd been long gone?), what illnesses she'd had, what operations. She wanted to know if Mavis smoked (ha!), if she had any food preferences, what her hobbies were. "I do my work at home and go to church," she told her. "That's all the hobbies I need." Finally she asked Mavis for her next of kin, and when she gave Dale's name, Barbara Santucci punched that information into her computer, too, red nails clicking on the keys like a hailstorm.

Finally, when she had finished, she looked up at Mavis and said, "You'll be in room 311 in the new wing. Paul at the desk can point you the way."

"I'm sure I can find it with no trouble," Mavis said, turning the wheelchair. She'd die if she got stuck here in Barbara Santucci's office and had to ask her for help. "I've been here on *numerous* occasions to visit the sick." She looked hard at Barbara Santucci, then said, "In fact, I was out here just a few days ago to see Miss Elgie Skinner—before she passed away."

Just the corners of Barbara Santucci's mouth turned down. "Yes, poor Miss Skinner. So unexpected. We just never know, do we?"

"I guess not," Mavis said, and wheeled herself out into the hallway. If Barbara Santucci smiled good-bye, Mavis didn't see it.

Dale was waiting for her with her packages from Penney's on the chair beside him and Mavis's bag on the floor. His worried look was gone. "That took a while," he said. "I thought maybe they'd already taken you away."

"I had to tell my entire life history," Mavis said in a loud voice, hoping Barbara Santucci would hear. "Asked me all sorts of foolishness. But come on now. Let me get upstairs. I know you've got better things to do than waste all Saturday afternoon with an old lady." Mavis headed for the archway leading to the new wing where the elevator was located.

Dale picked up the packages and the bag. " 'Bye," he called out to the young man at the desk.

"Take care of yourself," he answered back. "If we can do anything to help, you just let us know."

"So far so good," Mavis said as soon as the elevator doors had closed. "Nobody seems to suspect a thing."

"No, but promise me you'll be careful." Dale's face had a worried look again. "If there *are* killings going on, it could be almost anybody around here. You've got to be on guard all the time."

Mavis reached up and patted Dale's arm. "Don't you

worry, honey. I'll be all right. I've placed it in the hands of
the Lord.''

They left the elevator and paused a moment in the hallway,
letting their eyes adjust to the low light. ''That way,'' Mavis
said, and began to move the chair noiselessly over the polished floor. ''The nursing station is where the bright light is.
I remember from before.''

At first no one appeared to be there, but then a woman
stood up, looked over the counter, and said, ''You must be
Miz Lashley. We've been expecting you.'' Looking up, Mavis saw that it was the nurse who had come into Miss Elgie's
room while Mavis was there visiting, but if there was any
recognition in her pale gray eyes, Mavis did not see it. ''Estelle Overby, R.N., Nursing Supervisor,'' Mavis read again
on the pin on the front of her bright white uniform. ''Are
you kin?'' she asked Dale, but did not smile.

''Yes, ma'am. I'm her nephew,'' he said.

Nurse Overby walked down to the end of the counter,
raised a section, and came out into the hallway. ''Well, we'll
take care of your aunt,'' she said in a dismissive voice. ''You
can go now. It's better if she settles in right away.'' She took
the handles of the chair and began to push Mavis down the
hall.

''Hey, don't I even get a kiss good-bye?'' Dale stepped in
front of the chair so that the nurse had to stop. Her expression
did not change as he bent down to kiss Mavis on the forehead. ''Here, honey,'' he said, giving Mavis the packages.
''I'll be back to see you tomorrow soon as visiting hours
allow.'' To Nurse Overby he said, ''This is Mavis's bag,''
and handed the suitcase to her. She took it without comment.

Hurrying ahead, Dale pushed the elevator button. The
doors opened, and he got inside with a final wave. *Take me
with you!* Mavis wanted to cry out, but the doors were already closed and he was gone.

''Here,'' Nurse Overby said, pausing at a doorway, ''this
is your room.'' Looking inside at the empty bed, Mavis had
the sudden horrible thought that they were putting her into
Miss Elgie's room. But then she remembered that the sicker

residents were downstairs on the second floor, she was here on the third, and her heart stopped its brief thumping.

"I think you'll be comfortable here," Nurse Overby said, her voice suddenly warmer. "As soon as you get situated, I'll have them bring up a little snack from the dining room. You've missed lunch, and supper isn't for a while yet." She helped Mavis out of the wheelchair into a lounger by the side of the bed.

With a sigh, Mavis sank down into the cushions, leaning on the nurse's strong arms. Perhaps it was foolishness after all—suspecting that Miss Elgie and the others had been killed here in the home. How could anybody take care of a sick and needy person all day and then kill her in cold blood in the middle of the night? "Thank you," she said to Nurse Overby. "I think I'm going to like it here just fine."

Chapter
Eleven

When Mavis awoke the next morning and heard the ring of church bells, she thought at first she might still be dreaming. Even when she opened her eyes and saw the sharp sliver of bright light beneath the window shade, so different from the lacy pattern the curtains made in her bedroom back home, she was not sure where she lay. Then, shifting her body just slightly, she felt the heavy weight of the cast on her leg, and she laughed aloud and said, "Well, for goodness' sakes, welcome to Lakeview Nursing Home!"

She sat up in bed and looked around. It was a pretty enough room—pale yellow walls, white curtains patterned with blue and yellow flowers, dark wood furniture—but as anonymous as a hotel, no sign that any *person* lived there, except for Mavis's well-thumbed Bible and the book of daily devotionals she had packed in her bag before leaving home. Her clothes, unpacked efficiently by the nurse the evening before, were hung in the closet, and her toilet articles (toothbrush, toothpaste, the nightly cleansing cream she had used since before she was married, her little bit of makeup) were arranged on a shelf above the bathroom sink. She had everything she needed, but already she missed her own house. Thank goodness she wouldn't be staying long enough to acquire the personal items she had seen cluttering up the rooms of others she had visited who were in long-term care.

It was still quiet outside her door. Last night there had been the murmur of voices, laughter from a TV, and the whirring sound of the floor buffer, and at first Mavis had been afraid she wouldn't sleep. At Nurse Overby's suggestion, she had eaten dinner in her room ("It's a big adjustment coming in here," she had said. "Why not have a quiet little evening to yourself?") and then tried to watch TV. But the shows were foolish and her eyes grew tired, so she read one brief paragraph in the book of devotions, turned off the light, and said her prayers. Before she could get out "Amen," she was sound asleep. Now here she was, still lying in bed on the first Sunday morning within memory that she hadn't risen early to get ready for Sunday school and church. Just a few days ago she couldn't have imagined it!

"Knock, knock," came a voice from the hallway. Before Mavis could say, Come on in, the door was pushed open, a tray appeared, and then the black woman carrying it. "Well, Lord have mercy, look who's here!" the woman said. "Let me put down this tray before I drop it smack in the middle of the floor. I've never been so surprised."

It was the dining room attendant Mavis had talked to the day of the bazaar. Trying to remember her name, Mavis said, "Hey there, how're *you*?" and peered at the badge on the front of her pink uniform. DAISY, it said there in large letters beside a smiley face. The woman's own face smiled with pleasure, her gold tooth bright as sunshine; she still wore a flower in her hair. How nice, Mavis thought, to have someone around who isn't a perfect stranger.

"What happened to *you*?" Daisy asked, reading the ticket that had come with Mavis's tray. "That's it," she said, snapping her fingers. " 'Miz Lashley.' I couldn't come up with your name at first. Getting too old."

Mavis pulled back the bed covers, exposing her legs. "*I'm* getting too old to be falling about." She pointed at her cast. "That's the reason I'm here."

"Oh, you poor thing," Daisy said, coming closer. "What have you did to yourself?"

Mavis hesitated a moment. She hated to lie. But Dale and Charles Morgan had both told her not to trust anybody, so she would have to tell her story.

"One of those silly accidents," she said. "I was cooking up some collards on Saturday—they're good now after the frost has bit them—and when I went from the sink to the stove, I must have slopped some water on the floor, because the next thing I knew, my feet were up in the air and I fell on my leg with a thump. I tried to get up, but the pain was bad, so I kind of half crawled over to the phone and called my nephew and he came. Nothing would do but I had to come out here till I get the cast off. He wouldn't hear of me staying home by myself even though I can get around perfectly well in that wheelchair."

"Well, I don't blame him, honey. You don't want something else to happen, now do you? Think of it as a vacation. You just relax and let folks wait on you." She brought over Mavis's tray and set it on the stand by the bed. "You can have breakfast in bed every morning if you want to," she said. "There's a menu on the tray—pick out anything you want. Food's not bad here a-tall." Suddenly she looked at her watch. "Whew-eee!" she said. "I better not stand here talking any longer. There're some hungry folks on this hall, and they'll be complaining no end if their eggs is cold." She started to turn.

"You have the whole floor?"

Daisy nodded her head. "Right now I do. Used to be somebody else to help me, but he got fired. Not that he was worth the powder and shot to blow his head off. La-zy— you've never seen the like! I be up here passing these trays, and he be down yonder on the patio smoking a cigarette." She sighed. "Nobody much wants a job like this anymore. Don't pay much, and you have all sorts of hours. Me, well, I don't have much choice. No schooling to speak of, too old now to go back, and I've got a son to put through college. It's all I can do to make it." She backed away from Mavis. "I better get going," she said. "If the supervisor comes by and sees me a-talking, I might get fired. You take care now. I'll see you later." She went out the door, though Mavis, while eating her meal, continued to feel the woman's sunny presence in the room.

The food was good. Oatmeal with brown sugar on the side, grapefruit, juice, and coffee still piping hot in its little carafe—more than she would have eaten at home. She'd have to be careful not to gain weight here. The very idea—after nine o'clock on a Sunday morning, and her still lazing in bed with a breakfast tray in front of her. She smiled. John, in the year after they were married, had fixed her breakfast a few times and brought it to her in their bedroom. Poor man, he could hardly boil water, and the eggs he had cooked were tough, the bacon burned. After brushing crumbs off the sheets and washing up all the pans he'd used in the kitchen, she had finally told him, "It's sweet of you to do all this, but I didn't marry you to wait on me. You've got enough to do around the house—I'll cook." And he had looked relieved.

By the time she came out of the bathroom, the tray was gone. Mavis didn't know what to put on. Surely people weren't expected to sit around all day in their bedclothes, and since it was Sunday, she wondered if they would dress up. Finally she decided on a soft blue wool dress with three-quarter-length sleeves that looked nice with her pearls, the only jewelry she had packed for her trip out to the home. On one foot she wore a soft house slipper in blue satin; on the other, just a white sock where her toes stuck out of the cast. "Well," she said to her reflection in the mirror as she smoothed down the curls on the back of her neck, "I guess I'm ready." It would be her first full day of investigating the murders at the Lakeview Nursing Home. She wheeled herself out into the hall.

"Morning, dear." The nurse going by gave her a big smile and stopped in front of Mavis's chair. "Well, aren't you the smartest thing—getting yourself all fixed up this morning without a bit of help. I sure wish some of the other guests would take a lesson from you. Seems like they can't even brush their teeth without urging."

"I do for myself at home," Mavis said. "No need to be waited on out here long as I can get around."

"I'm sure not. I read your chart. You're Miz Lashley with the broken leg. I'm Lacy Pearl Williams, one of the day nurses.'' She gave Mavis a plump hand with rings on four fingers. ''Still, you let us know now if we can do anything for you. You might as well get your money's worth while you're here.'' She gave Mavis another smile and walked off down the hall, her uniform riding up on her haunches. Her rubber-treaded shoes made squelching sounds on the floor. Mavis turned her chair in the opposite direction and headed for the sun-room.

Even before she went through the doorway, she could hear the TV blaring—music with a beat no hymn writer ever intended, played in a style that Mavis associated with dubious supper clubs out on the highway—one of those TV evangelists' shows, she could tell without even seeing the screen. Maybe if no one else was there, she could change the channel and get a nice quiet service from one of the local churches. Shouting and carrying on gave her a headache.

It wasn't to be. As soon as she rolled into the sun-room, she saw a woman curled up in one of the big chairs with her head no more than two feet from the TV set, eyes never wavering from the figures there. She was as tiny as a child, her hands almost transparent, like baby birds'. Her dress was dark, and she wore a heavy knitted shawl around her shoulders even though sun poured through the windows and gave the small room the sultry feeling of a July afternoon. Well, don't let me *disturb* you, Mavis thought as she swung her chair around so that she could look at the TV.

''Ain't that precious?'' The woman pointed to the screen with her finger. Mavis looked. A little girl dressed up in ruffles and enough ribbons to get a person through an entire Christmas season had begun to sing in a whiny voice. ''One of the Lord's chosen,'' the woman said. ''She's the preacher's daughter. The whole family is on the show. You watch it?''

''No, ma'am. I go to my own church on Sundays. Leastways, when I can.'' Mavis pointed to her leg.

The woman looked at her for the first time. ''What's your name?'' she asked suddenly.

''Mavis Lashley.''

''I'm Swannie Hocutt. Lord knows whether I'll ever see

my church again except in a coffin. My children put me in this place and won't let me out. Never darken the doorway to pay me a visit, either—you'd think they'd be ashamed. You got any children?"

"No," Mavis said. She rolled her chair just a little away.

"Maybe you're lucky. Me, I raised four, and look what good it's done me. All of them hanging around, hoping to get something when I die. My young-uns spend every nickel they can get their hands on, and then some. Sin and degradation, that's all they're interested in. I don't know what the world is coming to."

Swannie Hocutt sank back against the chair cushions, nearly breathless. Lord, she can talk, Mavis thought. She looked at the TV where a shiny-faced man in a white suit had gotten up and had begun to preach in a singsong voice, but she didn't listen to the words. They were the same in every such sermon. She'd be better off going back to her room and reading her Bible in a little peace and quiet. She was just about to say, Morning, ma'am, to Swannie Hocutt and wheel herself back down the hallway when the other woman clicked up the volume on the TV and bent toward Mavis to whisper, "You're new here. You'd better watch your step. There's all sorts of things going on."

Lord have mercy! Mavis thought. Does she know something about the murders? Trying to appear calm, she asked, "What kind of things? Is there danger?"

"Of losing your mortal soul!" Swannie said. She looked at the screen a moment as if the preacher might echo her words. Then she turned back to Mavis. "Don't tell me you haven't seen it? How can you be so blind?"

"Seen what?"

"The lustful looks, the secret glances. They're all around!"

"From who?"

"Why, *every*body." Swannie bent even closer, her own eyes glittering. "The nurses, the attendants, the people in the office upstairs. Even some of the patients, fools that they are. I told my young-uns I didn't want to be in any home

where there were *men* around, but they stuck me in here with
a bunch of roosters. Everybody knows what they're after.''

Mavis sat up straighter. ''I can't rightly say I've noticed
anything,'' she said. ''I've been here only one night.''

''That's the worst time! I hear them sneaking up and down
the hallway, the doors opening and closing. It's a regular sex
ring. I wrote letters to the police, but I'm sure they were
intercepted. I'd try the president, but I know they'd get those
letters, too. You get out while you can, or you'll end up a
white slave like the rest of 'em.''

The room felt even warmer to Mavis. The noise from the
TV and Swannie's words had given her a headache. ''Thank
you for all the information,'' she said to Swannie, and started
to turn her chair. But before she could get to the door, Swannie jumped up and walked past her. She had on golden slippers turned up at the ends like some harem girl's, and Mavis
thought she might take off and fly down the hallway.

''I got to check my room,'' Swannie said back over her
shoulder. ''You never know who might be in there up to no
good. Lock up your stuff or they'll steal it.'' She disappeared
into the shadows.

Mavis sat for a moment in the sunny room, the preacher's
voice in the background wailing of sin and damnation. Well,
mercy me, she thought, what kind of a place have I got
myself into?

Dale visited that afternoon. Mavis was dozing over an
article in a magazine she had brought from the sun-room
(''How to Keep Your Husband Interested in Your Marriage!'') when the door suddenly swung open and in walked
a huge bouquet of flowers with two legs and feet attached.
She didn't even know it was Dale until he peeked through
the blossoms, head as golden as the yellow chrysanthemums
he carried. ''You rob a florist?'' she called out, tickled to
death to see him even though they had parted only yesterday.

''Not one bit,'' he said, dropping the flowers on the stand
by Mavis's bed. ''I bought them all for you. Thought you
might need a little cheering up by now.''

Mavis nodded her head. "You're right there. This is kind of a lonesome place."

"Let's get these in water," Dale said as he looked around the room. "Is there a vase in the bathroom?"

"Not that I noticed. Let me ring my buzzer. I haven't even tried it out to see if it works." She reached over to the bed and pushed the white plastic button attached to a cord. Outside her door there was a pinging sound and the reflection of a red light going on.

"Fancy," Dale said. "If the murderer stops by, you just turn that on and somebody will come running."

Mavis shuddered. "Don't even tease about such things, though I'm not at all convinced anything is going on around here."

Before Dale could ask her what she meant, the door opened and Lacy Pearl Williams, the nurse Mavis had seen that morning in the hallway, poked her head inside. "Can I help you with something, Miz Lashley?" she asked, coming farther into the room. Short as she was, she could hardly see over the bouquet lying on the stand. "Howdy," she said to Dale, and tried to pull down the skirt of her uniform, which rode right back up again. Don't tug on it too hard, Mavis thought, or those buttons will pop right off.

"Why, yes, ma'am, you certainly can help. My nephew here"—she pointed to Dale—"he's rounded up just about every flower in the country, and we need a vase, maybe even two."

"Let me take them. We've got a special little room for flower arranging. I'll bring them back pretty as a picture." Lacy Pearl reached for the flowers and almost dropped them, and Dale had to help her gather them up again in her arms. "Thank you, sir," Lacy Pearl said, smiling to beat the band. She looked at Mavis. "If you aren't the luckiest thing I know, with a handsome nephew to bring you all these pretty flowers." She winked, turned, and walked out of the room on squeaky shoes.

"Lord, I thought she was going to eat you up," Mavis said.

Dale pretended to wipe his brow. "Me, too. Poor thing, I bet it's a long time since anybody brought her flowers."

"Don't be mean. She may have a perfectly nice husband who brings 'em home to her."

"Not with all those rings, and not one of them a wedding band." Dale closed the door, then drew up a side chair and sat down close to Mavis, their knees touching. "But I didn't come out here to see how Lacy Pearl was doing. How are *you* getting along? What did you mean you weren't sure any murders were going on?"

"Well, I haven't seen a sign of anything. Everybody seems perfectly nice."

"How about Miss Glacier yesterday, the nurse that rolled you away? I felt like I was never going to see you again." Dale took her two hands in his.

"Oh, she's all right. Helped me unpack and sent off for a nice snack after you left. I suspect she just needs to show she's the boss." Mavis paused. "There *is* one person who's a little bit strange, though, one of the other patients."

"Who's that?"

"Her name's Swannie Hocutt, she said. I met her in the sun-room this morning. She told me a whole bunch of mess about how her children are trying to get everything she has and put her here against her will."

Dale shrugged. "That's not too weird. It can happen."

"But that's not all." Mavis took a deep breath and looked just a little to the side of Dale's face. "She thinks there's this big sex ring going on here, and everybody is involved, even the patients."

Dale broke out laughing, head thrown back, teeth flashing. Mavis couldn't help but join him, and they sat like two teenagers howling over some silliness until they nearly lost their breaths. "Well, wouldn't that be something?" Dale said when he could finally speak. "There was an article in the paper not long ago about how down in Florida these retirees mess around without benefit of matrimony because their social security benefits would be reduced if they walked down the aisle together. Why not here?"

"I've never heard of such a thing," Mavis said, her voice disapproving. "I'd march out of this place right now, murder or no murder, cast or no cast, if I thought such a thing was going on."

"Well, keep your eye out. You never know what might be happening."

Dale was quiet for a moment. His sunny face darkened, his smile was gone. "Something wrong?" Mavis asked.

"Well," he said, "I guess I've got some bad news."

"What's that?"

Dale pushed his chair back a little and crossed his legs. "I went down to the jail today to take them a set of pictures I took of Miss Luna out by the pond, and I found out what was in the autopsy report on her. She drowned. That lick on her head probably knocked her out, and even in a little bit of water, turned facedown, she could suffocate in just a few minutes. What Mr. Jesse was doing during that time, he won't say, still claiming that he let go of the chair hardly a second, it rolled down the hill, and he went down right after it. Of course, that detective, Wilton Early, is saying that Mr. Jesse hit her on the head and then pushed her in, even though she might just as well have banged against a rock when the chair turned over."

"Isn't he the meanest thing you've ever heard of? He'll get his comeuppance one of these days, you'll see."

"I guess he's doing what he thinks is right. They've indicted Mr. Jesse."

Mavis shook her head. She felt like crying. "That poor man. And Elizabeth Warren, too—she's suffering as much as he is."

"Who's she?"

"His niece—about all the kin he has. Great-niece, really, but she's been close to them most all her life. Her mother died early." Dale didn't answer. Mavis asked, "Was there any news about Miss Elgie?"

"No, not that I heard."

"Then you call Charles Morgan and see if you can find out anything. If she didn't die a natural death, then there'll be a lot more reason to suspect there's a murderer running loose in this place."

"You can't call him?"

"I don't know that somebody can't listen in on the phone. Remember, honey, I'm still undercover."

Dale's smile returned. "Yes, I know. We've got to keep up appearances."

The door swung open suddenly. Lacy Pearl Williams was there with two big vases of flowers. They hadn't heard the squeak of her shoes, and Mavis wondered if she had been outside the door listening. "Now, aren't they the prettiest *things*?" she said. She set one vase on the stand by Mavis's bed and one on the dresser on the other side of the room. "Must have cost a fortune." She smiled at Dale. "I'll come back tomorrow and be sure they have plenty of water. I put in some of that powdered stuff they give you, so they should last a right good time." She backed toward the doorway, her eyes still on Dale. "You come back to see us," she said, and then she turned around and was gone.

Dale got up. "I should go, too," he said. "You may want to take a nap."

Mavis gave a little sniff. "That's about all I do around here, eat and sleep. I'll be so lazy and fat by the time I get out of here, I won't want to do a thing."

"I seriously doubt it," Dale said as he bent over and kissed her on the forehead. "You'll be going like a racehorse till you're a hundred. You need anything else?"

Mavis shook her head. "Not a thing. But I *do* appreciate the flowers. You're just too sweet to me."

Dale smiled but didn't answer, waved to Mavis, and then went out the door. For a long time Mavis sat there, Dale's empty chair in front of her, and felt lonelier than she could remember feeling in a long, long time.

Mavis awoke in the middle of the night from a dream. She couldn't remember what it was, but it left her feeling weighed down, as if she were in a cast all over. Her head ached dully. Although she shifted her leg, plumped up the pillow, and tried to relax, counting backward, she could not fall back asleep. If she were home, she would fix herself some warm milk and read for a while, but here at Lakeview, there was no chance of that.

Finally she could stand it no longer. Sitting up in bed, she reached for her robe (the one Dale had bought her—she smiled to herself, remembering), put it on, then shifted to her chair. Without turning on the light, she rolled herself out into the hall.

There she paused, half expecting a voice to come, telling her to go back to her room. But all she heard was the sounds of the other sleepers—little snores, coughs, rattles of breath—a chorus in the background. Noiselessly, she turned the wheels of the chair and went toward the light at the end of the hallway where the nurses' station was located. Maybe there'll be someone I can talk to, she said to herself. Surely there'll be somebody on duty.

There was . . . but she was sound asleep. A slim woman with thick, dark hair pulled back in a bun, small eyes pressed shut (why, she's foreign, Mavis thought), sat perfectly straight up in her chair with her head thrown back, a copy of *Star* magazine resting on her lap. Anything in the world could have gone on, murder included, and she would never have known. Mavis decided not to wake her.

She was about to go back down the hall to her room when she noticed the doorway of the sun-room. It was empty, and maybe, she thought, if she turned on the TV without the sound so it wouldn't bother anybody, she could watch some old movie a few minutes and then get back to sleep. She rolled inside.

Moonlight poured through the windows, bright as day. Outside where the bazaar had been held (the tables gone now, the stage torn down), the grass looked frosted, and on the far hill, nestled between the dark rows of trees, the little pond was silver. Such a peaceful scene—it was hard to think that such a tragedy had occurred there just a few days before. Mavis was about to turn toward the TV in the corner when something caught her eye—just a flicker of motion, as if a

light had blinked, there beneath the trees. She moved closer
to the window and pulled aside the curtain.

There it was again, but this time she was sure she could
see a figure moving, slowly but steadily, as if it carried something very heavy. She watched and wondered if she should
give an alarm—go out there and tell the nurse that somebody
was sneaking across the hill by the pond. She could, but
maybe they'd think she was just an old fool, imagining things,
like Swannie Hocutt. And anyway, it might not have anything at all to do with what was going on at Lakeview, maybe
just somebody taking a shortcut on his way home. She shook
her head and peered again through the window; the figure
was gone. She dropped the curtain, wondering if she had
been visible sitting there in the moonlight.

The foreign nurse was still asleep in the same position
when Mavis rolled past her at the nursing station, and the
same chorus of nighttime sounds met her in the hallway.
After she got into bed, she tried to picture that darkened
figure in her mind, but it slipped away as sleep overcame
her, and she slept till morning, undisturbed by further
dreams.

Chapter Twelve

"Honey, you going to sleep all day long?"

The voice came to Mavis as if from a great distance. She struggled to open her eyes, but even when she did, she still had trouble remembering where she was. Then she saw Daisy's smiling face above the tray she was setting on the stand by Mavis's bed, heard somebody cough down the hall, felt a slight itch beginning under her cast, and she pushed herself up on her elbows to greet another day at Lakeview. "What time is it?" she asked.

Daisy looked at her watch. "Well, it ain't too late," she said, "nearly nine-thirty. But you just be as lazy as you want to—that's what you're here for."

"Lord, have mercy," Mavis said, pushing herself all the way up into a sitting position. "I don't know when I've lain so late in bed before. I couldn't half sleep last night, so maybe I was just making up."

"You wasn't the only one, looks like."

"What? What do you mean?"

"Seems like somebody was prowling around here last night. Wasn't you, was it?" Daisy laughed.

So I wasn't wrong, Mavis thought, there *was* somebody on that hill up to no good. She almost told Daisy, but then she remembered she was supposed to be investigating, so she said, "Not likely. I just lay here with my eyes wide open. What kind of prowling?"

Daisy looked around at the door, then moved closer to the

side of Mavis's bed. "Down in the storeroom," she said. "I'm not supposed to tell. But the food service director is having a fit about all the stuff missing—a carton of crackers, a box of hot dogs, some canned goods.''

"Who do they think did it?" Mavis reached up and began to undo the net she wore over her hair at night.

"Well, there wasn't no signs of a break-in, so they seem to think it was somebody inside. They been asking all of us questions—where we was last night, stuff like that. I said, 'Honey, I was at *church* all day yesdiddy, singing and testifying, and didn't get home till *late*. I went to sleep soon as I got home, tired as I could be. I couldn't have lifted a *package* of crackers, much less a box of 'em. You find somebody else to pin this crime on.' That sort of shut them up far as I was concerned, but they still going around to everybody else.''

"Even if they worked here, how would anybody get in?"

Daisy made a waving motion in the air. "Shoot," she said. "Half the folks around here got keys. People in the office downstairs, the nursing staff, Lord knows who else. They keep the door locked, but there's a key hanging right beside it since there's so much going in and out. Anybody in the world could take it and get a copy made on their lunch hour, and nobody would know the difference.''

"You have any suspicions?"

Daisy checked the door again. "Don't quote me," she said, her voice lower, "but if that Larry Lee Matthews was still around, I'd put my money on him.''

"Who's he?"

"I told you—he used to work in food service with me, took around trays. He got fired.''

"What for?"

"General sorriness. Late, laid out of work 'sick' a lot, sneaky. Some of the patients missed things from their rooms, and though everybody thought sure Larry Lee did it, they didn't have no proof. Good riddance, I say, but boy, was he mad, said they'd be sorry they let him go. But he was like that—all mouth and nothing much behind it.'' Daisy sighed and leaned against the bed. "I feel sorry for his wife and young-uns, though. I seen 'em a couple of times in his truck when he come to pick up his paycheck. She's nothing but a child herself, and I'd bet there ain't no framed marriage certificate hanging on their sitting room wall. And the children looked pitiful, pasty white, like they got worms."

"Miz Norris, I reckon there are others waiting for their breakfast, if you don't mind."

Nurse Overby stood in the doorway, one hand on her hip. Mavis and Daisy hadn't even heard the door open. A look of fear flashed in Daisy's eyes, and she pushed herself away from the bed. "Yes'm, I was just going," she said. "I was helping Miz Lashley here get situated."

"That's very kind of you," Estelle Overby said, "but we have to consider *all* our residents."

Daisy backed away from Mavis, not looking at Nurse Overby. Then she pushed the stand with the food tray on it closer to the bed. "You have a good day," she said, smiling at Mavis, the fear gone from her eyes. "I'll be back later to pick up your tray." Without a glance at the other woman who still stood in the doorway, she walked around her and went out.

Mavis began to tear open the carton of bran flakes, hoping that Nurse Overby would go away. She struggled with the cellophane, and suddenly the package burst, scattering little flakes of cereal all over the tray. "Well, damnation!" Mavis said, then looked up and saw that Nurse Overby was still there watching her. She pointed to the box. "I think they make those things on purpose so that nobody but King Kong could get 'em open."

The edges of Nurse Overby's mouth turned up in what might have been a smile. Then she looked over her shoulder, closed the door behind her, and came to stand by Mavis's bed. She did not look at the tray but stared at Mavis from beneath her thick brows. "Since you're new here, Miz Lashley, I just want to make a little request. It's not a good idea to get too familiar with the help. Now, Daisy Norris, she's a good worker—everybody would agree on that—but she *does* have a tendency to carry tales. She has her work to do, and if she gets behind, it just makes it hard on everybody else. I'm sure you understand.''

I understand that you're probably just jealous of somebody who hasn't got one mean bone in her body, Mavis would have liked to say, but instead, she began to push the cereal into a little pile with her fingers. ''I'll take that into consideration in the future,'' she said. She wasn't about to let that nurse get her goat. Estelle Overby didn't answer but turned and went out the door. My, she moves quickly for someone her size, Mavis thought.

Mavis enjoyed her breakfast in spite of her little run-in with Nurse Overby. She had just finished her second piece of toast and was pouring herself more coffee when she heard a commotion down the hall. First came a crashing sound like a tray falling on the floor, and then a voice that could have been heard all the way over by the pond. ''Tarnation, woman!'' it said. ''Haven't I told you before to leave me alone? Now, you just take that pretty little *be*-hind of yours out of my room before I throw it out. I'm not so senile yet, I have to spend my time making little doodads not worth a damn. I'm still a fit man. I could take on anybody here if they got a mind to do so. Take on you, too, honey, if you know what I mean.''

Darn this cast! Mavis thought. The voice had quieted before she was able to get out of bed into her chair and go to her door to see what the uproar was about. She looked right toward the nurses' station, then left, but at first nothing seemed amiss. Then she saw a figure sagging against the wall down by the elevator. Even in the dim light she could recognize Kimberly Collier's hair frizzed out around her head and the blue smock she wore with some sort of insignia on the sleeve. ''Anything I can do?'' Mavis called out, trying to keep her voice low.

Kimberly raised her head. No doubt about it, she had been crying. Pulling a handkerchief from her pocket, she wiped her eyes; then, trying to smile, she walked slowly to where

Mavis was sitting in her chair. "I'm sorry you were disturbed," she said. She pointed back down the hallway. "He's just so difficult. I guess I should stop trying."

"I wasn't bothered," Mavis said, "just curious. Who was it, anyway, making all the fuss?"

Kimberly took a deep breath, sniffing. Mavis rolled backward so that Kimberly could come into her room. "Mr. Alton Hubbard. I shouldn't talk about other guests, but I can't help it. He's just a wicked old man. I try to get him involved in activities, but he has a fit every time I come into his room. And it's not just me. He yells at everybody. Teases little Miss Hocutt to death, telling nasty jokes whenever she comes into view. Half the time, she puts her hands over her ears soon as she sees him. He's here for just a little while until they can get his medications adjusted—he's got heart problems and emphysema—but frankly, I don't see why it matters. He's too mean to die."

Poor Kimberly, Mavis thought. Probably all her life she'd go wandering around like a lost child. Some people just never grow up. Mavis patted her on the hand. "Don't you worry. Just ignore him. He's only trying to get attention—you know how men are. Talk and blunder about like wild animals, but underneath, half the time, they're scared to death. Leave him alone, and he'll come around when he gets lonesome enough."

"Why, I never looked at it that way," Kimberly said, smiling. "Maybe you're right. My way certainly hasn't worked." She glanced at her watch. "Speaking of work, I've got to be going. I still have to set up things in the activity room downstairs." Her face brightened. "*You'll* come, won't you? I just know you'll enjoy it, and it'll give you a chance to meet some of the other residents."

Well, I don't know that I'd *want* to meet Mr. Alton Hubbard, Mavis thought. But then, she didn't want to let poor Kimberly down. "Sure thing," she said. "What are you all going to be doing?"

"We're getting ready for Halloween day after tomorrow."

"Halloween? Lord, I'd forgotten all about it. The days sort of all run together here."

"Oh, we have the nicest time!" Kimberly clasped her hands in front of her. "In the afternoon the children from the nursery school at the church down the street come by for trick or treat in their little costumes. They're the cutest things! And then in the evening we have our own party with refreshments and costumes and all sorts of games We're making masks for everybody out of paper bags. It's so much fun."

Maybe, Mavis thought, but she wondered if Mr. Hubbard wasn't right about its sounding a little childish. Still, poor Kimberly Collier had had enough disappointments, what with the Fall Festival Bazaar getting rained out and turning into a disaster. So Mavis said again, "I'll come," and gave Kimberly a big smile.

"Thank you, Miz Lashley," Kimberly said, her face beaming now. She gave Mavis a quick kiss on the cheek, then turned and rushed out of the room.

Mavis washed up after that, changed out of her gown into a plain everyday dress—she had noticed that, except for the bedridden, most people wore their regular clothes at Lakeview—and rolled herself out into the hallway. From around the corner, down past the elevator, came the sound of a floor polisher, and she heard the murmur of voices at the nurses' station, but otherwise, a midmorning calm prevailed. The sun shone brightly through the sun-room windows where the curtains blew in a slight breeze, and the gaily covered furniture there looked soft and inviting. How different it had seemed the night before when Mavis was hidden behind the curtains watching the figure on the hillside by the pond.

She rode the elevator down to the ground floor, a little afraid. What if she got stuck? But that was a foolish thought. Surely it had an alarm she could sound, and someone would come and rescue her in no time flat. Perhaps she had been more upset than she had realized by what had happened last night and the report of a burglary this morning. A fine undercover agent you'd make, she told herself, frightened by every shadow. Just calm down. Putting on a smile, she rolled down the hall past the employees' locker room, where Zeena and the other Merry Makers had changed, to the activity room beyond.

It was large and colorfully painted; the sun shone in brightly here, too. Outside, the lawn spread toward the trees and pond, the grass beginning to yellow at the edges. There had been no rain, Mavis realized, since the storm last week, and most of that downpour had run off without soaking into the ground. At the doorway, Mavis paused. People were seated around the room at large tables working quietly, and a few of them looked up and smiled when they glimpsed her. Some she recognized from the dining room; others were strangers. Miss Swannie Hocutt sat at the far end of the room but did not let on she'd ever spoken to Mavis. Maybe she didn't remember. Just as well, Mavis thought. I wouldn't want the others to get the idea that I'm off in the upper story the way she is anyway.

Then Kimberly spotted her. She had been bent over a woman, helping her tie a ribbon, but seeing Mavis, she suddenly straightened up and called out (too loud; everybody stopped working and looked at Mavis), "Why, Miz Lashley, you *did* come! I'm so glad. Welcome to our little group. Now, everybody, let's all introduce ourselves. This is Miz Mavis Lashley. She's new. I just know you're going to like her."

The others mumbled their names, a little embarrassed, Mavis could see. She smiled and said, "How're y'all?" and was glad when they all bent over their work again.

"You find a place to sit, Miz Lashley," Kimberly said, coming toward Mavis. "I'll get you some materials. We're making little trick-or-treat items for the children when they come on Halloween—bags full of candy and some little toys they'll just love—and you can help fill them." She went to a cabinet near the door, opened it, and bent down.

"You can sit here." A woman to Mavis's right slid over her chair so there would be space. Mavis had not noticed her before, a solid-looking woman whose skin was covered in wrinkles, sun-darkened; her hair was still thick, pulled back into a bun, and though it was nearly all gray, it still retained a kind of golden sheen, as if a light shone on it from above. Her smile was as warm as the sunshine that came through the windows.

"I don't want to take your place," Mavis said.

The woman held up her hands. "I'm just sitting here for the company," she said. "I'm not much help with these."

Mavis looked at her hands. The fingers were all twisted like tree roots, the knuckles swollen rock-hard, painful just to see. Mavis didn't know what to say, so she pushed her chair up to the table and waited while Kimberly came over and gave her a supply of candy and toys, orange and black felt bags, and strips of ribbon to tie them with. When Kimberly had walked away again, Mavis bent over to the woman beside her and whispered, "Tell me your name again, honey. I couldn't keep everybody straight when we were going around the room before."

The woman laughed. "I'm not surprised," she said. "I'm Betty Williams. From over near Rocky Mount." She pointed to the ceiling. "I'm in the room right next to yours upstairs," she said. "I hadn't come in yet—thought you might want to get settled in before you had company."

"Well, I declare," Mavis said. "I wouldn't have minded a-tall. It seems sort of lonesome here, but maybe that's because I'm new."

The woman sighed. "No, it's just that way. I've been here almost a year—can't do much for myself; nobody at home left to do for me—and I still haven't got used to it. That's why I come to activities, just to be with the others. Why, I even come to bingo, even though somebody else has to play my card.

"Lord, when I think back about what I used to do. We had a farm, and I was up at dawn milking, saw to the chickens and did all my housework, not counting cooking for the hands when we was putting in tobacco, or fixing all the meat at hog-killing time. When the pain started coming in my fingers, I just ignored it at first, thinking it would go away. But it got worse and worse, and by the time my husband died, I could hardly do the dishes anymore. I went to the doctors, but you know how that is—they try this medicine and that medicine, and if it don't cause something else bad, it don't do you any good. Finally I had to sell the place—got a good price for the land; they wanted it for a housing development—and came on out here. I suppose it could be worse, but you're right, it does get lonesome.''

Before Mavis could answer, Kimberly Collier came over, looked at the unfilled bags that lay on the table in front of her, and asked, "You need some help, Miz Lashley?"

Mavis shook her head. "No, ma'am," she said, and pointed to Betty Williams. "We were just getting acquainted. I'll get those bags filled, don't you worry." Picking up one, she began putting candies inside. Kimberly smiled and walked away.

"I'm looking forward to seeing those young-uns on Wednesday," Betty said. "About all you see around here is old faces, except for some of the help, and they don't seem to last long. You got any grandchildren?" she asked, a serious look suddenly on her face.

With anyone else she had known so short a time, Mavis would simply have said, No, she didn't have a one. But sitting there by Betty, seeing those poor, distorted, useless hands, she felt already that she had drawn close to the other woman, and that they would be friends. She put down the bag and said, "I just had one daughter, but I lost her a long time ago. An accident. She was just going off to school, crossing the street right in front of the house while I was on the front stoop watching, when this crazy fool came roaring by in an old car and hit her. She was dead before I could scream." Mavis felt tears come to her eyes; she didn't know when she had last felt them there. "I guess I'll never get over it. Sometimes when I'm walking down the street, I'll look at young folks and think to myself, Now, that could be my daughter if she'd lived, that could have been her child.''

Mavis saw a glimmer of tears in the other woman's eyes. "Why, that's the saddest thing I've heard in a long time," Betty Williams said. She was silent a moment, but then she said, "But there are worse ways to lose your child, I expect. Ways that hurt even more."

Mavis was about to ask Betty Williams whatever did she mean, but at that moment she heard a boisterous voice behind her in the doorway. "Well, how're you folks this morning?" it bellowed. "So this is where everybody's hiding. I might have known."

"Why, Mr. Hubbard, I'm real glad you joined us," Kimberly Collier said in a voice sweet as syrup. Mavis looked at her just in time to see the bright smile fade from her face.

"I just bet you are." His voice was mocking, imitating Kimberly's sweetness. "You thought I'd come down here to make some of those foolish doodads. Ha! Don't hold your breath."

Well, isn't *he* a hateful thing, Mavis thought as she turned around to stare at the man in the doorway. But he was not at all what she had expected to see. Hearing about Alton Hubbard from Kimberly after his outburst that morning, how he insulted her and teased poor Miss Hocutt with dirty jokes, Mavis had pictured him as a dried-up old man, bandy-legged, foulmouthed, with three days' worth of whiskers on his chin and half his breakfast on his chest. Lord, was she wrong this time! Mr. Alton Hubbard was as handsome as could be. Thick silver hair that fell over his forehead, eyes as blue as a stained-glass window, a ruddy complexion (Mavis hoped it didn't mean he drank)—he could have walked right out of one of the afternoon soap operas. In spite of the frown she tried to put on her face for his mocking of Kimberly Collier, Mavis couldn't keep her hand from rising to smooth the curls on the back of her neck.

"Well, you can certainly visit with us," Kimberly said, her voice wavering.

"I intend to," Alton Hubbard said. "This is where all the pretty ladies have gone." Swannie Hocutt gave a snort and turned her chair so that she was facing away from the table. Moving farther into the room, Mr. Hubbard didn't seem to notice. "Well, my goodness," he said as he bent over, trying to catch Mavis's eye. "Here's a new face, and a mighty nice one, too. How come you haven't introduced me, Miss Collier? At least you could do *that*.''

Kimberly came over and stood by Mavis's chair. "You be nice to her," she said, her voice firmer. Why, she might even stand up to him, Mavis thought. "This is Miz Lashley. She's just come. It's her first day of activities."

Mavis felt herself go red. She ought to tell Alton Hubbard that at his age he should be thinking about getting ready to meet his Maker rather than whatever else he seemed to have on his mind. But with those blue eyes staring straight into her own, she couldn't get out the words, and all she could say was "I'm mighty happy to meet you."

He grinned, moved to the table, and leaned against the edge so that Mavis wouldn't have to turn around to see him. Kimberly stood her ground near Mavis's chair. Alton Hubbard pointed at Kimberly. "She'll have you down here working all the time if you don't watch your step. Me, I'm at Lakeview for a rest, not to spend my time messing around with 'projects.' Like I said, I came down here for the company.''

Mavis could feel Kimberly's tenseness next to her even though they were not touching, and she remembered the poor girl's upset this morning. For all his good looks, Mr. Alton Hubbard wasn't very polite, and Mavis decided she just had to speak up.

"Well, that's her job," she said, reaching over to take Kimberly's hand. "She's trying as hard as she can. I reckon you might be a little more cooperative—you might even enjoy it once you got started. I'm having a real nice time myself." (Lord, forgive me, she prayed to herself, for that little white lie.)

Alton Hubbard slapped his leg. "Well, what do you know?" he said. "Somebody with a little spunk. My, that's a change! Everybody else around here creeps about like they're going to be taken any minute and don't have enough strength left to open their mouths, let alone have a reasonable conversation." He gave a little bow to Mavis. "We'll have to talk some more, Miz Lashley. I'm real glad to meet you."

With that, he sailed out of the room like some figurehead on a boat, trailing a scent of cologne.

"Devil!" hissed Miss Hocutt at the end of the room, but nobody paid her any mind.

Betty Williams, who had sat through the whole conversation with a smile sparkling in her warm eyes, reached over and patted Mavis on the arm with her distorted fingers. "Looks like he's taken a real shine to you," she said. "He's hardly said two words to any of us the whole time he's been here, except maybe to tease."

Mavis shook her head. "Lord, I sure do hope not. Last thing in the world I need is Mr. Alton Hubbard sniffing around my door." But Mavis had to admit she was pleased. Beneath all that bluster, she sensed, Alton Hubbard hid feelings of warmth, even kindness, that he did not want to admit. Perhaps it was her Christian duty to try to bring them out.

It wasn't till much later, when she went back to her room to get ready for lunch, that she suddenly thought, Alton Hubbard could be the murderer just as well as anybody else. Maybe that's what he's hiding from view—evil—not kindness at all!

Chapter Thirteen

Dale bounced in late that afternoon, this time with a big box of candy. "I'm going to be fat as a pig," Mavis said, "sitting here on my rear end and eating all the time. They won't know me when I finally get back to my exercise class."

With a shrug, Dale put the box on the bedside stand. "Give it to the nurses," he said. "Sweeten 'em up. That Miz Overby could certainly use a little bit of it. She was on the elevator when I was coming up, and she couldn't help but point out it was after regular visiting hours. 'Yes, ma'am, I know,' I told her, 'but I couldn't get here any sooner, and my poor old aunt Mavis would be just *devastated* if I didn't get out to see her.' She looked like she'd sucked vinegar but didn't say anything else. I had a good mind to open that box and offer her a piece of candy, but I knew it would be a waste."

Mavis laughed and said, "I don't know what I'm going to do with you. She'll have you banned."

"Shoot," Dale said. "I'd climb in the window if I had to." Flopping down in the chair beside Mavis's bed, he let out a long sigh. "But thank the Lord I didn't have to come in that way today. I don't know that I could have made it."

"What's wrong with you?"

"Just tired. I spent half the day over at the Women's Club taking pictures of their annual flower show. If you think the Fall Festival Bazaar out here was bad, you ought to have been there. Ugliest flower arrangements I've ever seen! Each one had to have a 'theme,' so there were arrangements spray-painted silver in toy rocket ships, cutesy ones with calico ribbons and teensy bales of straw, more Bibles and praying hands than you'd see at a revival. And some smiling lady behind every one of them wanting her picture taken. I finally asked, 'Isn't there just a plain bowl of flowers around here?' and they looked at me like I'd passed gas.''

"Now, that's no way to talk at all," Mavis said, trying to give Dale a serious look.

He bent over with his elbows on his knees and his chin cupped in his two hands. "I was just trying to cheer you up a little," he said. "I'm sorry."

"Cheer me up? For what? Do I look down in the dumps?''

He shook his head. "No. It's just that I've got some bad news and I know you'll take it hard."

"What in the world?" Mavis said.

"Miss Elgie Skinner. She was murdered. Charles Morgan called to let me know. The autopsy report came in and showed she had been smothered to death."

"How?" Mavis's hand flew up, as if she wanted to take back the word.

"With a pillow, or a plastic bag. I guess it doesn't take long—if she was weak and the killer strong, no more than a few minutes." He sat back up. "I hate to say it, but it would be about as long as Miss Luna took to die, lying there at the edge of the pond."

"Now, how could there be any connection? Surely they don't think Mr. Jesse is some mad killer who has been running around Lakeview killing off the residents. And anyway, he was already in jail when Miss Elgie was killed.'' She felt such pain when she thought again of Miss Elgie. "That poor thing,'' she said, "just lying there waiting to die. Who could be so cruel?''

Sitting back in the chair, Dale crossed his legs and said, "Well, I reckon they're going to try to find out. They're launching a big investigation—Charles has been put in charge—so it won't be just Miss Elgie's death they're looking into. Already, Charles said, they've examined the death certificates of some of the others who died recently, but they didn't see any connections—all from different places, with different illnesses and reasons for being at Lakeview—except that they were women and they were all made-up when they were found.''

"Well, thank the Lord Charles Morgan is taking over. I hope that other detective—what's his name, Wilton Early?— will be out of it for good.''

"Well, don't forget, Mr. Jesse is indicted. He'll still go to trial if something else doesn't turn up in the meantime.''

"Charles will find a way to learn what really happened. You can count on it. And I'm saying a little prayer every night just as a reminder to the Lord.''

"Well, you'll get a chance to talk to Charles tomorrow. He wanted me to tell you he'll be coming out in the morning to question a lot of folks—the administrator, some of the other staff, even a few patients. That way, he said, it wouldn't seem odd for him to come in to see you. But if anybody else is around, you're to pretend you don't know him from before. Remember, you're still undercover.''

"Well, so far, I certainly haven't uncovered a thing. Maybe Charles will tell me to forget it, and I can get out of this cast. It's beginning to itch all the time.''

"I doubt it. You're still in a good position to learn what's going on. But that's all the more reason for you to be careful, now that we know that Miss Elgie was murdered—and probably some others, too.'' Dale looked at his watch and jumped up. "I've got to go now," he said. "Believe it or not, I have an invitation out to dinner.''

"Anybody I know?''

"Not hardly. Somebody new.''

"Seems like they're all new.''

Dale laughed. "I guess so. But I *try*—things just never seem to work out for me.''

"Well, *I'd* like to ask you for a date tomorrow night.''

"Why, Mavis Lashley, whatever do you mean?'' Dale opened his eyes wide as saucers.

"For the Halloween party here at Lakeview. Bring your

camera and take some photographs. Poor Kimberly Collier, she's worked herself half to death on it, and after the bazaar was such a bust, I know she'd be pleased to have some pictures."

"Long as you keep her away from me," Dale said.

"Be nice," Mavis told him. "She's all right—just tries too hard."

Smiling, Dale kissed Mavis good-bye, told her not to eat too much candy, and then was gone. Mavis sat a long time in the fading light, thinking about Miss Elgie Skinner and all those other poor dead ladies with their faces made up by their killer.

After supper Mavis went to play bingo in the activity room. It was strange to be there at night, the fluorescent lights above shedding an unreal brightness, the windows reflecting darkly. Figures bent over their cards as if guarding secrets. Up front, one of the night staff called the numbers in a flat, monotonous voice, flicking her cigarette in an ashtray beside her without looking even though just above her head hung a sign that said in big letters NO SMOKING. Every now and then a wavering voice would yell out, "Bingo!", startling the others every time, and they would all stop, complaining about their luck, while the winner read back the numbers to be sure they were correct. Kimberly had left a box of prizes—pocket combs, sample lipsticks, little bottles of perfume, bags of sugarless candy that nobody wanted—and the winners would each select an item. Mavis was surprised how eager they were to get them. Not worth five cents, she thought, but she had to admit she was disappointed when she didn't win.

When Mavis had first rolled into the room, Betty Williams had called out to her and pointed to the space beside her at the table. Mavis had stopped there, smiling, and Betty said to her, "I'm real glad you came. I wasn't sure who I was going to ask to play my card"—she held up her crippled hands—"but now that you're here, I wonder if you'd mind." She'd laughed. "They've got large-print cards, so I can see the numbers all right. It's the chips that I can't put on."

Mavis had picked two cards and grabbed a handful of chips from a container on the table. "Of course I will," she said. "Maybe together we'll get lucky."

They didn't. All around them, people kept calling out, "Bingo!" and claiming their prizes, and though Mavis and Betty both came close, with just one more number needed several times, neither won. When they stopped for refreshments (a pitcher of Kool-Aid from the kitchen and a box of cookies), Mavis pushed the cards away, said, "Maybe we need some new ones," and chose two more. "Next time around, we sure should win."

"I guess it's just luck," Betty Williams said.

"Yes, and I never had any." Mavis took a swallow of the pale pink Kool-Aid and leaned back against her chair. "My husband, though, he was about the luckiest person I've ever seen. We'd go to carnivals—they had a lot back then; I reckon television has killed them off—and they'd have these plain-out gambling games, not just bingo, and he'd win prize after prize. 'I just stand,' he'd tell me, 'and watch how the numbers go. It's not hard to figure out. Then I play when I know one is coming around again.' Worked every time, though he'd get such mean looks after a while, I'd give him a tug and say, 'Let's go,' and we'd walk over to another stand, me carrying all the loot. Back then, it wasn't all teddy bears and fancy dolls, but real things you could use, like blankets and housewares. Why, I bet I've got things up in a closet right now that John won twenty years ago at some carnival."

"Well, consider yourself lucky," Betty Williams said with a laugh. "I never got to go. I was raised up in the Holiness Church, and anything *fun* was *sin*; leastways, that's what I was taught. If I'd have set foot in a carnival back then when I was growing up, I'd have been sure I was headed straight for damnation. Much less gamble—that was so bad, it was hardly even talked about, like fornication. By the time I was old enough to figure a few things out on my own, I was already married, and we didn't have time or money to go gallivanting off to a carnival. Even then, I expect I would have thought it a sin."

They played a few more games. The prizes were almost gone, and the night nurse's voice was getting raspy from the cigarettes. Mavis and Betty still had not won. Then, hardly believing her eyes, almost letting it pass, Mavis looked at Betty's card and realized that the number just called completed a row there. "Hallelujah! Raise your hand, honey. We've just won!" Mavis jerked up Betty's hand and raised it in the air. She was so excited that she could hardly read the numbers back. When she had finished, she and Betty went to the prize box and looked at what was left. "Not much," Mavis said. "You want a pad-and-pencil set?"

"What's that?" Betty pointed to a small red box.

Mavis picked it up and turned it over; the side was cellophane. "Well, isn't that pretty?" she said. "A little figurine. I'm surprised it wasn't broken in the bottom of the box."

"I'll take that," Betty said. "You don't mind carrying it upstairs for me and putting it on my dresser?"

"You don't even have to ask."

After a few more games, when all the prizes were won, the nurse stubbed out her last cigarette, gathered up the cards and chips with help from some of the other residents, and then waited till they were all out in the hallway before she turned off the light. " 'Night," she said, and walked off toward the dining room to return the empty Kool-Aid pitcher. Betty rolled Mavis's chair up the hall to the elevator ("At least my hands are good for *something*," she said), and they went up with the others and then to Betty's room. "Right here okay?" Mavis asked after she had taken the china figurine out of the box, pointing to the dresser.

"That'll be just fine," Betty Williams said. "I appreciate your help."

Mavis went to her room, changed quickly into her gown, brushed her teeth, creamed her face, and then put the net over her hair. But she didn't feel a bit sleepy, she realized, when she got into bed and closed her eyes, ready to say her prayers. Too much excitement at bingo, she thought . . . and nothing to do all day to make her tired. She opened her eyes again and sat straight up in bed, listening. Was Betty Wil-

liams next door feeling the same way? Mavis felt as if the
two of them still touched somehow, her hand tingling the
way it had tingled when she had jerked Betty's arm into
the air to win her prize. "Honey," she called out tentatively,
"you still awake?"

"Sure am," Betty called right back. "You want to visit a
while?"

Mavis put on her silky robe and got off the bed back into
the chair. "You reckon they'll *get* us?" she asked as Betty
came through the door.

Betty laughed. "They'll never know. That little night nurse
sleeps like a log. Sometimes I wonder what I *would* do if I
really needed help in the night." She sat down across from
Mavis. "My, aren't those the prettiest *flowers*," she said,
pointing to the vase on the dresser. "They sure do brighten
up the room."

"My nephew brought them," Mavis said, smiling. "That
scalawag"—she pointed to the box of candy—"brought me
that, too. I told him I'd be so fat, I wouldn't be able to get
through the door if he kept that up." She reached over for
the box, removed the cellophane wrapper and then the lid,
and extended the box to Betty. "Have some," she said.
"Show me the one you like and I'll get it for you."

"That piece there that looks like sea foam," Betty
said. "It always was my favorite kind. It'll be worth having
to brush my teeth all over again."

Mavis took out the piece of candy and carefully gave it to
Betty, who put the whole piece in her mouth and chewed up
and down, grinning like Christmas morning. "You thank
that nephew of yours," she said. "I don't know when I've
enjoyed anything so much."

"I'll do that," Mavis said. "Maybe next time he comes,
you can meet him."

Betty sighed, her face sober again. "That'd be real nice.
I don't have many visitors. Most everybody's gone, or they
don't keep in touch."

"Why's that?"

"Bitterness, old bad feelings." She paused, as if she was

trying to decide whether she should say the words, then went on. "Maybe if you *had* to lose your daughter, it was better she went on when she did. At least you knew there was pure love in her heart for you when she died, not hate."

"Are you talking about one of your own?"

Betty nodded her head. "Yes, ma'am. My daughter, the only child I ever had, like you."

"Is she gone?"

"I don't even know! Isn't that the most pitiful thing? I suppose somebody would get in touch if anything happened to her, but I'm not sure."

Mavis looked at Betty's sad face, surrounded by the glow of her golden hair, and felt the other woman's pain. Mavis's own wounds had grown dull over the years, and though the sudden flash of her daughter's face before her eyes could still bring tears, she was more accepting now, hoping that, one day, the Lord would reveal to her why he had taken her child. But Betty's scars were raw still, unhealed, and though Mavis wanted to bind them up, she could think of no easy words of comfort to apply, so she simply said, "Tell me what happened."

Betty shrugged off her bedroom slippers and put her feet up in the chair beside her. "It's no new story," she said. "You've heard it before. You remember the war, how it was right after—everything changed? That's when Roxanne was born. Maybe it was just the *time* that was wrong, not anything I did." She shrugged her shoulders. "I tried to raise her up the best I could. We were struggling at first, with the farm, but when we began to have a little more, it was easier. We could buy her things, nice things like the other children. Maybe it was we got her too much, and it was something else she needed—who knows?

"I was still going to the Holiness Church then—she was, too, went every Sunday and got an award for perfect attendance—and though I guess I'd sort of broken with some of their beliefs, maybe I was carrying a lot of them around with me still. Anyway, we were okay till she got to high school, and then suddenly it was makeup and dances and revealing clothes—and fights once I tried to put my foot down. Overnight, it seemed, Roxanne had changed from the sweetest little girl you've ever seen into a you-know-what, and we couldn't seem to do anything about it. Her daddy tried—beat her once so bad that I was afraid we'd have the law on us— and *I* tried to understand her, but it didn't do no good. She was stubborn and bound and determined to have her way.

"You can imagine what happened. A week before her sixteenth birthday, she announced she was pregnant, and then it was hurry up and have a shotgun wedding so the neighbors wouldn't suspect. She didn't want it, and I knew it wouldn't work, but her daddy insisted, so we went through with it, just pretend. When they walked out the door of the church, it never dawned on me that would be the last time I'd see her, but that's what happened. That sorry thing she married decided he could get a better job up North somewhere, so they took off next day without a fare-thee-well in his rattletrap car with little more than the clothes on their backs. For a while she kept in touch with some cousins, too proud, too stubborn, to write me, I guess, and I know she had the baby without any trouble. The boy left her soon after, and that was the end of any kind of news."

Betty stopped speaking, her last words echoing slightly in the room. It was very quiet, as if she and Mavis were the only inhabitants of Lakeview Nursing Home, the rest of the world gone by. When Mavis spoke, it was almost a whisper.

"You didn't try to find her?" she asked.

Betty shifted in the chair, trying to cover her bare feet with the hem of her robe. "Not then. I expect Roxanne got her stubbornness from me. And I was too hurt. 'She's made her bed—let her lie in it,' my husband said, and though I knew he was as broken up about it all as I was, he didn't let it show. And I didn't push him, just went along, pretending everything was fine. Much later, when I couldn't stand it anymore, I did find out that those cousins had heard from her again, and they gave me her address, not a hundred miles away. But I couldn't get up the courage to go see her, felt that it was too late by then—too much water had gone under the dam—and she might hate me, nothing else. I stuck her address in my Bible, and I see it every day when I read it, like a sore you pick at and never let heal.''

They were quiet for a while. Betty's story rested on Mavis's heart like a heavy stone. Finally she said, ''Your daughter must have some of the same feelings. Maybe it's not too late. By now she's probably learned her lesson a dozen times or more.''

''I'd like to think so. I could rest easier in my grave if I knew my daughter didn't despise my soul.''

''You got the address?'' Mavis pointed next door to Betty's room. Betty nodded her head yes. ''Well, then, why not write her? What have you got to lose? You never know— she might be sitting in some lonesome room right now feeling the same feelings.''

Betty gave a sad little laugh. ''With these?'' She held up her hands.

''It's my *leg* that's in a cast, not my arms,'' Mavis said. ''I'll write the letter, you supply the words. Wait a minute.'' Mavis rolled past Betty's chair and went to the dresser. ''Seems like I remember the other day when I was putting my things away, I saw some Lakeview Nursing Home stationery in this drawer.'' She pulled it open. ''See?'' she said, holding up the sheets and an envelope. ''It's a sign. The Lord wants us to do it.''

''What in the world will I say?''

''It doesn't have to be fancy,'' Mavis said as she lowered the stand next to her bed and pressed out the sheets. ''Just say right out, 'I'm sorry about all that has gone before. I'd like to see you again,' and sign it, 'Love.' There's bound to be some little bit of that left even after all this time.'' Mavis bent over and wrote ''Dear Roxanne'' in her fine script, and Betty shifted around so that she could see the words spread out on the page. They sat there for a span of time composing the letter. And when it was finished and addressed and stamped, they both felt as if a great weight had been lifted from them, and they knew they would rest easy during the remainder of the night.

"You're one of the Lord's own chosen," Betty said as she bent down to kiss Mavis on the forehead.

"Not by a long shot," Mavis said, but she smiled.

Chapter Fourteen

Mavis was up, dressed, and waiting for her breakfast when Daisy came in with her tray. "Well, look at the early bird," Daisy said as she set the tray on the stand. "You must have been up at the crack of dawn."

"No, ma'am. Just decided I was going to stop lying up in bed late every morning. I never did it in my life before, and it's no time to start now." Mavis didn't look at Daisy. She hated to lie. Although she had no reason at all not to trust the other woman, she was still undercover and couldn't tell her that she was expecting Charles Morgan to come in to see her. "My, doesn't this look nice," she said, lifting the metal cover from her plate. "They cook right good here."

Daisy didn't seem to notice that Mavis had changed the subject. "Yes, ma'am," she said. "But you eat all of that. Lunch'll be light. They're busy fixing the refreshments for the Halloween party tonight."

"You going to be there?"

"I sure am. I volunteered to help with the serving." Daisy turned. "I'll see you there later." She flashed Mavis a smile and went out of the room.

Actually, Mavis ate little, excited by the prospect of Charles's visit. After she had pushed the tray on the stand aside, she went to the bathroom and brushed her teeth, smoothed down her hair once more, then returned to wait in the chair beside the bed. She tried to read her daily devotional but couldn't keep her mind on the words. Too bad she hadn't brought a good mystery with her, though Nurse Overby probably would have been shocked by the sight of a bloody cover. She jumped when a knock finally came on the door.

"Hey there," she said to Charles as he poked his head into the room. "I thought you'd never get here."

"I couldn't come to see you *first*, now, could I?" Charles sat down in the easy chair, his bony knees sticking up in front of him. "People would be suspicious if I made a bee-line for your door."

"Well, who *did* you go to see, then?"

"Clifford Joyner, the administrator. Barbara Santucci, his assistant."

"Lord, the gypsy lady," Mavis said.

Charles gave her a look. "Do I hear a little note of condemnation there?"

"No," she said. "But if I had to pick a suspect, she'd be at the top of my list."

Charles gave his funny laugh. "Well, I guess she does look like something out of a spy novel, the way she dresses and such." He turned serious again. "But you could be right. Some things I'm finding out about this nursing home make me wonder."

"What kind of things?"

"Mainly the finances. We've been looking into the other recent deaths, and there are some strange coincidences. All were women. All were sickly but not necessarily ready to go yet. All had given over their assets for lifelong care. And none of 'em had any really close relatives to watch over them."

"Which makes you think that the sooner they were gotten rid of, the more money there would be left for Lakeview." Mavis shook her head. "But you didn't mention one other coincidence."

"What's that?"

"They were all made-up, the bodies, I mean, even before the undertaker got hold of them."

Charles crossed his long legs and leaned back in the chair.

"That's the part that doesn't make any sense at all. You got any ideas?"

"I guess not. It doesn't fit, far as I can see." Mavis was silent a minute, then asked another question. "What about the doctors? Was it one or two who signed the death certificates?"

"No pattern there. It was a whole bunch. And I suspect most of them hardly knew the patients, just phoned in a prescription when it was needed. But it's a group of doctors that owns this place."

"You don't say?" It had never occurred to Mavis before to wonder who owned Lakeview.

"It's not unusual—a good investment for them. But maybe another reason nobody wanted to look too closely at why so many people were dying off."

"Did you get anything out of the people you talked to?"

"Mr. Joyner and Miss Santucci? No, not a lot. Naturally they don't want to say anything that would hurt Lakeview's reputation, but they gave me the charts on all the patients I asked for, and they all seemed in order. I couldn't go rummaging around in their offices for other evidence with no cause." Uncrossing his legs, Charles sat forward. "What about you?" he said. "You found out anything interesting?"

"Not much. Seems like somebody made off with a few supplies from the kitchen the other night, but I don't know how that could relate to murder."

"I'll check and see if there was a report. You never know." Charles looked at his watch. "I guess I'd better get going," he said. "If I stay too long in your room, it might be noticed. I'll have to go talk to some of the other patients just for show."

"Be careful."

"What do you mean?"

"Well, Miz Swannie Hocutt will probably think you're a sex fiend, and Mr. Alton Hubbard no doubt will try to wrestle you to the floor just to show you what a big shot he is. If you want to meet somebody *nice*, go next door and talk to Miz Betty Williams. She's the sweetest thing I've ever seen."

"I appreciate the advice," Charles said as he got up. "Keep your eyes open. And take care of *your*self. We know now that something pretty awful is going on. We don't want anything to happen to you."

Before Mavis could tell him not to worry, a knock came on the door. "Who in the world could that be?" she said, and then called out, "Come in."

"I hope I'm not disturbing you." It was Elizabeth Warren, Mr. Jesse Dixon's niece. She blushed when she caught sight of Charles standing beside Mavis's chair.

"Not a-tall!" Mavis said, rolling forward just slightly. Now, isn't this a nice coincidence, she said to herself.

"I was just going," Charles said. He looked as awkward as a little boy again sitting in a chair too small for him in a crowded Sunday-school classroom.

"It's nice to see you, Detective Morgan," Elizabeth said. (Lord, Mavis thought, how can Charles Morgan resist those eyes?) "I wanted to thank you for being so nice to my uncle."

Charles tried to smile. "You're certainly welcome," he said. "He's a right nice gentleman."

Mavis couldn't hide her curiosity. "What did you do?" she asked.

Charles shrugged. "Just talked," he said. "I drop in to see him every now and then."

"He still won't talk about bail?" Mavis looked at Elizabeth. She shook her head.

"No. I think he wants to be punished somehow. Someday soon I hope he'll tell you why."

"Maybe," Charles said. He looked at his watch again. "But I do have to go now. It was nice to see you, Miss Warren. 'Bye, Miz Lashley. You take care now." Mavis saw that his eyes were shining when he went out the door.

"He's a real nice man," Elizabeth said.

"Goodness yes," Mavis said, motioning for Elizabeth to sit down. "I've known him since he was a young-un in my Sunday-school class. He was good to his parents, would have been good to the girl who was to marry him except that she ran away and left him in the lurch. By now she certainly must know what a fool she was. He'd still make a mighty fine husband.''

Elizabeth didn't look up. ''Well, how are *you* doing?'' she asked, and Mavis knew she was changing the subject on purpose.

''All right, far as I know. Tired of being laid up. It can get pretty boring. It's a treat to have you come visit.''

''Well, I wanted to. I had to come out to get Uncle Jesse some more clothes, and I said to myself, I'm going to visit poor Miz Lashley while I'm at it. Detective Morgan told me you were out here the other day when I was down at the jail.''

Mercy, Mavis said to herself, they've been seeing more of each other than I thought. Elizabeth seemed not to know what to say next, and for a moment they sat in silence. Then at the window a ray of sunlight suddenly shone in, the sun shifting a billionth of an inch, and the whole room was lit with its brightness. ''My, isn't that pretty!'' Elizabeth said. Her own face suddenly lit up, too. ''How would you like to go for a little ride outside?'' she asked Mavis. ''It's pretty as can be, just a slight chill in the air, but all you need is a little something around your shoulders. I can roll you over to Uncle Jesse's apartment and back. Wouldn't you like that?''

Mavis was already on her way to the closet to get a sweater. ''I sure would,'' she said. ''Anything to get out of this room.''

Outside, the day was clear, the sun bright, though, as Elizabeth had said, there was a chill in the air, and Mavis was glad for the warmth of the sweater on her arms. Still, there had been no rain, and the lawn spreading back to the stand of trees by the pond had continued to yellow in spite of the arcs of water fanned back and forth by sprayers. In just one week the trees had lost most of their leaves, and bare black branches spread over the parking lot in front of the home. Rolling down the ramp, Mavis remembered again the lone figures who had sat there once in winter chill. Soon it would be that cold again.

"I've never been on this side before," Mavis said as Elizabeth pushed her around the other side of the building. A wide walkway went back past the nursing home to a long, low, U-shaped building, brick with Colonial trim, that reminded Mavis of a motel. "If I noticed anything back here at all, I would have thought it was just apartments, not part of Lakeview."

"They're new," Elizabeth said. "The apartments. I think Uncle Jesse and Aunt Luna were the first ones to occupy theirs. If Uncle Jesse doesn't come back here, I guess somebody else will be moving in soon."

Mavis heard a catch in Elizabeth's voice. "Well," she said, "since they gave over everything they had when they moved in, surely the Lakeview folks won't be putting their stuff out on the sidewalk right away. And anyway, shouldn't Mr. Jesse get something back if he doesn't return?"

"I don't know. I never saw the contract. My guess is Lakeview tied things up pretty tight."

Elizabeth turned left at the corner of the building under an overhang. In a center court, flower beds were laid out, but only a few chrysanthemums still bloomed there amid the dried stalks of faded marigolds and zinnias that had not been cleared away. Though aluminum folding chairs leaned against the walls, no one sat outside; at the windows, curtains were drawn. The whole place seemed closed up and deserted, and despite the brightness of the day, Mavis felt a sense of apprehension as Elizabeth stopped in front of one of the closed doors, searched in her purse for a key, and then put it in the lock. She paused before opening the door, as if she, too, felt a sense of dread.

"It's always strange, isn't it, going into somebody else's place when they aren't there?" Elizabeth rolled Mavis over the threshold to the center of the living room. The air was stale, the room dark, and even though Elizabeth went over to the window, raised the shade, and pulled up the sash, the room continued to feel closed up, unused, the corners shadowed. "We won't stay but just a minute," she said. "Uncle Jesse gave me a list of things he wants. I'll get them together

in the bedroom. You make yourself at home.'' Elizabeth
went through an archway to a little hall with other doors
leading off to the bedroom, the bath, the kitchen. Mavis heard
her opening drawers.

Mavis looked around. The room was small, the walls
painted a pale yellow that reflected no light. Dark green wall-
to-wall carpet covered the floor. Obviously Jesse and Luna
Dixon had brought their own furniture with them to this place,
favorite pieces, but they were too big, too fussy, for this
anonymous room. In some old house with rambling corri-
dors, high, wide windows that let in the sun, and wooden
floors polished by years of wear, they would look inviting.
But here, they simply looked shabby. Only the new TV set
sitting catty-cornered at the far end of the room seemed to
fit. The framed pictures sitting on a crocheted doily on top—
a yellowing photograph of Mr. Jesse and Miss Luna smiling
into the camera with young hopes spread across their faces,
snapshots of small children, a portrait of Elizabeth dressed
in a white summer frock, innocent, just blooming—could
not disguise its hideousness.

Mavis rolled over to a table at the end of the sofa. A week-
old copy of *Sports Illustrated* lay there beside a small Bible
with a worn cover and the same devotional tract that Mavis
had brought with her to Lakeview. Miss Luna perhaps had
held it no more than a week ago. Could she still understand
the words? Mavis wondered. Perhaps just the picture of Jesus
on the cover, the feel of the pages between her fingers, had
been comforting to her. Mavis shook her head.

It was then that she saw the box on a lower shelf, half-
hidden in the shadows.

She'd never pry. Leave an opened letter out all day in plain
sight and she'd never read it. But it occurred to her that there
might be something in the box that would help her understand why Mr. Jesse would not talk. Surely it would be all
right just to take a quick look. She glanced up as if the Lord
might be watching her. In the bedroom Elizabeth was still
moving about. I have to, she said to herself, and reached for
the box.

It was oblong, embossed with flowers—candy must have come in it on some long-ago birthday or Valentine's. The top slipped off easily, and Mavis laid it aside. Greeting cards filled the box, yellowed, old-fashioned, signed with love from Jesse and Luna to each other. On others, childish scrawls spelled out the names of children whose parents had made them remember, with a card at Christmastime, the couple who had taught them in Sunday school. Mavis had her own buried away at home somewhere. How sweet. She was about to put the cover back on and slip the box back beneath the table when a thicker edge caught her eye at the bottom. Brushing aside the cards, she pulled out a booklet.

At first the name meant nothing to her, but then—oh, dear Lord!—she remembered a show she had seen once on educational TV about a group that gave out information about how to kill yourself if you wanted to—or how to kill somebody else to put them out of pain. Hemlock. Poison! What in the world would such a thing be doing here? But then, hadn't that other detective, Wilton Early, accused Mr. Jesse of just that—killing off Miss Luna to put her out of her misery? She still wouldn't believe it. From what everybody said, the two of them had seemed so happy. Miss Luna wasn't all that bad, just forgetful, and Mr. Jesse could still take care of her.

But maybe he *did* worry about the future, maybe considered what he might have to do if Miss Luna became worse, or he himself got down sick and couldn't take care of her. Surely that was why he had ordered the pamphlet, not to plan her death over by the pond back of the hill. He would have found some smoother, easier way—pills, then sleep and silence. She slipped the brochure into the pocket of her sweater. No need to leave it here in case the police decide to search the place. Mr. Jesse was innocent. Nothing could make her think differently.

"Well, I guess I got everything." Elizabeth came back through the doorway just as Mavis sat up again from having returned the box to the shelf beneath the table. "You all right, ma'am?" Elizabeth asked. Mavis wondered what expression she showed on her face. She tried to smile.

"Yes," she said. "It's just a little stuffy in here." She waved her hand in front of her face. "You ought to tell them back at the office to come out here once in a while and air out the place."

Elizabeth came over and took the handles of Mavis's chair. She carried a canvas bag in one hand. "There's supposed to be maid service," she said, "but as soon as Uncle Jesse went away, I expect they decided they wouldn't bother anymore. I'll come back in a few days and give the place a good cleaning."

They went outside. Elizabeth locked the door, and they headed back to the walkway. Though the courtyard was still empty, shadowed now, the sun dropped lower in the sky, to Mavis the windows seemed watchful, as if eyes peered through the curtains in the darkened rooms. She felt the edge of the pamphlet in her pocket. Surely no one could know she had taken it, yet any moment she expected a door to open, a figure to emerge with a pointing finger, and a solemn voice to make an accusation.

Hurry! she wanted to say to Elizabeth. Let's get away from here. I have to hide this pamphlet in my room!

Right after lunch they began decorating the activity room for the Halloween party. Kimberly Collier ran around like a chicken with its head cut off, giving orders to two attendants who had been told earlier that morning that they were to help her, and now, with little enthusiasm, were tacking up black and orange streamers across the room. A volunteer was pasting cutouts of black cats and witches on the windows, and someone from food service was filling a tub with water for bobbing apples. A pin-the-tail-on-the-donkey board was tacked up nearby. Mavis and Betty Williams had worked together setting out jack-o'-lanterns on the tables, and when somebody called out, "They're coming!" Mavis hurriedly lit the candles in each one and then turned out the lights, so that the room had a sudden eerie feeling, the cutouts on the windows casting wavering shadows on the walls and floor, the smiles of the jack-o'-lanterns sinister.

Everyone went outside to the staff parking lot to watch the children as they came straggling across the lawn. With the trees nearly bare, the steeple of the church where the day-care center was located was visible, stark against the sky. Already they could hear the bright cries of the children and, as they drew nearer, could begin to identify their costumes—princesses and turtles and Supermen and ghosts—already stained with chocolate and soda from their party at school. Teachers' voices rang out, trying to keep them in a straight line and away from the street. "Aren't they the cutest things?" someone said, and everyone murmured agreement.

Just as the children reached the edge of the parking lot, Kimberly put a record on the record player, and ghostly sounds—whispers, cries—floated out into the bright afternoon. At first the children looked puzzled, stopped, and reached for one another's hands. But then they realized the joke and began to jump up and down, eager to go inside for the promised prizes and treats.

Kimberly led the way, and though she tried to interest the children in bobbing for apples and in pinning the tail on the donkey, they saw the pile of orange and black felt bags and grabbed them right away. Most were torn open immediately, and candy corn sprayed across the floor. The other items—small toys, candy bars—they put in the nearly filled plastic jack-o'-lanterns that they carried. Orange Kool-Aid ran in rivers on the refreshment table as the children grabbed for cups and overturned them.

It was then that two little boys decided that the tub full of apples might be fun after all, but instead of trying to bob for the apples, they simply fished out the hard, red, knotty fruit and began to throw it at each other. Naturally, somebody got hit—a princess whose tiara was knocked half off and who began to cry immediately.

"Stop it!" a voice rang out. Everybody turned; the children became silent. Swannie Hocutt, her wraithlike arm raised to the ceiling with a pointing finger as if to indicate

imminent doom, stood framed in the darkened doorway.
"You behave yourselves," she said. "Dressed up like hea-
thens—the devil himself will come and get you if you carry
on like this."

Thunder couldn't have scared the children more. The princess started up again with a yowl that could be heard out to
the street, and several other children began to tune up. The
two little boys who had started it all stood dripping wet with
wide eyes in the corner by the tub, as if they expected Miss
Swannie Hocutt suddenly to fly across the room and take
them away on a broom. "It's all right! It's all right!" Kimberly Collier ran around saying, but everybody knew the
party had been ruined.

Alton Hubbard saved the day. He must have heard the
commotion upstairs, and he came rushing into the room past
Miss Hocutt like the wind, gave a great laugh that startled
the children out of their fear, then picked up a crying child
and swung her to his shoulders. With that, he began to parade
around the room like some silver-haired Pied Piper, whis-
tling a happy tune, and in no time at all, he had all the
children following him as he wound around the tables. "I do
this all the time with my grandchildren," he said to Mavis
as he passed, and his eyes sparkled in the candlelight. When
the children started getting boisterous again, he led the whole
group outside, stopped, and helped the teachers get them in
order. With a bow, he backed away, out of breath, and the
children all applauded.

"Oh, Mr. Hubbard," Kimberly said. "We all do thank
you so much!"

He winked at her just before he turned to go back inside
and said, "You're welcome. Call on me again when you need
some help."

Mavis laughed. "Well, don't that beat anything?" she said
to Betty. "Who'd have expected Mr. Alton Hubbard to have
a way with children like that?"

Betty shook her head. "Not me. I'm surprised he didn't
scare them half to death. But the party turned out nice, didn't
it? I'm glad."

"Me, too, for Kimberly's sake if nothing else. She worked so hard."

They moved down the hallway together toward the elevator past the activity room, where the cleaning staff was already straightening up the tables for tonight's party. Neither spoke. What Betty's thoughts were, Mavis did not know, but her own went back to Halloween nights long ago when she dressed her daughter in the costume she had made her that year (just the sewing of it providing joy), and they had gone out together along the darkened streets with lanterns lit at every doorway, and she would say to her, "Go on up there, don't be afraid, you know them," and then watch while the child approached the house, rang the bell, and said, "Thank you for the treat," with a little bow just the way Mavis had taught her. Afterward, they would come home, and John would have returned from work by then, and they would empty her jack-o'-lantern on the kitchen table, separating out all the treats. What a joyful time, Mavis thought, and gave a great sigh. At least she had those memories. Perhaps poor Betty was thinking of *her* daughter, remembering pain. But there must have been good times, too. Wasn't everything a mixture? Nothing all joy, nothing all sorrow. Perhaps we were lucky simply if the good part outweighed the bad.

Chapter Fifteen

"Hold it!" Dale said. The camera flashed. Mavis and Betty, posed in front of one of the cutout witches, pulled away from each other, giggling.

"I'm surprised we didn't break the camera," Mavis said. She brushed her hand over her hair.

"You are the two prettiest ladies here—why wouldn't I want to take your picture?"

"I'm sure you can do better. Just look over there at Kimberly Collier." She pointed toward the refreshment table, where Kimberly was talking to two of the volunteers who were serving punch and cookies.

"You look at her." Dale glanced around, then frowned. "*I* could put together a better gypsy costume than that in just about five minutes. She looks about as authentic as Marlene Dietrich in that old movie *Golden Earrings*."

"She's going to be telling fortunes later," Betty said, her eyes sparkling. "Maybe she'll tell yours."

Shaking his head from side to side, Dale said, "No, thank you, ma'am. I wouldn't get near that tent with her, much less in it. No telling what she might do."

"Now, hush," Mavis said. "As soon as the children left this afternoon, Kimberly and the volunteers started working again to get ready for tonight's party, and they finished up just before supper. She deserves some praise. I think that tent's right cute even though it's just made out of bed sheets.

It wouldn't hurt you a-tall to pretend to get your fortune told."

Dale laughed. "Lord knows what the future holds. I'd better not know. How about some punch?" he said to Clara and Mavis. "You think it's spiked?"

"I sincerely doubt it," Mavis said. "They say in the brochure for the home that it has a 'Christian atmosphere'—that doesn't include drinking, in most people's book."

"I'll get us some," Dale said, and walked away.

"He's sweet as sugar," Betty said to Mavis as soon as Dale was out of earshot.

"Lord, I know it. I don't know what I would do without him. He's come to seem like my very own child."

They sat quietly for a while after that, watching the party. It's turned out to be right nice, Mavis thought. Once again candles flickered in the jack-o'-lanterns, and now that it was dark outside, the room was shadowed, even mysterious, the white tent glowing luminously in the far corner. Somewhere in the background music played—not some rock and roll number that would make a person deaf, but a song with strange foreign rhythms, a tinkling of bells, and a slithering of drums. Although none of the residents had worn a costume, Kimberly had made up their faces—Mavis had a rose on her cheek, and Betty had cat's whiskers—so that even *they* looked exotic, different from their everyday selves. Swannie Hocutt had taken one look and declared, "It's wantonness and the devil's work," but even she had worn a nice dress with a sparkling pin on the shoulder. Alton Hubbard had appeared long enough to bellow out, "I reckon my face is red enough already; I don't need no makeup to improve it," and then went out again. Mavis wondered where he had gone to.

Dale came back then with the punch and a plate of cookies that had been made by Kimberly's volunteers. "This stuff *must* be spiked," he said, "the way people are pushing and shoving to get a cup." He tasted it and shook his head. "Nope, I don't think so. I guess it's safe for you church ladies."

"Don't be a smart aleck," Mavis said. "You know how many cases of drunken driving there are. I don't want anything happening to you. You've got to drive home—all I have to do is push this contraption up two floors and roll into bed."

Dale laughed but looked a little ashamed. "Well, you won't have to worry about any of the visitors here getting high. This stuff isn't much more than fruit juice and a little ginger ale to give it bubbles, more than likely left over from the kids' party this afternoon."

"It's a right big crowd tonight," Betty said, changing the subject. "A lot of folks have visitors, and there's a bunch of volunteers. Just like at the Fall Festival."

Dale looked around. "I sure hope it doesn't end up the same way," he said.

"Don't say it!" Mavis declared. "Nothing like that can happen *here*." But in her own mind, she wasn't so sure. Someone right here at this party quietly eating a homemade cookie might be the murderer, might already be selecting his next victim. She gave a little shudder and almost spilled her punch.

Just then, the music stopped and the lights went up slightly. People stopped talking. At the front of the room, near the refreshment table, Kimberly Collier was waving her hand, gold spangles flashing and earrings atremble. "Can I have your attention for just a minute?" she called out. "I can see what a good time everybody is having, but Mr. Joyner, our administrator, wants to say just a word. I think we should give him and Lakeview a great big hand for making all this possible." With a big smile, Kimberly began to clap, and a few others joined her. Then she moved away.

Until that moment, Mavis had not seen Clifford Joyner all evening. But then, he wasn't very visible around Lakeview— probably busy in his office all day long trying to get people to sign over everything they owned before they could move in. He was dressed in a navy blue suit and dark tie (Mavis tried to imagine him in some kind of costume, but nothing came to mind), and his rimless glasses sparkled in the light.

When he spoke, the little pouches on his cheeks trembled like Jell-O in a bowl.

"I told Kimberly I just wanted a minute to say hello and tell y'all how pleased we are that you're here tonight—our residents, our volunteers, our relatives, and our friends. Now I'm going to turn right around and do to Kimberly what she did to me. Let's give her a nice hand for planning all this. I know that she and a lot of folks have been working behind the scenes for weeks getting ready." He clapped his hands, and this time, more people joined in. Mavis wondered if he was peeved a little bit because Kimberly got more applause than he did, but if so, he didn't show it. "That's all I had to say," he said, waving his hand good-bye. "Now you can go back to your fun."

He turned, spoke briefly to Kimberly, then walked toward the doorway. Just as he went through, Mavis saw Barbara Santucci waiting for him on the other side. Well, isn't she a sight? Mavis thought. With all that makeup on and wearing those funny clothes, she looked more like a gypsy than Kimberly Collier ever could without even trying.

"Isn't he the sweetest soul you've ever seen?" The voice at Mavis's shoulder startled her. Turning quickly, she saw Swannie Hocutt standing just behind her chair.

"Well, I don't know much about him," Mavis said, trying to be neutral.

Swannie looked smug. "I do. He goes to my church."

"That's nice," Mavis said, looking at her empty cup. If nothing else, she could say she had to go get another drink and move away.

"Yes." Swannie sighed. "So faithful. There every Sunday, and him with such a burden to bear."

Maybe she wouldn't go for a drink just yet. "What's that?" Mavis asked.

"His wife. You don't know?" Swannie didn't give Mavis a chance to respond. "So sad. Happened years ago soon after they were married. His wife was in an automobile accident, badly injured, and she's been in a wheelchair ever since, can't walk a step.'' Miss Hocutt gave Mavis a knowing look and said in a whisper, ''They never had children.''

''Well, that is a sad story,'' Mavis said, moved. How awful to be in a wheelchair half your life with no hope of ever escaping. Just the little while she'd been in her cast, she had come to realize how much she had to depend on others to take care of her, how much freedom she had to give up. Perhaps she shouldn't have been so critical of Clifford Joyner—he'd sacrificed his life taking care of his poor invalid wife. She might have said more to Swannie Hocutt, but just then, Kimberly's voice rang out again.

''It's fortune-telling time!'' she called, waving a deck of cards above her head. ''Mademoiselle Kimberly will answer all your questions—about the past, about the future. Come one, come all! Who'll be the first in line?'' With that, she ran across the room like some exotic dancer, ducked down, and entered the tent, bracelets jangling. A soft pink glow flared up inside.

''Well, I think she's pure lost her mind,'' Mavis said. She looked over to where Swannie Hocutt had been standing, but the other woman had disappeared.

Betty and Dale must have overheard her. Smiling, they came closer to her chair. ''Well, are you going to have your fortune told?'' Betty asked.

''Lord have mercy, no!'' Mavis said. ''I have no need to know what's ahead. The Lord will take care of that.''

''Oh, come on, honey,'' Dale said. ''Go ahead. I might just get in line myself. You wanted to help Kimberly make this party a success—here's your chance.'' He pointed over at the tent. ''I don't see anybody else lining up. She'll be disappointed.''

''I'm sure Swannie Hocutt would say it's the work of the devil,'' Mavis answered.

''You aren't Swannie Hocutt,'' Dale told her. ''It's just for fun.''

Mavis felt a tingle of excitement. It couldn't really hurt to have Kimberly tell her fortune, now, could it? Though she'd never told a soul—not even Dale, who knew most all her secrets—every morning she read her horoscope in the paper while she was having coffee, and sometimes it was right on the head. Maybe it was all superstition, but you never knew. "I reckon I could do it for Kimberly's sake," she said. "But if she starts to talk about a tall, dark man, I'll up and walk out."

Grinning, Dale bent down and gave her a kiss. "If she mentions a not too tall blond man, you can tell her you've got one already. In fact, you might want to ask her if she can come up with a cure for hair loss. Blondes may have more fun, but they get bald earlier."

"Ask her yourself, smarty-pants," Mavis said, and laughing, rolled away.

Up close, the tent was larger than Mavis had expected. Billowing slightly, a red curtain covered the doorway, and when Mavis reached over and pulled it aside, she could roll her wheelchair through the opening quite easily. Inside, the light was dim; a floor lamp stood in the corner, with a rose-colored scarf covering the globe so that the room had a soft pink glow, like the inside of some exotic flower. Behind a card table draped with an old shawl that swirled with color sat Kimberly in her gypsy finery, gold loops glowing in her ears. Bright banners hung above her head. Mavis moved closer, peering through the gloom, and when she saw that Kimberly was veiled (just her eyes showing above the soft fabric, dark and with a faraway look), she thought, I have entered another kingdom far from Lakeview Nursing Home. Kimberly spoke, and it might have been the voice of a stranger.

"What is your question?" she asked.

Mavis rolled her chair back just a bit. "Beg pardon?" she said.

"Your question," Kimberly said. "You are the Querent, I am the Reader. You must think of a question you want answered by the cards. Do not tell me, but think hard."

Mavis thought Kimberly was taking herself a little too seriously, but she might as well do her part. What question could she ask? Her mind was a blank. Any other time, she might have had a dozen. Then she thought about the murders. She shivered slightly even though it was warm inside the tent. Dare she do it? She could ask who the murderer was. Closing her eyes, she imagined some dark figure, his face unseen, bending over a bed with something in his hands. With her eyes open again, she looked straight into Kimberly's and said, "I'm ready."

"We must choose a card to represent you," Kimberly said as she began to look through the deck in her hand. "Here. The Queen of Cups." She laid it on the table. "Was your hair light brown before it turned gray?" she asked. "Your eyes hazel?"

"Close enough," Mavis said. She leaned over and looked at the card and saw a woman sitting on a throne, holding something in her arms. As far as she could tell, it didn't look like her at all.

"You want me to shuffle?"

"Yes, ma'am," Mavis said. "I've never been a card player."

"Then place your hand on the deck and repeat to yourself your question."

Mavis touched the cards briefly, remembering the dark figure; then Kimberly began to shuffle. The cards made a thumping sound on the table. Only then did Mavis realize how quiet it was in the tent in spite of the party outside. She felt strangely alone sitting there with Kimberly wrapped in veils. "Cut the deck," Kimberly said, laying the cards in front of Mavis. "Make three piles with your left hand, going to the left. It's the true gypsy way."

Mavis divided the cards, following Kimberly's instructions. She wanted to say something to indicate she thought this was all just a joke, but the words wouldn't come. As she drew her hand back while Kimberly picked up the cards again, she noticed that her own fingers were trembling slightly.

Kimberly dealt the cards faceup, covering Mavis's own Queen card first, with one card turned one way, one another, then dealing four cards out around them to make a kind of cross, and finally a line of four additional cards on one side. She bent over and stared at them. Then, after what seemed a very long time, she began to speak.

"The Ten of Swords," she said, pointing to the first card over the Queen. "This represents the general atmosphere that surrounds your question and the influence at work around it—pain, affliction, ruin, tears."

"Well, you sure nailed that one on the head," Mavis said without thinking. Kimberly did not look up at her but pointed at the second covering card. "The Ace of Cups—it's the force opposing the other influences and a good sign, a sign of beginnings, of love and abundance. Something good will happen in your life." She went next to the card at the bottom of the cross. "The Six of Cups also is a good sign. It's about the past. You've had happiness and enjoyment. And it may mean you'll make new friendships."

Mavis sat back, a little relieved. These were things she'd rather hear. Yes, her question about the murderer was surrounded with pain and tears, but she didn't like to dwell on it. Perhaps there were no murders after all—just a funny series of coincidences.

Kimberly pointed to a fourth card. "The Knight of Swords. He represents the influences that are passing away—conflict and destruction. That, too, is good news." She paused, tapping the card at the top of the cross. "Oh, dear, it's not for sure, but the future could hold something very unpleasant. The Moon card indicates unforeseen perils, secret foes, perhaps bad luck for someone you love." She hurried to the next card. "Let's see what the future *does* hold," she said, and then gave a sigh. "Ah, the Two of Cups, a sign of new beginnings, of friendship, possibly a love affair."

Mavis almost laughed out loud. A love affair! At her age! Well, here was Kimberly getting ready to tell her about a tall, dark stranger. She should have known this was all silliness—she'd never learn anything about the murderer by sitting beneath a pile of bed sheets!

It was then that they heard the scream. It pierced the tent like a knife and seemed to make the draperies flutter. Kimberly jumped up, knocking over the table, and the cards went flying. "Oh, what's happened now?" she yelled out. "I don't think I can take any more!" She pulled the veil away, and Mavis saw tears running down her cheeks.

Mavis reached up, ready to pat her on the arm and say, Don't worry, it's probably not as bad as it seems, but Kimberly brushed past her and ran out of the tent, calling, "What is it? Is anyone hurt?" and Mavis was left alone inside. Looking down, she saw that one of the cards had fallen into her lap. She turned it over.

Oh, Lord! She never should have done this! There in her hand was the picture of a skeleton dressed in a knight's armor riding on a horse. "Death" was the one word she read at the bottom.

Later, Mavis couldn't remember exactly what she had done during the next few minutes. Certainly she had dropped the card and rolled over the scattered deck outside the tent, her eyes clouded, surprised somehow to find herself still at Lakeview. Perhaps she had simply sat, along with the others, waiting for the scream to subside, as if they had all been stilled, like a moving picture suddenly stopped, and could not move again until released.

It was Kimberly who finally put the scene in motion again. Hurrying toward the front of the room, she reached the doorway, stopped, and then, in a perfectly calm voice, said, "What is it, Miz Hocutt? What in the world is the matter?"

Swannie Hocutt, standing all alone in the doorway, blinked at first as if she didn't know where she was, her mouth still open from the scream, and pointed into the darkness behind her. She moistened her lips, took a breath, and then, still pointing a trembling finger, she said, "He did it! That devil! There's no place that's safe!"

Mavis wondered if the answer to her question in the tent was about to be answered. Perhaps Swannie had uncovered the identity of the murderer and was about to reveal the name. Mavis rolled closer and heard Kimberly ask in a soothing voice, "What, Miz Hocutt? Who did what to you?"

For a moment Swannie looked as if she might scream again. Then, in a piercing voice, she yelled out, "Mr. Alton Hubbard—he exposed himself to me! Right down yonder in the hallway. He's drunk as a skunk, and he's got a whole bunch of men with him in the locker room drinking and playing cards. Oh, mark my words, the devil is in this place. But it won't be for long. The Lord will come and strike dead the iniquitous. Prepare to meet thy doom!"

She would have gone on—all night probably, Mavis thought—except at that moment a bellow came from the hall and Alton Hubbard appeared suddenly in the doorway. Swannie Hocutt gave another shriek and shrank back; Kimberly put her arm around her. "What in the world's the matter, woman?" Alton Hubbard cried. His face was redder than ever, his clothes rumpled, his great mane of hair in disarray. "I didn't do a thing to that fool," he said to the others. "Just forgot to button up after I took a leak, that's all." He turned to Swannie again. "Lord knows, if you ain't seen things a-dangling before now, it's about time you had a peek before you die." Laughing, he tried to hitch up his pants and tuck his shirttail inside, then started to turn, swaying just a bit, ready to go back down the hall.

Just at that moment, the figure of an angel emerged from the darkness behind him. Alton Hubbard drew back, a gasp went up from the crowd, and Swannie Hocutt had a look of dismay on her face, as if she was trying to decide whether the Lord really was about to fulfill her prophecy and destroy Lakeview with his messenger.

Then they recognized the angel. Even in a flowing white robe, with feathery wings and a golden halo around her head, Nurse Overby could not hide her identity. The way she moved, those heavy brows (even covered, like her face, with white makeup) gave her away. And her order to Alton Hubbard left no further doubt. "Mr. Hubbard, you're drunk," she said. "Go to your room this instant and simmer down. One of the attendants will bring you some coffee. I'll be up later to see that you're safely in bed." She pointed, and like a child being sent away without supper, Alton Hubbard slunk away.

Nurse Overby turned back to the group. "I'll find out who did it," she said to no one in particular, "who gave him and the others the liquor. It's a disgrace to Lakeview and all it stands for. I'll find out and turn out whoever it was if it's the last thing I ever do!" She whirled around, wings aflutter, and marched away, her huge figure luminous in the darkened hallway.

"Lord, Mavis honey, what kind of a place have you got yourself into?" It was Dale. At some point, he must have moved over to the tent to stand by Mavis's chair. "I wonder what will happen next," he said.

But Mavis didn't answer him, remembering suddenly the card that had fallen to her lap in the glow of the gypsy tent. Death!

Chapter Sixteen

The party ended quickly after that. Someone turned up the lights and blew out the candles, and Kimberly's tent was hastily taken down by two of the attendants. The volunteers carried empty cups and cookie plates back to the kitchen, self-conscious in their costumes beneath the bright fluorescent light. Catching sight of her reflection in one of the windows, Mavis was startled to see the twining flower still painted on her cheek, and she said to Betty, "Aren't we a sight? It's about time we washed this mess off our faces."

Dale was packing up his camera equipment. "I've got to go, too," he said. "I didn't get a whole lot of pictures. Seems like every time I come to Lakeview, something happens to cut the party short."

"Well, at least this time nobody got killed." Betty put her gnarled hands on the back of Mavis's chair, ready to push her away.

"When Swannie Hocutt let out that bloodcurdling scream, I wasn't so sure," Mavis said, shaking her head. "Poor lady, she's had a trying day."

"Sounds like she goes out of her way to make it trying," Dale said.

"Maybe, but Mr. Alton Hubbard had no business a-tall carrying on like that. I wonder if Nurse Overby's got him tucked in bed yet." Betty and Dale laughed. Betty pushed Mavis toward the doorway, and Dale followed. They stopped just outside in the hall.

"I'm going this way," Dale said, pointing to the outer door. Mavis wondered if anyone would remember to lock it later. "Nice to meet you, Miz Williams. You two take care of yourselves. You've had enough excitement for a while." He bent down to kiss Mavis. "I'll give you a call," he said, and then sauntered away.

"Seems late, don't it?" Betty said as she pushed Mavis toward the elevator.

"It *is* past my bedtime, but my goodness, we stayed up a whole lot later last night writing your letter. Did you send it off this morning?"

"First thing. Got down to the office and left it on the counter for the postman before anybody else was around."

Just then they passed the open door to the staff locker room. "Well, look at that," Mavis said, pointing to the litter of cups and ground-out cigarette stubs on the floor. "I reckon they had themselves quite a little party, didn't they?" She laughed. "I bet Nurse Overby nearly scared them to death when she came barging in in her angel outfit and broke up their game. There's going to be a bunch of peaked-looking fools around here tomorrow morning, Alton Hubbard in particular, I suspect. I wonder where they *did* get their liquor. Nurse Overby probably will be sniffing around all over the place trying to find out."

Back in her room, Mavis scrubbed the flower from her cheek and spread on her night cream. She peered into the mirror at her hair. It wasn't a mess *yet*, but she'd soon have to find some way to go down to Shirlee's Beauty Shoppe to get it done. Maybe Dale would take her. Turning out the light, she rolled back to her bed and was just getting up on the side when she heard a light tapping on the door. "Come in," she said, and wondered, now, who in the world can that be this time of night?

Daisy Norris poked her head in. Earlier in the evening, Mavis had seen her helping the volunteers set up the refreshment table, but she lost sight of her after that in all the confusion. Though she was dressed in her usual pink uniform, no doubt at the insistence of the dining room supervisor,

Daisy had, nonetheless, pinned two large gardenias in her hair and wore a jangle of bracelets on her arms. Her nails were painted a glowing red. "Can I come in for a minute, Miz Lashley?" she said, mumbling the words, as if trying to cover the gleam of her golden tooth. In spite of the finery, Mavis had never seen her look so sad.

"Why, sure," Mavis said, sitting on the side of the bed. "I'm not really sleepy—too much going on around here."

Opening the door, Daisy slipped inside, then waited to be sure that the door swung shut behind her all the way. She came closer but did not look at first at Mavis's eyes. Then the tears began, great, silent drops that rolled down her cheeks and fell onto her high, pink bosom. Mavis reached out, but Daisy was too far away for her to comfort, so she said, "What in the world is the matter?", her own tears threatening to fall at the sight of the other woman's distress.

"I didn't mean to do no harm," she said, inching closer. Mavis grasped her hand. "I was just trying to help folks have a good time."

Mavis pressed the damp palm with her own two hands. "What do you mean?" she asked, baffled.

"Mr. Alton asked me to do it. I brought him his tray the other morning, and as I was about to leave, he said, 'Wait a minute, Daisy, I want to ask you to do something for me.'

"I looked at the door. I always leave it cracked since you never know what that old man might do. He's throwed plates at Miss Kimberly. I calculated I could get out if he tried something funny.

" 'We got this Halloween party coming up,' he says.

" 'Yessir,' I answer him back.

" 'Won't be much of a party with nothing to drink, now, will it?'

" 'There'll be punch,' I tell him, still not knowing what he has in mind.

"He says, 'Oh, shoot, that's not what I mean. Me and some of the other fellows around here want to get us a friendly card game going, and we want something a little stronger than *punch*. You think you might buy us a bottle? There's some money in it for you.'

"Just then he whips out these two twenty-dollar bills from under his pillow and says, 'One for you, one for the bottle. How about it?' "

Daisy's tears had stopped while she was talking, but now they began again. "You don't know how hard I tried to resist, but the devil tempted me. Like I told you, I got this son in college, and he don't never have anything extra. I thought, With that twenty dollars, he can go out and have him a good time, buy him a nice meal and go to a movie. It won't hurt nothing if I take it. That was the devil's talk, and I let it get me." She shook her head. "Now it looks like I'll have to pay."

"What do you mean?" Mavis was still holding Daisy's hand. She gave it a final pat and let it go.

"Nurse Overby. You heard what she said. She'll find out what I did and get Mr. Joyner to fire me. He does anything she tells him."

"Who else knows?" Mavis asked.

"Just Mr. Alton, far as I know." Daisy's eyes were pleading. "And now you." She began to talk very fast. "I just had to tell somebody, and I didn't know who else to turn to. I could have gone to my preacher, but he'd just say it was a sin and I'd have to bear my punishment."

Well, thank the Lord I'm not a preacher, Mavis thought. Daisy had suffered enough already. Certainly Alton Hubbard was far guiltier than Daisy ever was, and Mavis was not about to cast more guilt. "I'd just keep quiet," she said. "*I'm* not going to tell, and I doubt that Mr. Alton Hubbard will either. He strikes me as the type that nobody could drag something out of if he didn't want to let go." Before she even thought, she said, "I'll have a word with him if I get a chance."

Daisy smiled; her tooth glowed. "You think it'll be all right then?" she said. "Nothing'll happen?"

"Wait and see," Mavis said. "I expect things will simmer

down. There's a lot else going on around here to occupy folks' minds.''

''Lord, you're right about that.'' Daisy looked solemn again.

''What do you mean?''

Daisy stepped closer, lowering her voice. ''Meanness,'' she said. ''Too many people dying unexpected, particularly those that ain't got no kinfolks around. There was this policeman here this morning asking questions. I know it must be about all the ones that died.'' Daisy suddenly stopped talking, looked at the closed door again, and moved even closer to Mavis. ''I'm going to tell you another secret,'' she said.

''What's that?'' Mavis felt a tightness in her chest.

''I called 'em.''

''Who?''

''The police. Called up and didn't say my name but told them that there was some funny goings-on out here. I'd seen too many nice folks die when it didn't seem like they had to that soon.''

''Whew-ee!'' Mavis said. ''That took a lot of doing. But don't tell anybody else. You never know who might be involved.''

''Yes, ma'am. I know. That's why *you* need to be careful. I sure don't want nothing to happen to you.'' Daisy began to back away. ''I've got to go now,'' she said. ''They'll be wondering downstairs where I've been all this time.'' She gave a last smile, though her face remained solemn. ''I thank you for listening,'' she said. ''Now I can rest easy.''

Ah, maybe you can, Mavis thought, but I'm not so sure about myself.

And, indeed, she couldn't get to sleep. For at least an hour after she turned out the light and went to bed, she tossed and turned, faces flashing before her eyes—Miss Elgie Skinner's painted features, Kimberly's eyes behind her veil, the Death's head on the card, Daisy's teary cheeks, Clifford Joyner and Barbara Santucci's bent heads—they were all there. And no matter how hard she tried to find some order in her visions, nothing fell into place. Finally, sitting straight up in bed, she said out loud to herself, "I have to take some action. I can't sit around and wait any longer."

But what? She would still have to keep her cover, so she couldn't just start going around asking people questions. Charles had done that, and if he had found out any great secrets, he certainly hadn't told Mavis about them. And his examination of the charts Clifford Joyner and Barbara Santucci had provided him with downstairs in the office had been unrevealing. Of course, they showed him only what they wanted him to see. There could be all sorts of records in their files that might be interesting, but he'd never lay eyes on them without a search warrant, and with no real evidence to go on, he'd probably have a heck of a time getting one.

I don't need one, though, Mavis thought with a shiver of anticipation. Who was to stop her from rolling herself to the elevator, riding downstairs, and taking as long a look as she wanted at the files in the office? Though no voice answered her out loud, all the warnings that she had heard from Charles and Dale, and even Daisy Norris—*You need to be careful, there are dangerous things going on around here*—came to her ears, but she decided to ignore them. Nobody was up. Half the residents would be in a drunken stupor, thanks to Alton Hubbard's liquor, and the other half would be exhausted from all the excitement of the party. And if it was like usual, the night nurse would be sound asleep at the desk.

She flung off the covers, reached for her robe, and slid into the chair. Her heart beat with excitement. Rolling to the door, she pulled it open and sat for a moment, listening; but then, hearing nothing except the usual night sounds, she rolled down the hallway to the elevator. When she pushed the button, the green light for her floor came on immediately and the doors opened. She went inside.

The ground-floor hallway was just as deserted. But that was no surprise—who else would be there at this hour? Mavis looked at her watch. The volunteers, the food service workers, and any other staff who had been at the party would all have driven home long ago, and she would have the office to herself. But still, she would need to be careful—not turn on any lights that could be seen from the outside, remember to leave everything just as she had found it in the files. She'd show Charles Morgan what a good detective she was! Wouldn't he be surprised if she discovered some important evidence?

The EXIT sign over the front door dimly lit the lobby and cast strange shadows on the wall from the plant near the window. Noiselessly Mavis rolled over the thick carpet to the other doorway, which, if she remembered correctly, led to Barbara Santucci's office—perhaps that way she could go behind the counter where the young man sat, too. That's where the files should be. Grasping the wheels of the chair, she began to go forward, then stopped all of a sudden when she heard the sound.

Soft, almost a moan, it could be someone weeping. But where was it coming from? She listened carefully. There was silence for a moment; then the sound came again, this time louder, and she knew it came from one of the offices in the rear.

Surely she should go! Turn right around and roll herself through the lobby back to the elevator and up to her room. And even if she didn't sleep one wink all night, it would be safer than remaining here and trying to find out who made that sound. But she couldn't. She had to know. If she was discovered, well, that was all right—she'd pretend she was losing her mind and had gotten lost trying to find her room. Swannie Hocutt went around half the time with her marbles rattling; Mavis could, too.

Thank goodness for the carpet. She moved forward without a sound to the hallway that led to Barbara Santucci's office. The EXIT sign gave a little light, and she could see that Barbara's office was dark. But the one behind it wasn't. Light streamed from a crack in the door and lit the sign on it: CLIFFORD JOYNER, ADMINISTRATOR. Well, for goodness' sake—was he in there all alone, crying in his misery? Mavis remembered Swannie Hocutt's sad story about his wife's ac-

cident. She moved closer to the light, pity in her heart for
Clifford Joyner's unhappiness.

The moan came again, louder, then louder still, and there
was a great gasping for breath and the sound of sofa pillows
bouncing up and down in a regular rhythm. Through the
crack in the doorway, Mavis saw enough—saw too much—
to know that Clifford Joyner and Barbara Santucci were in
there fornicating on the sofa while Clifford's wife sat at home
alone in her wheelchair, waiting for his return.

She whirled around in her chair, at that moment no longer
caring whether she could be heard or not, and raced out into
the waiting area and across the room. As she turned the
corner leading out to the hallway where the elevator was
located, she cut too sharply and banged into a wooden table
that stood there. The sound rang out like a shot. "Damnation!" Mavis said, and backed up, then went forward again
to the elevator.

Thank heaven it was still there; no one else upstairs had
pushed the buttons since Mavis had come down. She rolled
inside, hit number 3 as hard as she could, and waited, breathing hard, while the doors slowly closed, half expecting Clifford's pale, naked arm to reach in and grab her. Because at
that point she realized that she did not want to be discovered.
She was shaking all over—partly from fear, partly from em-
barrassment—and she felt that she could never look Clifford
or Barbara in the eye again. And what if they were the mur-
derers? She could imagine them downstairs right now, half-
dressed, watching the elevator light flashing upward to the
third floor. Perhaps they would come running up the stairs
to find out who had seen them in their sin.

The doors opened. She rolled out. Down at the end of the
hallway the light still burned at the nurses' station, but otherwise the hall was dark. If she could only get to her room,
get inside, she might take one deep, peaceful breath again.

Finally she was there. Opening the door, she went inside,
stopped, pushed the door closed behind her, and then sat
listening for the sound of racing footsteps. None came. The
only sound she heard was the pounding of her own heart

and, when it finally quieted, the ticking of the clock on the stand beside her bed. Wearily she pulled off her robe and climbed into bed, too tired for prayers except for one word of thanks to the Lord for taking care of her.

And she *had* learned something that night, even though her plans for looking through the records in the office had been thwarted. Clifford Joyner and Barbara Santucci carrying on like that—if there was anything going on at Lakeview, they would be in it together. You read about such things all the time—pillar of the community running off with some young thing, taking the company's money. Maybe the two of them already had plans for a voyage to some tropical island with wide beaches and endless days of sun, like those ads you saw on TV.

Just wait until she told Dale and Charles about it!

Chapter Seventeen

Mavis called Dale as soon as she got up the next morning. From his sleepy "Hello?" she could tell she had awakened him, and she knew that he would be lying in bed, hair standing on end and his eyes puffed up. "I am *not* a morning person," she'd heard him say many times before, and the few occasions he had spent the night in her guest room, she'd had to give him three cups of black coffee next morning before he was able to put three words together that made sense.

"Honey, I'm just as sorry as I can be," she said, "but I wanted to catch you before you went to work."

"Work?" he said. "It's the crack of dawn. What are you doing up so early after last night's party?"

"I couldn't sleep. I've found out something I think you'll want to know."

"What's that?"

"I want to tell you in person."

Dale was silent for a minute. She could see him rubbing his eyes. "Well, I guess I could come out again tonight," he said, but didn't sound too enthusiastic.

"I've got a better idea."

"What's that?"

"I need a little break from this place. I'm tired of this chair and of so many sick folks. Reckon you could come by this morning on your way to work and take me down to Shirlee's Beauty Shoppe? By the weekend this hair's going to look like a rat's nest, and I could go ahead and get it done today. I'm sure she'd work me in. As many permanents as I've paid for all these years, she'd better try.''

Dale sounded a little brighter. ''I think I can arrange that. I've got a job to do—photograph the cast in a little theater production—so I can do that while you're getting pretty at Shirlee's and then pick you up. What about lunch?''

''Lord, I don't need any more food. My clothes are already getting tight.'' But she smiled, thinking how much she would enjoy sitting in a real restaurant, away from the dining room at the home, where the residents constantly complained about the food, worrying whether or not they were getting enough fiber. ''We'll see about lunch,'' she said, but knew that she would go.

By eight o'clock she was dressed and ready even though Dale had said it would be at least eight-thirty before he could pull some clothes on, swallow a glass of orange juice, and get out to Lakeview to pick her up. But she couldn't bear to sit in her room and wait, so she put on her nice spring-weight coat, tied the pretty print scarf that Dale had given her on her last birthday around her neck (pure silk and too expensive; she'd never buy it for herself), checked the mirror one last time, and rolled out into the hallway.

She almost ran into Nurse Overby.

''Well, where are *you* off to this morning?'' she said. Nurse Overby raised her eyebrows for a moment, and Mavis could see her pale eyes.

''I'm going to get my hair fixed,'' Mavis said. ''My nephew's picking me up out front.'' She started to roll again.

''Well, now, I wonder if that'll be all right with your doctor. I'll go check the chart.''

''You don't need to bother. He said I could get out anytime I wanted to.'' Mavis hadn't really asked. She hoped that Charles had given the doctor at the hospital instructions about what orders to give to the staff. But whether there were proper orders in her chart or not, she was going on her outing with Dale today, even if it meant running over Nurse Estelle Overby in the process with her chair. ''You have a nice day,'' she called back as she rolled toward the elevator. Nurse Overby didn't move the whole time Mavis sat there waiting for the car to come.

The waiting area downstairs was empty. How innocent it seemed in the early morning light that streamed through the windows—the plant no longer menacing, the only sounds the clicking of computer keys in the front office and the voice of some morning show host played low somewhere on a radio. As she passed the table that she had rammed with her chair the night before, Mavis quickly glanced at the leg to see how badly it was scratched. There was a nick, nothing more. Thank goodness there was no damage to her chair. "How're you this morning?" she called to the nice young man at the reception desk.

"Just fine, Miz Lashley," he said, and smiled.

Wasn't it nice of him to remember her name? She might have chatted with him longer, but just then the front door opened and Barbara Santucci came in. Mavis checked her watch. Right on time, even after last night's debauchery. Well, that was *one* thing in her favor, Mavis thought. She looked up and smiled at the other woman and said, "Isn't this lovely weather we're having? Good *sleeping* weather. I had such a nice rest last night."

Barbara Santucci didn't glance at Mavis. "Yes," she said as she passed by. She disappeared through the doorway at the back of the room.

"I'll see you later," Mavis called out to the man at the desk, then waved and rolled outside into the welcoming sun.

"So what's your big secret?" Dale asked as he pulled out into the lane of early morning traffic in front of Lakeview. His hair was still wet from the shower, and Mavis could see two bloody little nicks on his cheek, the result of hurried shaving. When a car tried to cut in front of him, he speeded up, opened his mouth (almost surely, Mavis thought, to swear at the driver), but then, catching her eye, closed it again and sat back against the seat with a sigh, slowing down.

"Thank you, sir," she said. "I'd like to get where I'm

going in one piece. I certainly don't need a cast on my other leg to match this one.'' She tapped her bound leg with her purse. ''One's enough to run you crazy.'' Any other time, if she had made some remark about his driving, Dale would have come right back and told her with a grin that she could just get out and walk if she didn't like his chauffeuring, but now he was silent, waiting for her to answer his question.

She didn't know how to begin. Maybe Dale would think she was taking an awful chance, wandering around the halls of Lakeview in the middle of the night. She might have met the murderer face-to-face, or at least made people suspicious, wondering what she was up to. But she *had* learned something. Clifford Joyner and Barbara Santucci were having an affair—who knew what else they might be involved in? Anyway, no harm had come to her. Let Dale fuss if he wanted to fuss. It wouldn't be the first time.

''I couldn't go to sleep after the party last night,'' she began, looking straight ahead through the windshield. ''Something just told me that I might find a clue in the office downstairs if I poked around a little bit.'' Already she felt that Dale's eyebrows were rising, but she would not look at him. ''There wasn't any danger—people all around sleeping. One good holler and they'd wake up. So anyway, I got up, put on that pretty new robe you gave me, and took the elevator downstairs. The office was deserted—or at least that's what I thought at first.''

''What in the world did you think you'd find?'' Dale interrupted her.

''I don't know. Charles Morgan got to see charts on some of the patients who died, but who knows what might have been taken out of them? I thought there might be incriminating papers, something relating to those folks' estates, a clue. But I never got far enough to look.''

''You *didn't* get caught?'' Dale was staring at her; she could feel it.

''Of course not,'' she said, rubbing her hand over her purse. ''I heard this noise first and went to investigate.''

''What kind of noise?''

"Well, one that wouldn't leave you any doubts about what was going on if you heard it. You'll say I should have turned around right then and gone back to my room, but I couldn't do it. I had to see who it was. It was obvious where the sound came from—back near Barbara Santucci's office where she asked me all those questions the day I came in—so I rolled my chair in that direction. But it wasn't Barbara's office that was busy; it was Clifford Joyner's just behind. I pulled up close to the door and looked through the crack, and you'd never guess what I saw"—she didn't give Dale time to respond—"Clifford Joyner and Barbara Santucci on the sofa going at it like two dogs in heat. It was a sight, let me tell you."

"Well, I'll be damned!" Dale exclaimed. Mavis finally looked over at him and saw that he had a big grin on his face. "That prissy old fart—you wouldn't think he had it in him, would you?"

"No need to talk dirty," Mavis said.

She knew Dale was ignoring her remark. "Poor Barbara," he said. "Wonder what she sees in him."

"Maybe she's the one who led him astray."

"Noooo, I don't think so. Clifford Joyner looks like the kind of sanctimonious ass that points out everybody else's transgressions while covering up his own. I expect it's more like Barbara had to do it to keep her job."

"Well, it's all disgusting," Mavis said. "But it does make it seem more likely that those two are up to something in the home. If I could get back to that office, I might find out what."

Dale's face lost its silly smile. "No you don't," he said, his voice quite serious. "You've had enough nighttime adventures. Next time you might not be so lucky and get caught. Promise?"

Mavis nodded her head up and down but didn't actually say the words. Thank goodness she hadn't told Dale about banging into the table in the waiting area when she was making her escape back to her room.

* * *

When Dale pulled up in front of the beauty shop, Mavis noticed that Shirlee still had her Halloween decorations in the window. "Want me to push you inside?" he asked as he unfolded the wheelchair from the backseat and helped Mavis slide into it.

"No, I can do it myself. Lord knows, I've had enough practice." She tucked up her coat so that it wouldn't drag on the sidewalk. "You go on and get your work done. I've taken up enough of your time. It's real sweet of you to do this."

"Can't think of a thing I'd rather do," he said, patting her shoulder. Then he got back into the car and drove away.

"Lord have mercy, what happened to you?" was the first thing Shirlee said when Mavis opened the door and rolled her chair inside the beauty parlor. Rayette made a beeline from the back, where she was sweeping up, and rushed to help her. Mavis could see tears welling up in her eyes.

"It's not the end of the world," Mavis said. With Rayette's help, she struggled out of her coat and tucked the scarf in the sleeve, and Rayette hung it on the coatrack. "I can get around pretty good." And then she told them about the accident, how she fell in the kitchen and managed to call Dale, who came over and took her to the hospital, and she'd have to wear the cast for six weeks. By now, she had told the story so many times that she almost believed it, almost seemed to remember the feeling of falling and the pain in her leg as she crawled across the kitchen floor. Everyone in the shop— Shirlee, Rayette, two women who had poked their heads out from dryers, and another one sitting in Shirlee's chair with her head half-rolled—listened to her raptly until she mentioned staying out at Lakeview.

"Mavis, honey, are you sure that's *safe*?" Shirlee came closer and bent down in front of Mavis, reeking of cigarette smoke.

"What do you mean?" Mavis asked.

"Haven't you seen the paper?"

"Not this morning. And even if I'd have had time before I came down here, there'd be no chance of getting it out at that place. The men hog the paper half the morning reading the sports page so they can discuss ball scores the rest of the day. What's in it that's so interesting?''

Shirlee stood back up and put her hand on her hip. ''Just that they're investigating what they think is a whole series of murders out at Lakeview. It's all over the front page!''

''Oh, that.''

''What do you mean, *'Oh, that'?* Mavis, you could have been *killed*!''

''Not likely.'' Mavis leaned back in her chair. All eyes were on her face. ''From what I gather, they were all old and feeble. Like Miss Elgie Skinner. And they don't know for sure whether the others were murdered.''

Shirlee made a clucking sound with her tongue. ''Well, it says they might exhume some bodies. Sounds like they've got a pretty good idea.''

''Maybe so, but I don't think anything's going to happen to me. And if it does''—she laughed—''I don't want to go looking like I'm a fright already. You got time to do something with this hair?''

''Why, sure, honey,'' Shirlee said, waving her hand. ''Rayette, you push Mavis over there to the sink and get her washed while I finish up Miz Springle. It won't take but a minute.''

Dale came for Mavis at eleven-thirty. Long before then, Shirlee had forgotten about the murders and the possible threat to Mavis, telling her in great detail about Bonnielee's Halloween costume and how pretty she looked in it, and wasn't it a shame she didn't have her pictures back yet so Mavis could see? Mavis grunted a few times and almost went to sleep under the dryer, the quiet drone of the machine soothing, her mind freed of all thoughts of murder. ''You take care now,'' Shirlee said in a voice of real concern as Dale pushed Mavis's chair down to the curb and helped her into the car. Just before they pulled away, Rayette came running out of the shop with Mavis's scarf, which must have dropped out on the floor.

''Thank you, honey,'' Mavis said. ''I wouldn't want to lose that for anything.''

"I suppose it'll be all over town now," Dale said, starting the engine.

"What?"

"About your 'accident' and the fact that you're out at Lakeview, where all the murders have occurred."

"You must have seen the paper."

Dale shook his head. "It's in the backseat. You can take it if you want."

"I don't suppose it says anything I don't know already. And if Shirlee wants to talk, then let her. Maybe with all the publicity, the murderer will stop, or somebody might remember something they saw or heard that might be a clue. You never know."

Dale treated her to lunch at the cafeteria in Burke's Department Store, where she and that sweet Elizabeth Warren had had tea. To Mavis, everything looked especially appetizing, and she took more items than she should have. At the home, the food already seemed bland—margarine instead of butter, no salt, and not a speck of seasoning in the vegetables, most of them right out of a can. "This *was* a treat," she said to Dale as she scraped up the last crumbs from her strawberry shortcake. "I don't know when food ever tasted so good."

He dipped his head as if he were bowing. "Thank you kindly. I aim to please."

Mavis laughed, but before she could say anything further, a girl came over and asked them if they were finished. They both nodded, and the girl took up their plates and placed them on a tray, and before she went off to another table, she told them to have a good afternoon.

Mavis thought of Daisy Norris back at Lakeview and her tearful confession the night before. Poor thing. Mavis hoped Daisy wasn't in trouble because of buying liquor for Alton Hubbard. Surely they wouldn't fire her over such a little thing as that after she had been such a good worker all these years, not like that sorry one—what was his name? Larry Lee Matthews—they'd had to get rid of. "Well, my goodness," Mavis murmured to herself as an idea came suddenly into her head.

"What was that?" Dale asked.

"Just talking to myself," she answered, but then she said, "What have you got going the rest of the afternoon?"

"Nothing much. Some pictures to develop. Why?"

Mavis leaned closer, looking around to see if anyone was near enough to hear. "I didn't tell you about this figure I saw sneaking off over on the hill behind Lakeview the other night. Well, this real nice lady that takes around trays, Daisy Norris, told me the next day some things were missing from the kitchen, and she suspected one of the employees who had been fired not long before, said he'd sworn he'd make them sorry. Ever since, I've been wondering if he's the one I saw over on the hill. *He* could be the murderer . . . if he's warped enough to kill old ladies just to get even."

Dale looked skeptical. "Maybe," he said, raising his eyebrows. "But what can we do to find out anything more about it?"

"Give him a little surprise visit."

"A surprise visit? Honey, we aren't the police, even if you're working undercover. We can't go waltzing into his house and tell him we want to talk to him about murder. And what if he *is* the murderer? He could kill us both."

"He's got a wife and children. They'd be there. And it's broad daylight—he's not going to do anything. Anyway, I have an idea."

"I should have known," Dale said, and took a drink of water.

"It may be a sin to lie, but since it's for a good cause—trying to find a murderer—I don't think the Lord will mind all that much." She took a breath. "We could say we're out visiting for the church. There's bound to be one nearby, and folks go out all the time. He won't think a thing about it."

"You *are* something!" Dale said. "Once they let us inside—assuming they don't call the police on *us*—just what do you hope to find out? It's going to sound kind of strange to tell this guy he ought to come to a revival to repent all the murders he's committed.''

Folding her napkin, Mavis placed it on the table. ''Don't be silly,'' she said. ''We'll just observe, see what the two of them are like. You can tell all sorts of things just by keeping your eyes open.''

Dale grinned. ''Lord knows, *that's* true. I never could hide a thing from you. Come on,'' he said as he got up from the table. ''We might as well give it a try.''

They found the address in the telephone book. ''Isn't that Hillsborough Court Apartments?'' Dale said when Mavis read the street.

''Lord, I think it is,'' she answered, wondering whether they should go after all. If she were alone, or actually going out to visit for the church with some of the other ladies, she wouldn't set foot in the place. Everybody knew about Hillsborough Court. Built just after the war not far from downtown and bordering one of the nice old neighborhoods, it was the first public housing for low-income families in Markham. At first it was nice as could be, rows of yellow brick apartments with two rooms up and two rooms down, not big enough to skin a cat in but a godsend to the elderly folks and decent young families who couldn't make it otherwise on a small income. The grounds were landscaped nicely then. Every summer you could see slow arcs of water going back and forth across a thick green lawn, and roses bloomed at the corners of the buildings where benches were set for people to rest. Mavis had gone there many a time to visit a shut-in or bring a Christmas basket of food from the church.

But at some point—nobody could say exactly when—Hillsborough Court began to change. ''Have you been by there lately?'' people said to one another. ''Why, it looks real trashy. I guess they have to let just about anybody in. It's a shame.'' The windows and doors went unpainted, the lawn died and turned to dust, the roses failed to bloom, the benches were covered with words that made you blush to read. And the people—well, even though they seemed to be younger and younger, with hordes of children running wild all over the neighborhood, their faces looked very old, as if this was the end of the line for them and they already knew it. There were reports of crime at Hillsborough Court in nearly every edition of the paper, and nice folks stopped going there.

Larry Lee Matthews had a corner unit. When Dale stopped the car out front, Mavis noticed that there was still a white paper ghost in one of the windows, and two sagging pumpkins with cutout faces were sitting by the door, leftovers from Halloween. Somebody had made an effort to brighten up the yard, she thought as Dale helped her out of the car. The litter was picked up, and pretty colored coleus, gone now to seed, were set in cans along the front wall. She couldn't imagine Larry Lee doing something like that, at least not from what Daisy had said about him. "Reckon they're home?" she asked, pointing to the drawn shades at the windows.

At first no one answered when Dale knocked on the screen. Then the door opened just a crack and a voice said, "Who is it?"

Mavis rolled as close as she could to the door. "We're from the church," she said in a loud voice. A TV was blaring inside. "Can we come in for a minute?"

The door opened wider. A woman stood there. She looked first at Dale, then at Mavis, with a blank look on her face, as if she didn't understand, but then she said, "All right," and held the door open for them. Dale maneuvered the wheelchair inside.

It was dark there with the shades pulled, the only light coming from the TV in the corner, where two children sat on the floor watching cartoons. "Turn it down," the woman said, and one of them obeyed, looking with vague interest at Mavis's wheelchair. "I hope we're not interrupting," Mavis said.

The woman shook her head. "I was just changing the baby," she said, and walked around a partition to the kitchen.

"Take your time," Mavis said, and looked around the room.

Here, too, some attempt had been made to fix up the surroundings. Shiny plastic protected the silvery upholstery of the sofa and the two matching chairs, doilies sat atop the tables and TV, and a bunch of artificial flowers was arranged in a glass vase on the dinette table that stood near the kitchen partition. In a gold picture frame hung high on the wall out of the way of the children was a photograph of a young couple (surely Larry Lee Matthews and the woman changing her child a few feet from them) in happier days, Mavis thought. The two of them were smiling at the photographer, children, nearly, themselves, with nothing in their eyes to suggest that they suspected anything at all of what the future held.

"I'm sorry," the woman said, coming from around the partition. She carried a child dressed in overalls, gnawing on a chicken bone, his face shiny from the grease. Carefully she sat on the edge of one of the chairs, as if she weren't used to sitting there, afraid to mar the shiny surface.

Mavis brushed her hand in the air. "Oh, that's all right, honey. We didn't mean to butt in. But we did want to tell you about Bethel Baptist Church—it's not far a-tall—and invite you to come. They've got a nice nursery and everything for the children." She smiled at the baby, and it looked back at her with weak eyes. Then it occurred to her that they hadn't introduced themselves. "I'm Miz Mavis Lashley," she said. "That's Dale Sumner, my nephew."

"Hi," Dale said, and then went over to where the two children sat in front of the TV. Bending down, he asked, "What are y'all watching?" When the children didn't answer, only stared, he sat down next to them and picked up a GI Joe that lay on the floor. "I used to have one of these," he said. "I bet it's still at home somewhere." The children continued to stare at him, as if he had dropped from the moon.

"How do?" the woman said. "I'm Tammy Dawson." She looked down and blushed, and it was then that Mavis noticed that she had no ring on her finger and probably never would, at least not from Larry Lee Matthews. Those poor little children—she wondered what last name they used. Probably their mama's. It would say "Dawson" on the welfare checks. Tammy had straight, pale hair and small eyes too close together, and she wore a pair of shorts two sizes too small for her, cutting across the mottled white flesh of her legs.

"Are you churchgoing at present?" Mavis asked, trying to get a conversation going.

"No, ma'am, not in a long time. I was brought up as a Baptist, though, and that's where I'd go if I went."

"Well, you just come next Sunday, and bring the children. They need to be raised up in the Lord from the beginning. What about your husband?" Mavis would go along with the pretense. From what she read in the papers, half the world was living in sin.

If Tammy noticed a change in her voice, she didn't show it. "He's not one for church," she said. "Had to go too much when he was little, he says. But he probably wouldn't care if we go, particularly if he was working."

"What's his job?"

Tammy jiggled the baby on her knee. He was getting restless. Finally she took the chicken bone from him and put him on the floor, and he crawled over to where Dale was playing with the other two children, who seemed brighter now, giggling at his antics. "He ain't got one now," Tammy said. "He's out looking."

"Why, that's a real shame," Mavis said, hoping that she looked innocent. "What happened?"

"He was working out at Lakeview Nursing Home, in food service. But somebody got it in for him, and he got fired." Tammy's voice sounded angry, in imitation of Larry Lee's complaint, Mavis would guess. "With all these young-uns to feed, it makes it hard."

"That's the place where they are suspecting murder, isn't it? Lakeview, I mean."

"It sure is. This morning, when Larry Lee saw it on the news on TV, he said, 'Serves them right. There's a lot of stuff going on out there that nobody knows about. I could tell them a thing or two.' "

Why, I bet he could, Mavis thought. Aloud she said, "I

wonder what he could mean. Do you think he knows anything about the murders?''

Tammy shrugged her shoulders. ''I don't know. He didn't say anything else. He gets upset when he thinks about Lakeview, and the young-uns start screaming. I don't need it.'' Tammy bent over, her elbows resting on her knees, hands dangling, her eyes on the three giggling children and Dale, as if they were strangers to her. She didn't speak.

Finally Mavis said, ''Can I have a drink of water? Then we've got to be going.'' She looked at Dale.

''I ain't got no ice,'' Tammy said, pushing herself up.

''From the tap's just fine. Ice water hurts my teeth.'' Mavis followed Tammy behind the partition into the kitchen area. Here, too, things were neat and tidy, the dishes washed and draining and the dishcloth hung up to dry. It was then that Mavis noticed a large box and several tin cans lined up on the counter, institutional size, the box plainly marked with a saltines label, and the cans all different kinds of fruit, no doubt taken right out of the storeroom at Lakeview. Larry Lee Matthews *was* the weighed-down figure that Mavis had seen on the hill by the pond. Was he also the murderer? Tammy handed Mavis the glass of water, and Mavis looked at her face.

Enough pain already rests there, Mavis thought. I don't need to add more. Not to excuse his crime, but what if Larry Lee did take some food for his family? She was surprised they even missed it out at Lakeview. Half of what they put on the table got thrown away. No, she wouldn't tell, and if Larry Lee did turn out to be the murderer (and nothing she had learned today seemed to point in that direction), then she would have one small soft spot in her heart for him and Tammy Dawson. ''Thank you kindly,'' she said as she gave the poor girl back the glass.

Dale was lying on his back, and the three children were astraddle his chest like a horse when they got back to the living room. ''They'll mess up your clothes,'' Tammy said in alarm.

Dale poked his head up. ''Oh, it doesn't matter. This shirt's ready for the laundry anyway." He looked at Mavis. "You ready to go?" he asked her.

"I reckon so. We've got more visits to make."

She thought she saw him wink. Gently shifting the children from his chest, he sat up, pushed back his hair, and said to Tammy, "They're nice kids."

At first Mavis thought Tammy was going to cry. Her face wrinkled and she looked puzzled for a moment, but then her frown dropped away, like the outer covering of a flower to reveal a bloom, and she smiled. "That's right nice of you to say," she replied. "Sometimes they can be real sweet."

When Mavis and Dale pulled away in the car, Tammy Dawson remained in the doorway with the children clustered around her and gave a lonesome wave.

Chapter Eighteen

A TV van was parked in front of the administration building when they got back to Lakeview. "Lord," Mavis said as Dale pulled in to the drive, "I bet Clifford Joyner is in there right now, all puffed up and feeling important, telling some interviewer nothing like *murder* could ever happen at the home."

Dale laughed. "They should get *you* on. You could give them some hot news about Clifford and Barbara. Not to mention your undercover police work."

"Humph," Mavis said, swinging her cast around so that Dale could help her from the car into the chair, "I wouldn't lower myself to discuss such carryings-on . . . and I haven't exactly found out a whole lot of information that will shed some light on the murder."

"Well, you've found out a few things—Barbara and Clifford's little affair, if nothing else. And who the figure on the hill in the middle of the night was, and that Daisy made the call that first got things going. The police haven't done any better, or if they have, Charles Morgan hasn't told us about it. You just go on keeping your eyes and ears open. Something is bound to pop up soon. But you be careful—you never know who might be the killer."

Before Mavis had a chance to tell Dale she was tired to death of being told to be careful, a voice said, "Well, son, let me help you there," and she felt a sudden jerk of her chair. Looking around, she saw Alton Hubbard's bright face, his gleaming hair, and thought, Where in the world did *he* come from? Had he heard any of her and Dale's conversation? Alton gave her a big smile and took the handles of the chair away from Dale.

"Why, Mr. Hubbard," Mavis said. Dale gave her a look that asked, Who the heck is he? so she introduced them.

"I'm right glad to know you, son," Alton said, letting go of the chair long enough to shake hands with Dale. "I'm mighty proud to be acquainted with any relative of this fine lady."

Lord have mercy, Mavis thought. I never heard such sweet talk. Maybe he was still drunk. She asked him, "What are you doing out here this time of the day?"

"Going for a walk. It's a real fine day for one." He pointed at the bright sky through the trees. "I can't sit inside all day with those sick folks complaining. It's no place for a healthy man."

Mavis wanted to ask him why he was there if he was so healthy, but instead she said, "I'm surprised you're feeling so bright after last night." Looking around again, she saw that his face had turned a little redder.

"Oh, that wasn't anything a-tall, just me and some of the other fellas having us a good time. What's wrong with a card game and a nip or two from a bottle? Been doing it all my life, and I can't see it's done me one bit of harm. This place isn't a thing but a prison if we can't have *some* enjoyment. But I do apologize to the ladies—you in particular—if I upset 'em. Of course, nothing will satisfy Swannie Hocutt. She sees sin in every corner. I just wish I had a chance to do all she thinks I'm doing!"

"Well, there may *be* something going on in the corners," Mavis said, thinking of Clifford Joyner and Barbara Santucci. "You never know."

Alton gave her a wink and then turned her chair. "You go on," he said to Dale. "It'll be a pleasure for me to roll your aunt inside."

"That okay with you, honey?" Dale asked in a serious voice.

"Why, sure," she said, smiling at him, "I've taken up enough of your time today."

He kissed her good-bye. "I'll give you a call," he said, getting into the car and starting up the engine.

"A mighty fine boy," Alton murmured as Dale drove away.

Jerkily Alton Hubbard pushed Mavis's chair around to the side of the building. Lordy, she thought, I hope he's as fit as he thinks he is. I wouldn't want him to drop dead of a heart attack pushing me up the ramp. But instead of going to the ramp, he suddenly turned the chair and they started bouncing across the lawn.

"I thought we'd go for a little stroll," Alton said. "It's too pretty to go inside yet. And besides, I'm enjoying the company."

"Well, you might ask someone else's opinion first," Mavis said in a short voice, and clutched her purse tighter.

He apologized. "I'm right sorry. It seemed like such a good idea to me, I forgot to ask your permission."

"That's all right. Where are we going?"

"Over by the pond. See?" Mavis looked up and saw Alton's finger pointing over her head. "There's a bench there by the trees. We can take us a little rest."

Lord have mercy, Mavis thought as her heart began to beat, he's going to take me over there where Miss Luna Dixon got killed! But surely he wouldn't try to do anything to *her*. She did see the bench—before today, unnoticed—and it was out in broad daylight where anybody could see. If nothing else, she had a good pair of lungs and could yell if Alton Hubbard did anything untoward. Though he drank too much perhaps and had his mind too much on bedroom functions (but that could just be all talk), he didn't seem like a murderer to her. Still, she would have to be careful. You never knew.

They didn't speak again during the ride across the lawn. Above, the sun shone brightly, with only a small bank of clouds on the horizon. The grass was drier—Mavis could smell its warm scent—and insects flew up from the wheels of her chair. As they progressed toward the stand of trees, Alton's pace slackened, and she could hear his heavy breathing. That and the sound of birds flittering along the treetops were the only sounds.

Finally they were there.

"Whew-ee!" Alton said, wiping his brow. "That was a longer trek than I'd thought it would be." Turning Mavis around so that she faced in the direction of the home, he sat beside her on the bench.

"You rest," she said. "We don't want another death over here." Alton gave her a funny look but didn't say anything. Mavis looked around. Though she had never crossed the lawn this far before, the place seemed familiar to her—the stand of trees, the pond sparkling in the sunshine, its marshy edge—and then she remembered that Dale had described it all to her when he had told her about Miss Luna's death. Looking back now at the Lakeview buildings, she thought again of poor Mr. Jesse Dixon running toward them in the rain (how far away he'd seemed), shouting for help too late for Miss Luna, already dead. She shook herself to wipe away the picture from her eyes.

"You're not too chilly here in the shade?" Alton asked her.

"No," she said, "I wore my coat this morning and it feels right good."

He smiled at her, his face more relaxed than she had seen it, the furrows between his brows gone. He *was* a right nice-looking man, she thought. "I'm glad I ran into you like this," he said. "Over yonder"—he pointed to the home—"it's hard to carry on a decent conversation, everybody listening in. And now with all this murder business going on, there's not one minute of peace and quiet."

Mavis could have told him that all his carrying on didn't help any, but she decided to hold her tongue. Instead she said, "I saw the TV van when we drove up."

"Yes, it's been there all the morning, and the police were out yesterday. Did they talk to you?"

"Yes," she said, remembering Charles Morgan's visit. "Just for a minute."

"Did you tell them anything?"

Mavis paused. For some reason she wanted to tell Alton Hubbard about Daisy's call to the police, about Larry Lee Matthew's theft, about Clifford and Barbara's sporting on the sofa. But she held back, Dale's warning for her to be careful still loud in her ears. In spite of all his warm words, Alton Hubbard might be the killer. Sometimes the most innocent-seeming were the ones who did the direst deeds. "I didn't have any news to tell them," she said at last. "How about you?"

"Nothing for sure. I suppose there's gossip, but I'll let them hear that from somebody else." Alton stopped speaking for a moment, his eyes turned back toward Lakeview across the lawn. "I've got a funny feeling, though," he began again, "that we're all waiting—waiting for something else to happen—like being in a bad dream when you can't wake up."

"Lord, what do you think it might be?"

"I don't know. If I did, I guess I could do something. But I wanted to warn you. I don't want anything to happen to you especially."

Had Alton Hubbard turned even redder? Mavis wasn't sure, and she didn't want to turn her head to look directly at him, afraid she might catch his eye. She tucked her scarf closer around her neck and said, "Well, I surely do appreciate that, but I think I can take care of myself. Besides, I haven't signed over what little bit of money I have to Lakeview for lifelong care the way most of the people who died had done. Soon as this cast comes off, I'll be right back home."

"I know," he said. "You'll surely be missed."

Mavis still couldn't look at him. "What about you?" she asked. "You don't plan to stay on, do you?"

"No longer than I have to in order to get my medicine straightened out, though that may be a while yet."

"Well, then, maybe *you* need to be careful. You think the murderer will be after you?"

Throwing back his head, Alton Hubbard gave a hearty laugh, and the tension that Mavis, at least, had felt between them evaporated like water on a hot day. "I'm still strong as an ox," he said, "and I make enough noise to scare most anybody away, even a murderer."

Mavis looked into his bright blue eyes then and smiled. "Yes," she said, "I've noticed the noise. You scare poor Swannie Hocutt and Kimberly Collier half to death."

"Aw, those two," he said, waving his hand. "It does 'em good. And I enjoy getting Nurse Overby's goat. But you know what—mainly I do it for myself. Most folks, they come to a place like this, settle in, and before you know it, they're dead. And I don't mean murdered, either, just given up. *I* don't intend for that to happen to me. I'll fight every step of the way, and anybody that tries to help me along with dying better watch out."

Mavis thought, My goodness, he's going to rise up and start marching around like he was still in the war. I've never seen a man so excited. But Alton did not get up. His breathing slowed, he folded his hands in his lap, and he began to stare off across the lawn. When he stared to speak again, his voice was quite soft, almost as if he were talking to himself.

"My wife," he said, "she wouldn't stand for my carrying on one minute. I'd get to going, and she'd say, 'Now, Alton, that's about all I want to hear of that. If you must shout, go in yonder and close the door so nobody else can hear you. It's too disturbing.' She always knew it was just my bark. I think you do, too."

"Has she been gone long?" Mavis asked gently.

"Thirteen years next December. The seventh. It was cancer and it took a long time. All I could do was sit by and watch her fade down to just a little bitty thing I could pick up in one hand, but the one thing I can thank the Lord for is that she had no pain. Me, I felt like there was a pair of pliers twisting inside of me that never let up."

"You didn't find anyone else?"

Alton broke his stare, sat up, and brushed back his hair. "No," he said, then laughed. "But others tried to find *me*! Two days after the funeral, I got an invitation out to dinner, and several ladies would drop by to see me every chance they got to find out how I was 'getting on.' One even pressed her telephone number into my hand while I was standing in line at the post office buying some stamps. But I didn't take to them. I never saw a single person who I thought could come close to my wife. That is, until lately."

Oh, Lordy, Mavis said to herself, what have I got myself into? Had she encouraged Alton Hubbard? Surely she hadn't said anything misleading. He had needed to talk. She had listened. Who in the world would ever have expected it to turn out like this? She was too flustered even to answer. Finally, in desperation, she looked up at the sky and saw that the bank of clouds had drawn a little closer. "Goodness," she said, pointing upward, her voice quite hoarse, "look at those clouds. I think it might rain. Maybe we should be getting back to the home."

Alton barely glanced at the sky, the expression on his face like that of some old dog that's been yelled at for no good reason. Getting up slowly, he said, "Yes, ma'am, I reckon so," and for the first time since she had met him, Mavis thought that he looked a little frail. He, too, might need protection against a murderer.

They went back across the field in silence. The sun had sunk low in the sky, and there was a chill in the air. Mavis was glad she had her coat to cover her arms. Back inside the building, they could heard the noise from the kitchen, where the evening meal was being prepared, and as they passed the activity room, they could see a few heads bent over some project. "I guess I can take over now," Mavis said, touching the wheels of her chair. "You'll spoil me."

"I don't mind a-tall," Alton said, and sounded a little brighter. "Maybe we can have us another little visit."

"That would be nice," Mavis answered, and then began to wheel herself toward the elevator. How lucky she'd been! She'd had her hair done just that morning and around her neck she had worn the pretty silk scarf Dale had given her. Smiling to herself, she wondered if Alton Hubbard was still watching her as she rolled away.

Chapter Nineteen

"That you, Mavis honey?" Betty William's voice called out from her room as Mavis passed by in the hallway, returning from supper. The door was almost closed, and at first Mavis didn't see anyone inside until she pushed open the door and then, surprised, grabbed the wheels of her chair to stop it. Who in the world can *that* be? She wondered, staring at the woman sitting there by Betty's bed. Her hair was bleached silver, her clothes clung to her buxom figure like something painted on, and despite the heavy makeup, the lines on her face revealed the sorrows of her life plainer than Kimberly's fortune-telling cards ever could. And yet when Mavis said hello, the woman smiled a smile so warm that it seemed to fill the room with light, and Mavis knew at once that she had found great happiness there. "This is my daughter," Betty said. "The one you wrote to for me, Mavis. She got the letter this morning and drove a hundred and fifty miles this afternoon to see me. Ain't that something?" Betty's face, too, shone with joy.

"I sure do appreciate your writing that letter for Mama," the woman said, getting up. She shook Mavis's hand. "I'm Roxanne Dunn. You come on in." Pushing the chair she had been sitting in aside, she made room for Mavis, then sat down again closer to the bed.

"Wasn't anything a-tall," Mavis said, and smiled at Roxanne. "I was glad to do it. Your mama's been a real comfort to me since I've been here."

Roxanne pushed back her hair, and Mavis wondered why it didn't break right off and fall on the floor, it was so dry. Her eyes had a faraway look for a moment. "You don't know how much it means. I've been looking for that letter half my life, and when it finally came, I couldn't believe it, kept reading it over and over again just to be sure."

Betty had a pained look on her face. "You could have written, too," she said. "No law against it."

"I know, but I was afraid to."

"Afraid of what?"

"That it might not be welcome. Stubbornness, too, I reckon. You always did say I was the stubbornest child you ever did see. A lot of that's gone now, but I guess I've still got some left over."

Betty's smile came back. "Well, I'm just glad one of us did it before it was too late."

"Too late for what?" Roxanne asked.

Lying back against her pillow, Betty said, "I'm not getting any younger. I could go any minute. And if I stay in this place, I might just get helped along."

Roxanne bent toward her. "What in the world do you mean?" she said.

"You haven't read the papers?" Betty asked, and then went on when Roxanne shook her head. "There's been some deaths here, mysterious deaths, they think. The police are investigating, but nobody knows who might be next."

"Well, I'll just move you right out. You can come home with me." Picking up her purse from the floor, Roxanne looked as if she might start out right then.

"Now, sugar, I wasn't hinting around for anything like that. I'm safe enough here with Mavis right next door. And you know it would never work, the two of us together. Besides, you've got your own life to live."

Roxanne pulled a tissue from her purse and blew her nose. She didn't look up at first. "I've pretty much made a mess of it so far," she said. "I'm alone now. Been through more men than I care to remember, and though none of them stuck, I'm still looking—like a bad habit, I guess." Suddenly her face became radiant again as she began to rummage around in her purse. "But I *am* proud of something in my life," she said, pulling two pictures from her wallet and handing them to Betty. "We were so excited at first, crying and hugging, that I didn't even tell you I had two daughters. That's them there."

"Oh, my goodness," Betty said as tears formed in her eyes, too. "Think how many years it's been, and we never knew each other."

"I'm real ashamed," Roxanne said. "They wanted to meet you and Daddy, asked me all sorts of questions about what it was like when I was young. But I never got in touch. It's a shame you can't go back and undo the years."

"Aren't they sweet?" Betty said to Mavis, handing her the photographs.

She took them, looked at each one, the two girls a lot alike, not pretty but with good plain faces that still looked hopeful about what was to come. Perhaps they would escape some of the scars of living that showed so plainly on their mother's face. "That's Luanne," Roxanne said, pointing to the picture of the girl with the darker hair. "She's married to a nice boy. And that's Patricia Jean, who's just gone off to college, it surprises me to say. Where she got her brains, I don't know. Certainly not from her mama."

"Now, you hush," Betty said to Roxanne. "You always made good grades till you got to high school and it was all boys and nothing else."

Roxanne sighed and took Betty's hand. "Yes, I reckon things could have been different. But that's all water over the dam now. No point in talking about what might have been."

Mavis was about to say that it was never too late to make a fresh beginning, but just then the door opened. "Well, my goodness, we're having a little party," said Nurse Overby, who stood there with a tray of medicines in her hand. "I won't interrupt but a minute. Miz Williams, I'm going to leave your pills there on the stand if you'll promise me you'll take them before bedtime." She started to walk past Mavis but then stopped dead in her tracks when she saw Roxanne in the chair by the bed.

"Well, my goodness, Estelle Overby," Roxanne said. "Isn't it a small world?" Mavis could have sworn she had a glint in her eye.

For a moment, Nurse Overby turned as white as her uniform; the tray shook in her hand. Then, when she regained her composure, she gave a sickly smile and said, "Lord, yes. It *has* been a long time, hasn't it? I didn't know you were a friend of Miz Williams."

Roxanne gave a laugh that seemed too loud for the little room. "That's my *mama*!" she said, pointing to Betty and giving her a smile. "We've had a regular reunion here, thanks to Miz Lashley. And now that we've got together again, I aim to come see her every chance I get."

"Won't that be nice?" Nurse Overby said, but Mavis could tell by the tone of her voice she didn't mean it. She became very businesslike. "I've got more medicines to distribute," she said, leaning over to place a little cup on Betty's stand. "Remember, now, you're supposed to take it before you go to sleep." She started to back away toward the door.

"I'll be sure she gets it," Roxanne said with a big smile on her face. "It was nice to see you, Estelle. I'm sure we'll see each other again."

"No doubt," Nurse Overby said, and went out the door.

"Well, isn't that a coincidence?" Betty said.

"Yes," Mavis added. "How in the world do you know Nurse Overby?"

Roxanne settled back in her chair and, as she spoke, began to twirl the little pill cup that the nurse had left on the stand. "We lived down the street from each other years ago," she began. "I can't remember how long, but my girls were little then—us in this dinky apartment (all I could afford in those days with no husband in sight and two babies to take care of), and Estelle and her mama in a house that seemed to me big enough to be a mansion. Looking back, I expect it needed work, and later the whole neighborhood got run-down and that old house was full of boarders who were about as trashy as you can get.

"But back when I'm talking about, I envied Estelle Overby more than anything, though she hardly knew I was alive. I did her mother's hair. I was a beauty operator then—came to the house every week after the old lady got down sick and couldn't get out anymore—to give her a wash and set. Poor thing, she hardly had any hair left. But Estelle always indulged her mama, and Lord knows I needed the money, so I came there every week regular as clockwork to do my little job. Estelle would come into her mama's room and leave the money on the dresser, but if she said hello, it was a rare occasion. I knew she thought I was dirt." Roxanne laughed. "Imagine what it was like for her when I started dating her ex-boyfriend. I'm sure she hates my guts to this day."

"Boyfriend!" Mavis and Betty shouted out the word at the same time. Mavis went on. "That's the last thing in the world I'd ever expect that woman to have. I can't imagine her any way but starched."

Roxanne shrugged her shoulders, shifting in her chair. "It was a long time ago—she was different then, not so heavy, a permanent in her hair. I did that, too. And she always did dress nice, worked in an expensive ladies' store downtown and got all her clothes there, her mama's, too. Every time I'd go to do the wash and set, her mama would be sitting up in bed all dolled up in a new bed jacket—pretty little thing, I was sorry when she died, though that was long after Estelle and I had our little falling-out."

"Who was this man, pray tell?" Betty sat up straighter in bed and stared at Roxanne's face.

"Mr. Ray Hedgpeth. Real nice, and a pillar of the First Baptist Church. That's where Estelle met him, I heard. They went together for years. Church each Sunday, every social they had in the church basement, once in a while a movie if it wasn't too nasty. People said he proposed more times than you could shake a stick at, but Estelle always said wait. Her daddy had run off when she was young—that house was her mama's old homeplace—and so by the time Estelle and Ray

Hedgpeth got together, her mama was already down sick and just got worse and worse, water around her heart, as time went on. Estelle had to take care of her.

"Maybe Ray just got tired of waiting; who knows? Anyway, he and Estelle weren't seen around town together so much—no more church socials, no more movies—and all of a sudden everybody was saying he'd started dating other girls. That's where I came in. Don't laugh, but I met him at the church, too. My landlady was one of those people who are always trying to save somebody's soul, and she pestered me so much that I finally agreed to go with her to a Wednesday night prayer service. Ray was there, and we got to talking at the social hour afterward. Needless to say, nothing much came of it—a few dates, and then no more telephone calls. I guess Ray realized I wasn't exactly an outstanding prospect for the First Baptist Church. Soon after, he married some other girl, plain as wallpaper, who had been hoping to be a missionary to China but couldn't get in. I hope he's happy.

"Estelle never called again, either, after she found out I'd dated Ray those few times, so somebody else must have fixed her mama's hair. When old Miz Overby finally did die, Estelle sold the house quick as she could and left town. Much later, I heard she'd gone into training to be a nurse. Lord knows, she'd had enough experience, taking care of her mama all those years."

For a long time there was silence in the room after Roxanne finished speaking. Outside, the day had dimmed, and the shade at the window was golden with reflected light. Finally Mavis said with a sigh, "Well, isn't that a sad story? You'd never know from looking at her, would you, that she's seen so much sorrow. Maybe working here makes up a little for what she lost. Ministering to others in need can bring a person joy."

Roxanne said, "Maybe," but didn't sound convinced. She looked at her watch, then turned toward the window, where the light was fading, casting shadows in the corners of the room. "It's getting late," she said. "I'd better be going." She bent down to get her purse.

Betty's face looked stricken. "Lord, it seems like you just got here," she said. "Can't you stay a little longer?"

Standing, Roxanne smiled. "I've got a long ways to drive, Mama, but I'll be back. I know the way now, and know that I'm welcome. I'll bring the girls next time. They'll be tickled to death to finally meet their grandmama." She turned to Mavis. "I'd like for you to meet them, too," she said. "After all, if it hadn't been for you, none of this would have happened."

"It wasn't much a-tall, but I'm glad everything turned out the way it did." Mavis started to pull back, ready to turn the chair around, but before she could move away, Roxanne put both hands on the arms, bent down, and kissed Mavis on the forehead.

"It was a lot," Roxanne said, her eyes blurred with tears, "and I'll be eternally grateful."

Mavis moved out then, her full heart almost overflowing with joy. And much later, after she had gone to bed and had finished her prayers, she asked God a special favor: Take care of that Roxanne Dunn, and give her at least some few years of happiness.

Chapter
Twenty

Mavis was never quite sure what awakened her in the middle of the night. Perhaps it was a sound, like the fluttering of leaves. She almost turned over, dragging the cast, thinking that the wind must have risen and branches were blowing against the screen outside her window. But then she remembered that her room was high above the shrubbery and no tree sheltered that side of the building. When she opened her eyes to look, the window shade, illumined by the moon, showed no wavering shadows.

It came again, a whisper, a moan. She sat straight up in bed. Betty's room? Was that where the sound came from? She called out, "Betty, honey, you all right?" and waited, with a feeling that someone else also waited in the shadows. Once more she called, "Betty?" but still no answer came. "I've got to go see," she said out loud as she slid her legs off the side of the bed. Taking no time to put on her robe, she reached over for the chair, shifted her feet to the floor, then leaned forward. "Oh, dear Jesus!" she cried as the chair spun away and she fell, her cast crashing against the metal feet of the bed. She had forgotten to lock the wheels when she got out earlier in the evening.

Now what will I do? she asked herself. She had to get to the chair. She felt her body gingerly for pain, but nothing seemed broken. Perhaps the cast had even protected her leg from injury. Rolling sideways and drawing up her legs, she managed to get to her knees, then began to crawl toward the chair. Help me, Lord, she prayed. Let me make it in time. Her progress was slow—the cast dragged her down and her arms felt weak—but finally she was able to touch the cool metal of the wheels with her fingertips. She felt like shouting, Hallelujah! Locking the wheels this time, she pulled herself upward with shaking arms, twisted her body, and sank into the seat. The Lord was with her.

There came a sound again! Quite near, but different this time, the swish of a door opening and then closing. She rolled to her own door, turned the chair so that she could push against it, pulled back, and then moved out into the hallway. Darkness surrounded her. She looked both ways— to the right where the light in the nurses' station glowed, to the left past the elevator. Did she see movement there, some- one turning the corner to the other wing? She couldn't be sure, but she had no time to go chasing after anyone. She had to see about Betty.

At first she thought everything was all right. In the bright moonlight from the window, she could see Betty lying on her back in bed, with one poor, twisted hand flung out beside her head. Mavis wasn't close enough to listen for her breath- ing, so she rolled herself nearer to the bed, saying, "Betty, Betty," in a low voice, not wanting to frighten her. But no answer came, and when she pulled up beside the bed so that she could see Betty's face, pale in the white light, a look of horror on its distorted features, she realized that those poor hands were drawn up into tiny fists, as if she was trying to ward off an attacker. "Help! Help!" Mavis cried out, and reaching up behind Betty's head, grabbed the call button and pressed it as hard as she could. "Please don't let her be dead," she prayed. "Oh, please!"

"What in the world?" the nurse said, bursting through the door. She switched on the light, and Mavis could see the worry in her pretty eyes.

"It's Betty!" Mavis yelled. "I think the killer's been here. See if she's alive!"

Giving Mavis a look that said as plain as day she thought Mavis might just be crazy and wandering around in the middle of the night, she leaned over, pressed her ear to Betty's chest, then raised the thin wrist with her fingertips. "She is all right," she said in a slightly accented voice. "What happened?" she asked, looking as if she still wasn't quite sure she could believe what Mavis might tell her.

"I heard a sound," Mavis said. "It woke me up. I'm not sure what it was, maybe Betty moaning. But somebody was in here a minute ago—that's for sure. They came out just before I got my door open and disappeared down the hallway. Whoever it was, they were up to no good. I think you should go call the doctor."

Glancing first at Mavis, then at Betty's inert form, the woman wavered. She's afraid she'll get in trouble either way, Mavis thought. If she calls and it's nothing, she'll get yelled at. If she doesn't and something happens to Betty, she'll be in mighty big trouble. "You go on ahead and do it, honey," Mavis said in a soothing voice. "If anybody gets upset, you can say I'm to blame." Without answering, the nurse turned and walked out of the room. A minute later, Mavis heard her murmuring voice from the desk down the hall.

"Oh. . . ." Mavis jumped at the sound of Betty's voice, so small, it was hardly more than a sigh.

"Is that *you*?" Mavis cried out, swinging around to the bed again. She picked up Betty's hand and felt it relax slightly. Her heart was filled with praise for God's goodness. "Are you all right?" she asked. "Can I do something?" Then she pulled back, afraid she would frighten Betty all over again.

Betty's eyes opened, fluttering like a butterfly's wings. For a moment they seemed unfocused, but then she saw Mavis and smiled. "What happened?" she asked.

"Only the Lord knows for sure, but I think whoever has been killing folks around here was after you. Can you remember?"

Betty closed her eyes again; her lips trembled. "Oh, Lordy!" she cried out. "I do."

Mavis knew she shouldn't push Betty after such a fright, but she had to know. "Tell me," she said, and pressed Betty's hand in hers.

"I woke up," she said, "and knew right away somebody else was in the room. I sat half up but couldn't see anybody—they must have been sort of behind the head of the bed—and then there was this bag over my face." She shivered. "Oh, it was so awful, Mavis, everything blurred, my breath cut off, a warm feeling like fire spreading over me! I tried to push the hands away, but I didn't have the strength. I think I must have fainted away right then." Betty pulled Mavis's hands closer to her. "When did you come in?" she asked.

"Not too long after, thank the Lord. I heard something, too, woke up, and then I think I heard you cry out. That must have been when they were trying to pull the bag over you. Anyway, I tried to get in my chair, but I fell and had to crawl across the floor to get to it. If it hadn't been for that, I might have seen the killer running away."

Betty rose up, and her eyes looked afraid. "Oh, I'm glad you didn't. They might have come after you."

Mavis would have told her it wasn't likely, she could take care of herself, but just then the nurse came back. "I have called the doctor," she said. "And the police. They will be here any minute." Mavis breathed out a sigh of relief. At least she had been believed. She backed a little away from the bed as the nurse came up to check Betty's pulse again, then stopped as the woman called out, "What in the world is that?" pointing to the side of the bed.

"What?" Mavis said, trying to see around her.

The nurse moved backward. "There," she said, "on the coverlet. Did you spill something?" she asked Betty.

Mavis followed the pointing finger and saw the large spot of color—bright red and blue-green—and knew at once what it was. "Oh, Lord, it's makeup. Whoever tried to kill poor Betty was going to make up her face after she was dead just like all the others."

The nurse looked at Mavis as if she thought Mavis had lost her mind. "What do you mean?" she asked.

"I guess you don't get in on a lot of the gossip here, working nights," Mavis said. "The others who were killed, the ladies, all of them had been made up when their bodies were found. I must have scared the murderer away, and they dropped whatever they were holding, rouge and eye shadow. I wonder if there's a lipstick on the floor.'' She looked around but didn't see anything there. She might have searched more, but just then a buzzer sounded somewhere off in the distance, and the nurse hurried away to the desk. In no time at all, she returned with a policeman and policewoman trailing behind her.

"Evening," the woman said. Mavis thought, Well, isn't she a pretty little thing, nice red hair that looks natural, and the whitest skin I think I've ever seen, not at all the kind of person I'd expect to see in a policewoman's uniform. She walked over to the bed and touched Betty's hand, not even noticing, it seemed, the twisted fingers. "You want to tell us what happened, ma'am?" she said, and her voice was as gentle as if she were talking to a child.

Betty told her story, her voice growing stronger with each word, while the policewoman stood by the bed making notes on a little pad, and Mavis sat resting in her chair. The policeman had already gone off with the nurse to search the home to see if the killer was still lurking in some hallway. Watching them leave—her the tiniest thing, pretty as a doll, and him just an overgrown boy who looked as if he might still be afraid of the dark—Mavis thought, They won't find anything. If the murderer broke in from the outside, he'd have had plenty of time to escape by now, and if it was somebody here in the home, who's to say they shouldn't be there? She smiled at Betty to give her courage to continue.

When Betty had finished telling how she had struggled with the murderer, trying to push the plastic from her face, and then passed out, to be saved, surely, by Mavis, the policewoman turned to Mavis and asked, "Is that you?" and wrote something on her little pad.

"Yes, ma'am," Mavis said. "Miz Mavis Lashley. L-A-S-H-L-E-Y. My room's next door. Something woke me and I heard a noise in here, but by the time I got out of bed, the killer had escaped.''

Betty beamed at Mavis, all trace of the horror she had just

experienced gone from her face, and then said to the police-woman, "She's my best friend. She reunited me with my daughter. Wait'll I tell her Mavis saved my life again."

Mavis almost blushed in front of the policewoman, who had a puzzled look on her face. "You want me to call Rox-anne?" she asked Betty. "Tell her you're all right?"

"No. But thank you, honey. Roxanne's old enough to re-member when a long-distance call in the middle of the night meant only one thing—death. And though it did almost hap-pen, I'm safe enough. No need to add one more worry to her life."

The policewoman had no more questions, and when the policeman came back (of course, he hadn't found anything), she said they had to be going. "We'll keep cruising by to-night," the policeman said. "Don't you ladies worry none." Mavis thought, Fine lot of protection you'd be able to give with that baby face of yours, but she said, "You inform Charles Morgan first thing in the morning of what happened out here tonight. He'll want to know."

The two officers looked at her in surprise. "You know Detective Morgan?" the woman asked.

Lord, she had almost revealed she was working for Charles! She'd have to be more careful. "He was in my Sunday-school class a long time ago," she said. "I read in the paper he was working on the case, that's all. 'Night now," she said, and moved away from the door to let them pass.

"Thank y'all for coming," Betty said, and the officers smiled and left the room, turning right, no doubt headed for the nurses' station to have a last word with her before they left. Mavis was all ready to say, I bet they're down there asking the nurse if we're both crazy, but before she could open her mouth, the doctor poked his head in the door.

"Well," he said, "I hear there's been a little excitement tonight." He was young-looking, too, Mavis thought, sleepy-eyed, obviously dressed in the first thing that came to hand when he got out of bed—sweatshirt and khaki pants. He went up to Betty and asked, "How are you feeling, ma'am? Any pain? You want to tell me what happened?"

Mavis spoke up. "I guess I'll be going."

"That might be best," the doctor said, turning his head around to see her. "I'm just going to check this little lady over and give her a sedative so she can get some sleep during what's left of the night."

Mavis gave Betty one last smile. "You rest," she said. "If you need me, give a call." And with that, she turned and rolled out into the hallway to her room.

An hour later she was still wide-awake. The police and doctor had gone, and in the quiet she could hear Betty's light snore coming from the room next door. No doubt the nurse was busy writing up an incident report at her desk. "*I* need a sedative," Mavis said out loud, turning on the light. She sat up in bed. But even that might not help. Something was bothering her, something important, and she'd never sleep until she figured out what it was.

Sitting there, she went over everything that had happened in the last week—the bazaar and Miss Luna Dixon's death, the revelation that Elgie Skinner had been murdered, the investigation of the other deaths, all the things that had happened to her at the home—but nothing quite fit together. It was some small thing that bothered her, something recent, but she couldn't put her finger on it.

Maybe it would help to read just a minute, get her mind off everything. Sometimes answers popped up when you least expected them. Turning, she reached toward the bedside stand for her book of daily devotions. Then she caught her breath. There on the sleeve of her gown was a stain, a trace of makeup that the killer had dropped on Betty's bed. Mavis must have brushed against it when she was ministering to her. That was it! That was what she was trying to remember. Surely the killer's clothing, too, had been stained, perhaps even more obviously than the spot on Betty's bed, and if Mavis could find some garment that could be identified, then the murderer would be revealed.

She knew at least one place to look.

Reaching for her robe, she put it on and tied it securely,

then swung her legs over the side of the bed, made sure that the chair was steady to prevent another fall, and slid into the seat. When she switched off the light, the room was still bright with moonlight. At the door she paused a moment, hearing in her ears all the warnings she had been given—*Be careful!*—and she wondered if she should wait till morning when Charles Morgan came and let him search for the telltale clothing. But by then, it might have been taken away and they would have lost the chance to identify the killer. No, she wouldn't wait. Surely there wasn't much danger—who'd suspect an old lady riding around in the middle of the night in a wheelchair of looking for clues to a murder?

The hallway was brighter than usual, the sun-room at the end flooded by the moon, and the light from the nurses' station adding a golden cast. If the nurse was awake, she would be busy with paperwork, and listening, Mavis heard no sounds from the other rooms except the usual sighs and snores, murmurings from dreams. Betty rested peacefully next door. Quickly Mavis turned left, rolled to the elevator, and pushed the button. The doors opened at once, and she got on, nearly blinded by the bright fluorescent light. Thank the Lord the doors made only a light swishing sound when they closed.

When she got off on the ground floor, it was quite dark, the moonlight visible only through the doorway of the activity room and at the far end of the hall where breakaway doors led to the patio. Mavis wasn't going that far. Moving slowly along the wall, she peered upward, looking for the sign, not quite sure she remembered where the door was located, though she had passed it dozens of times on her way back and forth to the dining room. Finally she saw it, just a pale square on the wall, though the letters were quite visible: EMPLOYEES' LOCKER ROOM. She rolled over to the door and tried it. Thank goodness it wasn't locked! With a sudden feeling of excitement, she opened the door and went inside.

Windowless, the room was completely dark, and Mavis had to feel around on the wall by the door to find the light switch. *Was* she in some danger? she wondered just before her fingers found the switch and flicked it on. But then the room was suddenly filled with light, revealing its ordinary, everyday appearance—a little disorderly, locker doors hanging open, chewing-gum wrappers on the floor, a cigarette butt lying there even though there was another sign that plainly said NO SMOKING. Lord have mercy, was it only a week ago that she stood here helping Zeena with her costumes while the other Merry Makers chattered around her? How much had happened in that time.

She shouldn't linger. It wasn't *that* long till dawn, and some of the food service workers might arrive early to start getting ready for breakfast. Though she might have found the contents of the lockers interesting (she read the names as she passed—Kimberly Collier, Barbara Santucci, Clifford Joyner, Daisy Norris, members of the nursing staff), she didn't think she would find what she was looking for behind the metal doors. No, her goal was the corner where the bins of dirty uniforms stood waiting to be taken away and laundered and returned to the staff the next day, starched and pressed, in plastic bags. *Plastic bags!* Of course—the murderer could easily have found them here. Why, one of those torn bags that lay on the floor right now might have been pressed against poor Betty's face! Such an awful thought. Mavis shuddered.

She began to go through the pile of dirty uniforms. Goodness, people made a mess of them. She touched the fabric gingerly, slightly repulsed. When she recognized a name (they were printed on the collar), she looked at the uniform carefully, but then she thought, The killer could be a perfect stranger to me, someone who cleans in another part of the building, a dishwasher in the kitchen. But somehow she didn't think so. There had to be a reason for the murders other than just randomness. She was sure the killer knew the writhing features beneath the layers of plastic film, knew them quite well, but because of madness, didn't care.

She was right. Stuffed down near the bottom of the first bin was a rolled-up uniform that had a familiar name on the collar. Mavis held it up, let it unroll, and there right in front was a large smudge of makeup, the very same colors that marked Mavis's gown. She didn't even have to take off her robe to see. Of course, she thought, beginning to understand. It would make sense. Who else would have a better opportunity? She rolled up the uniform again, ready to take it back to her room. Wouldn't Charles Morgan be surprised when she handed it to him in the morning?

"Were you looking for something?"

The voice came from the doorway. Whirling around, Mavis remembered, too late, that she had forgotten to close the door. "No," she said, with a smile she knew looked foolish. She tried to hide the uniform beside her in the chair. "I couldn't sleep and was just poking around."

"I suppose you thought you'd help us with the laundry in the middle of the night." The lips turned up, but not in mirth. Mavis could not see the shaded eyes.

"Well, no," Mavis said. "I was missing this little sweater of mine, and I wondered if it might have gotten mixed up with the laundry."

The person closed the door and moved closer. "That's just the uniforms for the staff, not laundry from the rooms. Surely you can see that."

Mavis didn't answer at first, turning her chair. She leaned over slightly to one side in the hope that the uniform would not show. "Well, I declare," she said. "That never did occur to me." She tried to act as dense as Swannie Hocutt.

The lips turned up again. "Miz Lashley, I don't think you were looking for any sweater at all. In fact, I think you have what you were looking for right there in the chair beside you."

Mavis sighed; she knew she couldn't pretend any longer. Pulling out the uniform, she unrolled it and pointed to the name on the collar. " 'Estelle Overby, R.N.,' " she read. "It's your name plain and clear."

"Yes," Estelle said, pushing back her hair, "but what do you think it proves?" For a moment her face looked softer, the pink sweater she wore becoming to her. Mavis had never seen Nurse Overby out of uniform before, and remembering Roxanne Dunn's words that Estelle had once been almost pretty, enough so, at least, to catch a man's interest, she searched the face to see some trace of that lost time. But Estelle's face was a blank now, the eyes, revealed briefly, clear as water.

Mavis pointed to the stain on the skirt. "It's makeup," she said, "from where you tried to kill Betty Williams tonight." She pointed to her arm. "I got some on me when I was trying to help her out."

Estelle Overby was closer now. Her mouth was slightly open, and Mavis could hear her taking short, shallow breaths. Looking around, Mavis tried to find a way to escape from her. She couldn't roll back—the uniform bins were in the way—and rows of lockers blocked her on either side. She would have to go forward in the path where Estelle Overby stood.

Reaching around as far as she could, Mavis grabbed the wheels of the chair, turned with all her might, and zoomed forward, her leg in its cast held up like some giant weapon in a joust. She caught Nurse Overby just at the waist and sent her spinning. "God damn you!" Estelle cried, hands reaching out as she tried to regain her balance.

"I don't think he'll hear you," Mavis said. "Not after what you've done." She wheeled forward again, headed for the door. But then she heard Estelle panting harder and, looking back for just a moment, saw that the woman had righted herself and was starting after her again, the look on her face one of pure hate. In three bounds she would be across the floor and could grab the handles of Mavis's chair and stop her.

She had to do something quickly. Still rolling, she reached out and grabbed the door of one of the open lockers, pulled, felt the whole row jiggle slightly, then jerked as hard as she could. The lockers teetered for a moment, then swayed, and finally, with a crash, fell across Estelle Overby's path. Well, I think the Lord heard *me* this time! she thought, and almost smiled.

She was out the door then and whizzing down the hallway. She remembered that the fire alarm was just on the other side of the door to the activity room, and as she drew closer, she could see it, bright red, in the moonlight coming through the windows of the breakaway doors. Even if no one was awakened by the crash of the lockers, the entire building would be aroused by the alarm. Reaching out, she felt the cool metal of the little hammer that dangled beneath the glass shielding the alarm. One quick pop to shatter it and she could push the button inside.

But she didn't have a chance. Suddenly the chair was stopped, jerked backward and Mavis's fingers were left reaching into the air. The little hammer swung back and forth like a toy teasing a child. Estelle Overby had caught up with her. Mavis could feel the heat of her body just behind her, hear her breath. She did not even think to scream as Estelle turned the chair and began to push her as hard as she could toward the doors.

They burst through. Outside, the lawn was brightly lit and the air was cool. Mavis pulled her robe more closely about her as Estelle, struggling only slightly, pushed her up the hill from the patio. Still it did not occur to her to cry out; perhaps she did not want to disturb the stillness. Strangely, she settled back, almost enjoying the swift ride across the lawn, the wind fresh with the scent of leaves blowing against her face. Finally she asked, almost dreamily, "Where are we going?"

"Over there by the pond," Estelle said, speeding up just slightly.

Mavis was instantly awake. Oh, dear Jesus! Where Miss Luna Dixon drowned. Estelle Overby would kill Mavis and make it look like another accidental death. And she might even get away with it! Who was to say that Mavis hadn't gone out for a ride sometime in the night and then tumbled into the pond? She wanted to scream, but now it was too late. If people at the home even heard her, they would think it was some animal howling in the night or a cry from someone else's dream. Maybe if she got Estelle talking, she would at least slow down so that Mavis might have a chance to work out some plan of escape. Trying not to show her fear in her voice, she said, "Why did you do it?"

"Do what?" Estelle's voice revealed no emotion. She might as well have been telling Mavis the time of day.

"Kill all those people. Try to kill Betty Williams. It *was* you, wasn't it?

Estelle went on in the same tone. "Oh, yes," she said, "I killed them. But you have to understand—it was out of pity, no other reason."

"How can you call it pity, smothering somebody to death?"

Mavis could almost feel Estelle shrug her shoulders. "It was quick. They felt little pain. And they were so near dying, anyway, that it seemed a blessing to put them out of their misery. I felt so sorry for them lying there, all hope gone, everything they ever had given over to Lakeview, and no chance of returning home again."

"Not all of them."

"What do you mean?"

Mavis tried to look around so that she could look into Estelle Overby's eyes, but she could not turn that far. "Betty Williams wasn't anywhere near death. Crippled maybe, sad and lonely, but she was as healthy as could be, as far as anybody knows. And her life was about to change, now that she had found her daughter again."

"Yes. Roxanne." Estelle's voice was bitter. She almost stopped pushing the chair for a moment, then sprang forward even faster.

"It wasn't mercy that made you try to kill Betty," Mavis said, "but pure blind hate. And those others, too, you killed them for the same reason."

"I don't know what you mean."

"Roxanne told us about you. How you waited on your mama hand and foot all those years before she died, had Roxanne in every week to fix her hair, makeup on and everything. You sacrificed your life for her, and in the process, lost the one man you thought would wait for you. But it was too late by the time your mama died—he'd already found somebody else, and you were all alone."

"That bitch Roxanne!" Estelle said. "I'll kill her, too!"

Mavis went on as if she hadn't heard. "You went away, got your nurse's training, tried to care for others the same way you had cared for your mama. But that didn't take away your anger at her, did it? In fact, it might have made it even worse, those old people—constant reminders of all you had given up for her. So you started to kill them off, little old ladies that you made up to look like your mother, but it was in anger, not in love. You killed them the way you must have wanted to kill your mother a hundred times before she died. There's no mercy in you, Estelle, not one speck."

"Noooooo!" Estelle's scream filled the night, but no one would hear. Already she had pushed Mavis behind the rim of trees, and now she stopped the chair at the edge of the hill just above the pond that lay sparkling beneath them in the fading moonlight. It would soon be dawn. The sky had already turned deep blue, and in the trees the first birds were awakening with hoarse cries. Mavis gave up all hope of rescue. Estelle would do something soon.

"It's a lie," she whispered into Mavis's ear. "I loved my mama to death. You and that Roxanne made it all up."

With a sigh, Mavis said, "Look into your own soul, Estelle. Then you'll have to admit it."

"I don't have to admit anything," Estelle said, her voice loud again. "You're the only one who's suspected it was me, and you won't tell. There'll be another drowning, like Miss Luna's death—not my way, but good enough. Let's go."

Mavis felt the chair move forward again. In one last desperate effort, she swung both hands back behind her head, hoping to strike Estelle's chest and stun her for just a moment. And she must have hit her just slightly, because she heard Estelle give a groan, but the chair continued to move forward. Already she could feel herself begin to pitch over. "Oh, God!" she cried out loud, and then she heard another groan from Estelle, louder this time, in pain.

But the chair had tipped over the edge of the hill. Mavis tried to grab the wheels, but they turned too fast and scraped the skin from her palms. Wind fanned past her face, though the night was calm, and she could see below the silvery surface of the pond, the dark cattails, rapidly coming nearer. Then the chair must have hit a rock. It stopped with the sound of cracking wood and metal, twisted around, and Mavis felt herself being propelled through the air.

"Let me land in the bosom of the Lord!" she cried out. And then there was total darkness.

Chapter
Twenty-one

Mavis felt incredibly light, as if she were still flying. Though she had never thought about it before, she wondered now just how long it might take to get up to heaven— assuming, of course, that was the direction she was headed. Then she heard voices. Could this be a group excursion? She had to look. Opening one eye just slightly, she was at first aware only of a blinding golden light. But then she saw the outline of a figure (surely one quite familiar), and peering closer, she realized it was Dale's bright head she saw there, lit by the morning sun shining through the window of her room. "Well, I guess I won't see heaven just yet," she said, and sat straight up in bed. Immediately her head began to pound.

"Take it easy, honey!" Dale's worried face faded in and out of focus. "Don't move around like that."

She dropped her head back down onto the pillow, and the throbbing eased somewhat. Still, she felt a lightness about her, as if she might rise up and float above the bed. Feeling gingerly, she touched her chest, her stomach, her thigh. Oh, my goodness, the cast was gone! That was why she felt so weightless. She ran her hand down past her knee to her calf. Yes, it was all there—scaly, dry, no doubt as white as biscuit dough—but her leg was still attached to her body. She would have jumped up and danced if it hadn't been for her head.

Dale's voice came again. "You all right, honey?" he asked. "You want me to call the doctor? He said he'd stay around till you woke up. He's probably right down the hall at the nurses' station.''

Raising herself up slightly on her elbow, she said, "I think I'm all in one piece. Give me a minute." She looked around the room. "He take the cast with him?" she asked.

Dale laughed for the first time, his face relaxing. "Well, if that isn't something," he said. "You get banged on the head and nearly killed, and you're worrying about what happened to that fake cast."

"I'm just curious. I might want it for a souvenir."

"I'd think you'd want to forget about this place, after all that's happened."

She reached up and touched her head. A lump as big as an egg bulged on the side. "Lord, have mercy," she said, lying back down. "What did happen?" She tried to remember, but all that came was the sensation of flying, the wind whipping past her face. The effort made her head ache.

"You fell," Dale said as he pulled a chair close to Mavis's bed and sat down. "Your wheelchair must have gone whizzing down the hill and hit a rock, and then you went sailing right into the pond and banged your head. You're lucky you didn't drown."

Mavis gave a shiver. "Just like Miss Luna Dixon," she said.

"Well, not quite. You had a bit more help than she did. Nurse Overby gave you a big shove."

"Oh, dear Jesus!" Mavis said, remembering now what had happened. The long flight over the lawn, Nurse Overby's words trying to justify her deeds, the sparkling pond and the dark hilltop where the two of them had stood. And finally, Mavis's plunge down the embankment toward the water before she finally passed out. "Where is she?" Mavis called out, half-afraid that Estelle Overby would walk through the door with a plastic cleaning bag in her hands.

Before Dale could answer, a light knock came on the door; it opened, and Charles Morgan stuck his head inside. "You feeling like a visitor for just a few minutes?" he asked. "I came by a little while ago, but you were sound asleep."

"Or still knocked out," she said, trying to smile. "You come right on in. I want you to tell me what's happened to Nurse Overby. I hope she's not still running around loose."

Charles came into the room and pushed the door closed behind him. He nodded to Dale. "No," he said, "she's already on her way downtown. She won't be running around anywhere anymore."

"Did she say anything?"

"Oh, yes, talked a blue streak, all about how she had killed all those folks to put them out of their pain. Mercy killing, she said, but I think it was more," Charles said.

"No doubt about it. Pure outright meanness—that's the reason. When I'm feeling a little better, I'll tell you the rest."

Charles reached over and patted her arm. "You take your time," he said. "We've got plenty on her already."

"Did you get the uniform?"

Charles's face looked blank. "What uniform?" he asked.

"Estelle's . . . down in the employees' locker room. It's lying in the hamper for dirty clothes. That's where she came after me, there in the basement. I'd found something that linked her to the attempt on poor Betty William's life."

"What was that?" Charles leaned forward, his eyes intent on Mavis's.

"Makeup. Don't you remember? All the other ladies who were killed had been painted up. She was all ready to do it for Betty, but then I interrupted her and she dropped the makeup. It was all over the bed, and it seemed likely to me that some stain must have got on whoever it was that tried to kill her. I didn't know who that might be, but I remembered seeing those laundry bins in the locker room last week when the Merry Makers were down there changing for their number, so I decided to look. I'd just found Estelle's uniform with a big stain on the skirt when she walked in the door. I tried to hide it, but she saw what I had in my hand. I dropped it trying to get away."

"So that's why she went after you," Dale said. "We wondered. It didn't seem like she'd all of a sudden guessed your cast was a fake."

"What I want to know is why she didn't succeed in killing me." Mavis rose up again. Her head ached dully, but she did not lie back down, her eyes moving from Dale to Charles and back again. "You said I fell out of the chair into the pond and might have drowned—why didn't I? Nobody knew that Estelle was around last night, and even if they did, they wouldn't think anything about it. If I turned up dead, they'd just think I was off in the head like Swannie Hocutt, went for a midnight ride, and fell in and drowned."

"You had a rescuer," Dale said.

"Who?"

"Mr. Alton Hubbard."

"Lord, have mercy!" Mavis said, afraid her head would begin to swim.

Dale shook his head and grinned, and she knew he would tease her later.

"Yes, ma'am, that's right," Charles said. "We talked to him a little while ago. He said he couldn't sleep, tried to read, walked up and down, but nothing helped. He just happened to look out the window and saw you and Nurse Overby going over the hill lickety-split. He thought something funny must be going on, so he lit out after you, going around a different way to that little stand of trees on the hill above the pond."

"Where we talked," Mavis murmured.

"Ma'am?"

Mavis shook her head. "Nothing," she said. "Go on."

"He just stood there in the woods, says he could hear the two of you talking plain as day on the other side, so there's another witness to Estelle Overby's confession, though I don't think we'll really need it. As soon as he heard the two of you struggling, he ran out on the other side, but when he hit Estelle (he said it was the first time he'd ever hit a woman in his life), she let go of your chair, and you went plunging over the edge of the hill. Then you hit a rock and went flying off into the water. He says he thought you were a goner for sure, but he rushed down the hill and pulled you out and carried you all the way back here to Lakeview. Estelle Overby was still lying there on the hill knocked out cold when the police arrived.''

Mavis had a strange sensation, like a tingling all over her body. The very idea—Alton Hubbard's arms around her, and her soaking wet—but at least she had on one of her pretty new gowns and the robe Dale had bought her. Alton had saved her life. Strange how things turned out. ''I'll have to thank him,'' she said, ''but not now.'' She realized that she was suddenly very tired.

''No,'' Dale said, and his voice made the word sound like an order. ''You've got to rest now. The doctor says in a day or two you can probably go home, but he wants you under observation till then.''

''That's right,'' Charles said. ''You don't need to do any more undercover work.''

Mavis smiled at him from her pillow. ''Nothing turned out like we thought it would, did it?'' she said. ''Barbara and Clifford weren't killing people off for their money, Larry Lee Matthews didn't do it just to get even, and it wasn't one of the residents that had plumb lost their mind. You know what? I even suspected Alton Hubbard for a little while, and he's the one who saved me. I feel almost ashamed.''

Charles patted her arm again. ''Don't worry,'' he said. ''In this business you *do* have to suspect 'most everybody. The important thing is finding the one who did it.'' He moved back a step and looked at his watch. ''I've got to be getting downtown,'' he said. ''There's still a lot of work to be done even though the case is solved. You call if you need me. And take care of yourself. You don't need any more wheelchair rides.''

Mavis laughed. ''That's for sure.'' And she would have said good-bye then, but suddenly she thought, Charles Morgan is going back down to the jail; I wonder if they've still got poor Mr. Jesse locked up there in a cell. ''Hold on,'' she said to his back just as he opened the door. ''Tell me what's become of Mr. Jesse Dixon.''

Charles turned. ''Oh, he's out now. His niece, Elizabeth Warren, picked him up last night. I guess he's going to stay with her a few days, then move back on out here to his apartment.''

''Well, thank the Lord for that! I'm glad somebody finally got some sense. How did it come about?''

Coming closer again, Charles said, ''I just kept on talking to him, friendlylike, not asking him any questions at all about what happened over by the pond. Every chance I got, I'd drop by his cell, and we'd have a little chat about nothing in particular—the weather maybe, or something in the news. He read the paper cover to cover every day and was up on 'most everything. I enjoyed talking to him.''

''But you must have gotten more out of him than the weather report, else you wouldn't have released him.'' Mavis knew that her impatience showed in her voice. Probably, to Charles, she sounded the same way she did when he was in her Sunday-school class and she was trying to help him memorize the books of the Bible. But she couldn't hold back; she had to know what had happened.

''Yes,'' Charles said. ''He finally blurted it out. I think he was just waiting for a chance to get it off his chest. Once he did, everything made sense, and there didn't seem to be any kind of a case. Nobody much thought he'd done it, anyway, except Wilton Early.''

''But what *did* he say?''

Charles actually blushed. ''It's a little embarrassing to tell,'' he said. ''I hope you won't mind.''

Mavis could have given him a smack. ''Of course not,'' she said. ''Just go on.''

Charles took a deep breath, then began. ''You know a lot already. Mr. Jesse had pushed Miss Luna over to the hill above the pond, and they'd spent quite a little spell there, just enjoying the scenery. Mr. Jesse said he wanted to get her away from the crowd at the bazaar as much as possible since things like that upset her, kept her from sleeping at night unless he gave her a pill, and he didn't like doing that. Still, when they saw the cloud coming up so fast, he decided that they should go back anyway, even though there was still a bunch of people there, and he turned Miss Luna's chair, ready to push her back.

"That's when it happened." Charles blushed again. "Mr. Jesse had a call of nature—he's got sort of a problem that way—so he left Miss Luna sitting there in the chair while he went in the bushes. He wasn't gone more than two or three minutes, and he still doesn't know what happened—whether he hadn't put the lock on the wheels or she'd taken it off somehow—but anyway, she had rolled down the hill, turned over, and drowned before Mr. Jesse could get to her. He turned her over, but he'd never had any kind of lifesaving course, so he wasn't able to do a thing for her. That's when the cloud came and he started running back to Lakeview, yelling for help."

They were silent for a moment. Then Mavis said, "That poor man. Why in the world didn't he tell somebody right away?"

Charles shrugged his shoulders. "Embarrassed, I guess. Didn't want people to know about his little trip into the woods. He said he thought people would think he was awful for leaving Miss Luna alone and letting her drown. And he felt so guilty about it himself that he didn't care what happened."

"Lord, you men!" Mavis said. "You act like nobody knows a thing about how your bodies function. Who do you think changed your diapers when you were a baby, or put you on a pot to train you? I never thought I'd live to see the day when I'd hear of a grown man who'd rather be accused of murder than let on he had to water the shrubs."

Dale laughed. "Why, Aunt *Mavis!*" he said. "I've never heard you say such things before."

"Well, maybe it's time. I'm getting too old for it to matter any longer."

"Any maybe *we'd* better get out of here before she scandalizes us even more," Dale said to Charles. "If that doctor hears her, he'll think that lick on the head loosened up her inhibitions and he'll keep her here longer."

"Heaven forbid!" Mavis said. "I'll keep my mouth shut

around him. I don't want anybody to think I'm another Swannie Hocutt seeing sex rings in every corner.''

The two men laughed. Dale kissed Mavis good-bye, opened the door, and started out. Just as Charles Morgan was about to follow him, Mavis called him back one last time.

''How is that sweet Elizabeth Warren?'' she asked him.

''Fine,'' he said. ''We're having dinner on Saturday night.'' A look of surprise came on his face, as if he hadn't planned to say those words at all.

''Well, that's real nice,'' Mavis said. ''I thought something like that might happen.''

''How did you know?''

''Just call it woman's intuition,'' she said.

Smiling, Charles gave her a little salute and closed the door.

Chapter
Twenty-two

"Can I pour you some more wine?" Alton Hubbard reached for the bottle and raised his eyebrows at Mavis.

"You certainly cannot," she said. "I told you I'd take two sips, and I meant it. And if you have much more, I'll be looking for another ride home."

Alton laughed, set the bottle back down, and pushed his chair back slightly so that he could cross his legs. "You want some dessert?" he asked, but the waitress came over to the table before Mavis could answer. "You must have read my mind," Alton said to her, and winked.

"You just looked like you were ready," she said. She turned toward Mavis. "We've got some mighty good pecan pie tonight. Can I interest you in a piece?"

Mavis smiled at the girl, just a bit of a thing, probably working her way through college. She had on a white shirt with a little black bow tie and dark trousers, and her long, honey-colored hair was pulled back in a ponytail. "I'm tight as a tick," Mavis said, smiling up at her. "I shouldn't."

"Aw, go ahead," Alton urged her. "You can find some room. I'm going to have me a piece. And you can put some ice cream on it, young lady," he said to the waitress. "I'm not going to worry about any cholesterol tonight."

"Just bring me a little piece," Mavis said, and the waitress went hurrying away.

Mavis looked around the restaurant at the other diners. She didn't know a soul, and it was a good thing, too, with a bottle of wine sitting on the table and a glass half-full at her plate. If anybody down at the church saw it, she'd be disgraced. But it *was* a real nice place, each table with a little candle and a vase of pink carnations, and napkins so soft and snowy white that you hated to use them. Alton had said, "Order anything you want," and she'd had a shrimp cocktail and filet steak with a salad and baked potato, and she really was too full for dessert, though she'd have a bite or two just to please Alton.

Strange how things happened. A week ago, the last thing in the world she would have predicted was that she would be sitting here tonight with Alton Hubbard in this fine place. When the knock came on her door the day after Estelle Overby had taken Mavis on her little ride to the pond, Mavis had been pleased to see Alton standing there. Lord knows, she needed to thank him for saving her life, so she had given him a big smile and said, "You come right on in," and had told him how much she appreciated what he had done.

"Lord have mercy," he'd said, "I couldn't let that—well, you know, I can't say it in front of a lady—that *thing* get away with what she did. I just flattened her out and then brought you back here and called for help. My blood pressure didn't go up one bit." It was what he had said next that caught Mavis by surprise.

"I guess you'll be going home soon." He had pointed to Mavis's bag in the corner of the room.

"Yes sir," she had said. "This afternoon, if the doctor says it's all right. The lump on my head has gone way down, and I can get around as well as I ever could, now that I've got that cast off."

Alton had moved a little closer to her bed. "I'm leaving, too," he had said. "Tomorrow or the next day. They think they've got my medicines adjusted." He had paused then and looked down. Mavis had wondered if his face was becoming flushed. "Could I call you one day next week?" he had finally said.

You could have knocked her over with a feather! Alton Hubbard wanting to call her—would wonders never cease?

"I'm in the book," she had said, never expecting to hear from him again, but she had been home no more than two days when he had called her and invited her out to the Rustic Inn Steak House for a meal. When she called Dale and told him, he had said, "Why, Mavis, honey, I never thought I'd live to see the day when you'd be going out on a date!" She had shushed him, but the very next day she went downtown and bought herself a new dress—sheer black with a satin bow at the waist. Her one strand of good pearls set it off just perfectly.

"You're not eating your pie." Mavis jumped at the sound of Alton's voice.

"I told you I was too full," she said, pushing a small piece around with her fork. "And my mind was wandering. It must be the wine."

"Not on the little bit you've had. I hope you're not bored with the company."

"Of course not," she said. She almost reached across the table to touch him. "This whole evening has been a special treat."

Alton leaned forward; his voice was lower when he spoke. "It *has* been nice, hasn't it?" He didn't give her time to answer. "The nicest I've had since my wife died. It gets lonely in that big house when you're all by yourself. Oh, I have a housekeeper, but she's no real company. A person needs someone to share things with. You can have all the money in the world, travel up and down, but if you don't have someone you can say to, 'Well, look at *that*—did you ever see anything like it in your whole life?' where's the pleasure? You know what I mean?"

For a moment, Mavis considered what he was proposing (only a fool wouldn't know what Alton Hubbard was leading up to)—a fine house with somebody else to take care of it, a big car to ride around in, no more worries about whether or not she was spending too much money or how long what she had might last. How nice all that would be! But in her heart she knew that such a life hadn't been meant for her. Touching her pearls, a gift from John on their last anniversary together before he died, she remembered an earlier time, just after they were married, when they were trying to save for a house and had no extra money for gifts. He had given her a single rose and a note that said, *I love you with every beat of my heart; you are and always will be my one true joy*, words that he would never in a million years have been able to say out loud. That had meant more to her than all the jewels in the world, and she still had the note carefully folded in the bottom of the old candy box that contained her important papers, hidden away at the back of her closet. Theirs had been a life of small pleasures, treasured moments, and nothing could ever replace those memories.

Before Alton could ask a question that she would have to respond no to and embarrass them both, she said, "Well, yes, I do get lonely, but I don't know that I could ever get used to living with anyone again. I'm sort of set in my ways. Get up when I want to, go to bed when I want to—without having to be worried about somebody else's wishes. Maybe I'm just too old to change."

She got up then, excused herself, and went to the ladies' room. When she got back, Alton had paid the bill and was sitting at the table looking like a whipped dog. But he'd get over it, Mavis thought. Alton Hubbard had survived all this time without her help, and he had a lot of good years ahead of him if he'd take care of himself. One of these days, when some lady came up to him in the post office and pressed her telephone number in his hand, he'd keep the paper instead of crumpling it up and throwing it away, and give her a call. Who knew what might happen after that?

But when they pulled up to her house, and Alton stood at the bottom of the stoop while she found her key in her purse and unlocked the door, he looked up at her (those two pretty blue eyes shining in the porch light), and said, "Can I call you again sometime?"

Not wanting to hurt him more, she said, "Yes sir, I'd be right pleased," then smiled, turned, and went inside.

She had left one low light burning on the desk, and the house seemed warm, welcoming, when she closed the door behind her and stood for a moment leaning against it. The stiffly starched crocheted doilies that covered the tabletops and the backs of the chairs glowed, and the dish garden sitting on the coffee table looked slightly mysterious, like some small jungle, in the shadows. The recliner by the fireplace—John's chair—waited expectantly. "Well," she said out loud as she brushed her hand over the smooth leather, "I guess I almost slipped up tonight, didn't I? It *was* a temptation, but nothing more. I won't ever leave this house till they carry me out feet first. I'm just fine here by myself." Then she laughed and thought, What would people think if they could see me here talking to the air? They'd say I was as crazy as Swannie Hocutt and put me right back out at Lakeview!

Quickly she switched off the lamp, went to her bedroom, took off her dress, and hung it carefully in a canvas bag. It *was* pretty, wasn't it? And she had the feeling she might wear it again soon.

Before she was half-finished with her prayers, she had fallen fast asleep.

About the Author

Robert Nordan was born in Raleigh, North Carolina, and attended Duke University. After working as a sales promotion copywriter in New York, he completed graduate studies in psychology at the University of Chicago and is now employed as a clinical child psychologist in an urban medical center in Chicago. He is the author of *All Dressed Up to Die* and *Death Beneath the Christmas Tree*.

Fawcett Rounds up

The Best of The West